Praise for the Ivy Meado

THE SOUND OF M

"The setting is irresistible, the mys beguiling as ever, but what I real complexity of painful human relation of a sparkly caper. Roll on Ivy #3!"

– Catriona McPherson,
Anthony and Agatha Award-Winning Author of *The Day She Died*

"It is not easy to combine humor and murder, but Cindy Brown does it effortlessly. Who else would think of combining *The Sound of Music* with *Cabaret* with a serial killer? The result is such fun."

– Rhys Bowen,
New York Times Bestselling Author of *Malice at the Palace*

"The author blends theater lore with a deeper psychological layer, and always on stage is her delightful sense of humor. The concept of a mash-up of *The Sound of Music* and *Cabaret* is as brilliant as it is ripe for absurdity, and readers will thoroughly enjoy this extremely fun mystery that entertains until the final curtain call."

– *Kings River Life Magazine*

"The mystery kept me glued to the pages and I enjoyed all facets as each clue got me closer to the killer's identity...had me roaring with laughter...A delightful read and I can't wait to see what happens next in this amusingly entertaining series."

– *Dru's Book Musings*

"Brown's books are well-designed cotton candy, page turners sprinkled with genuine character-based humor and delightfully bad jokes. I greatly enjoyed both *Macdeath* and *The Sound of Murder*, and I look forward to the next one." – *Show Showdown*

MACDEATH (#1)

"This gut-splitting mystery is a hilarious riff on an avant-garde production of 'the Scottish play'...Combining humor and pathos can be risky in a whodunit, but gifted author Brown makes it work."

– *Mystery Scene Magazine*

"An easy read that will have you hooked from the first page...Brown uses what she knows from the theater life to give us an exciting mystery with all the suspense that keeps you holding on."

– *Fresh Fiction*

"A whodunit with a comic spirit, and Ivy Meadows has real heart. You'll never experience the Scottish play the same way again."

– Ian Doescher,
Author of the William Shakespeare's Star Wars Series

"Funny and unexpectedly poignant, *Macdeath* is that rarest of creatures: a mystery that will make you laugh out loud. I loved it!"

– April Henry,
New York Times Bestselling Author

"Vivid characters, a wacky circus production of *Macbeth*, and a plot full of surprises make this a perfect read for a quiet evening. Pour a glass of wine, put your feet up, and enjoy! Bonus: it's really funny."

– Ann Littlewood,
Award-Winning Author of the Iris Oakley "Zoo-dunnit" Mysteries

"This gripping mystery is both satisfyingly clever and rich with unerring comedic timing. Without a doubt, *Macdeath* is one of the most entertaining debuts I've read in a very long time."

— Bill Cameron,
Spotted Owl Award-Winning Author of *County Line*

The Sound of Murder

The Ivy Meadows Mystery Series
by Cindy Brown

MACDEATH (#1)
THE SOUND OF MURDER (#2)
OLIVER TWISTED (#3)
(Summer 2016)

The Sound of Murder

AN IVY MEADOWS MYSTERY

Cindy Brown

HENERY PRESS

THE SOUND OF MURDER
An Ivy Meadows Mystery
Part of the Henery Press Mystery Collection

First Edition
Trade paperback edition | October 2015

Henery Press
www.henerypress.com

Cover art by Stephanie Chontos
Author Photograph by AJC Photography

This is a work of fiction. Any references to historical events, real people, or real locales are used fictitiously. Other names, characters, places, and incidents are the product of the author's imagination, and any resemblance to actual events or locales or persons, living or dead, is entirely coincidental.

ISBN-13: 978-1-943390-01-4

Printed in the United States of America

For my favorite posse members,
Mom and Dad

ACKNOWLEDGMENTS

The idea for this book began with my dad, when he told me about an unusual day at the Sun City West posse. Dad's also the catalyst behind my love of mysteries, having introduced me to John D. MacDonald many years ago. My mom also encouraged my love of reading, and has been an enormous help with research. Best of all, they've both given me lots of love and support.

I've had a lot of support from others too, and would like to thank.

Everyone at Henery Press, especially: Art, for helping me navigate my new author world; Stephanie Chontos for the incredible cover art; Kendel and Anna and Erin for great editorial advice delivered in a positive, encouraging manner; and the Hen House authors, the most welcoming group I've ever had the pleasure to meet.

The people who helped me get the details right: Sterling Gavette of the Arizona Department of Insurance; Shelly Jamison of the Phoenix Fire Department; D.P. Lyle; the crimescenewriter listserv; and Roger I. Ideishi, JD, OT/L, FAOTA, Associate Professor, Dept. of Rehabilitation Sciences, Temple University. I'd like to give a special shout-out to John Hopper, Director of Investigative Services at JB National Investigations. I called him up out of the blue when I needed to talk to an Arizona PI. He's been gracious and informative, and patient with all of my questions. Any mistakes are my own.

Bill Cameron, for telling me about his fire-prone VW, and the great guys at Metro Car Care in Portland, OR, for discussing the finer points of car fires with me.

My early readers and writing friends, including Lisa Alber, Delia Booth, Jennie Bricker, Jane Carlsen, Judy Hricko, Bernice Johnston, Ruth Maionchi, Janice Maxson, Shauna Petchel, Donna Reynolds, Rae Richen, and Angela M. Sanders.

The good folks of Oregon Writers Colony, who are unfailingly supportive of me.

Fellow author Shannon Baker, for offering me time and space to finish my edits at her beautiful Arizona writers' retreat.

My friends who've helped me with the promotion pieces of the puzzle: Bruce Cantwell, Pam Harrison, John Kohlepp, Lindsay Nyre, Anthony Petchel, Orit Kramer, and Tricia Serlin.

Holly Franko, writer, editor, and friend. This book (and life in general) would not be as good without her.

Hal, always.

I can't thank you all enough.

CHAPTER 1

I should never do anything pre-coffee.

"It was only a teeny fire," I told my uncle over the phone. I sat outside on the steps of my apartment complex, watching the Phoenix Fire Department carry equipment out of my second-floor apartment. Black smoke trailed behind them. The air smelled awful, like the time I'd fallen asleep in front of a campfire and melted the bottom of my sneakers. Except this smelled like an entire Nike factory.

"Teeny fire?" Uncle Bob said. "Isn't that an oxymoron or something?"

"Nah," I said. "That's firefighter language for no one got hurt. Right?" I asked an especially cute guy carrying a heavy-looking hose.

"Yep," he said over his shoulder as he passed me. "Teeny. No one hurt."

I smiled at him again and watched him descend the stairs. On the back of his firefighter's helmet was a sticker that said, "Be Nice."

"Olive," said my uncle with a sigh. "Stop flirting with firemen and tell me what happened."

"I'm not entirely sure." I was not a morning person. "I got up early to go to that meeting you put on my calendar."

Since acting didn't always pay the bills (okay, rarely paid the bills), I worked part-time at my uncle's private investigation business. Right now I was mostly filing and writing reports, but

Uncle Bob promised he was going to give me some real detective work soon.

"You got up early?" I could hear the skepticism in my uncle's voice. "What time?"

"Eight." There was a pause on the other end. "Ish," I finished.

"To go to this meeting that starts in..." I could almost see him squint at the old clock on the office wall. "Twenty minutes?"

"Uh huh."

"Right. Go on."

"I put the kettle on the stove." When my old coffeemaker bit the dust, I had replaced it with a French press, a much better fit for my minuscule galley kitchen. "Then I got in the shower."

Another pause. Then, "You usually do that? Turn on the stove and get in the shower?"

"Sometimes. Then when I get out, the kettle's boiling and I make coffee. No waiting." Not only was I not a morning person, I was not a patient person. Especially in the morning. "Since the water was running, I didn't hear the smoke alarm."

"That's why you didn't hear the alarm? You were in the shower?" said the cute fireman, who was going back up the stairs. I nodded, though it did seem sort of obvious. I was wearing only a towel.

"So you turned on a gas stove, left the room, and put yourself in a situation where you couldn't see or smell smoke or hear an alarm," said Uncle Bob. I could tell he was trying to make a point. "And what happened when you got out of the shower?"

"The apartment was full of black smoke. Really nasty. I could taste it." I scraped the top of my tongue with my front teeth. I knew I probably looked like a dog that just ate peanut butter, but I really wanted the greasy bitter smoke taste out of my mouth.

"Here," the cute fireman came back and sat down next to me on the stairs, pulling a Day-Glo green bottle of Gatorade from a pocket in his voluminous fireman's coat. "Helps with that awful taste," he said, opening the bottle for me. Not only was he chivalrous, he was even better looking up close, with light brown eyes and the longest lashes I'd ever seen. I was wowed and envious at the same time.

"Thanks." I hiked up my towel, grateful I'd sprung for the large bath sheet. I twisted open the Gatorade. It was lukewarm, but it did make my mouth taste better. Like pleasant, lemony-limey smoke. The fireman shrugged out of his heavy firefighter's coat. The t-shirt he wore underneath showed off strong muscled arms. I tried not to stare.

"Olive?" Uncle Bob was still on the line. "Was it really a teeny fire?"

I looked at the big fire truck and the half dozen firefighters going in and out of my apartment. "Yeah," I replied, sticking with my definition of "no one got hurt."

"Good. I want you at this meeting. Can you make it?"

"I think I need to talk to the firefighters now."

The fireman, whose name was Jeremy (it was stenciled on his t-shirt), nodded.

"I'll be there," I said. "A little late, but I'll make it."

"Glad you're all right. See you soon."

Uncle Bob hung up, which was good because I was having a hard time holding my cellphone, the Gatorade, and my towel, which I thought I'd secured pretty well. I was in an awkward position. The stairs outside my apartment were shallow, which was nice for carrying groceries, but not for sitting in a ladylike position wearing a towel and nothing underneath. I made sure to keep my legs together.

Jeremy smiled at me. He had dimples.

"Is this," I held up the Gatorade, "part of 'Be Nice?'"

"Sort of," he said. "It's part of the Phoenix Fire Department motto."

I tried to figure out what Gatorade had to do with fires. I figured it wasn't flammable, but that seemed like a stretch.

"'Prevent Harm, Survive, Be Nice.' The Phoenix Fire Department motto," he explained. "Now, Miss..."

"Meadows," I said brightly, "but you can call me Ivy." The

green Astroturf covering the stairs tickled my hiney. I tried not to think about it.

"Ivy Meadows?" The smile stayed on his face but his eyes narrowed a fraction.

"That's my stage name." Not sure if it was the good-looking fireman or the lack of coffee, but I wasn't at my sharpest. "My legal name is Olive Ziegwart."

Jeremy laughed, one of those snort laughs that can make milk come out your nose if you're not careful. I didn't laugh.

"Really," I said. "That's why I changed it."

He looked properly chastened. "How do you spell that?"

"It's 'Olive' like in a martini," I said. "And Ziegwart is spelled Z-I-E-G...wart."

Another snort laugh escaped his lips. I laughed with him. I was trying for that one.

Two other firemen came out of my apartment and began the trek downstairs. Sweat trickled down their faces, courtesy of the eighty-degree spring morning. One of them, an older guy with a big gray mustache, punched Jeremy good-naturedly on the shoulder as he passed. "Watch out for this one," he said to me. "He's crazy about blondes."

I smiled and nodded, glad my roots weren't showing.

My phone chimed. A text from Uncle Bob: "Client here early."

"Any chance I could make a meeting pretty soon?" I asked Jeremy.

"I only have a few questions. But you might want to get dressed too."

There was that. I wondered if all my clothes smelled like burnt Nikes.

"So I overheard what you said on the phone about turning on the stove. We know the fire started there. Maybe you turned on the wrong burner? One that had something lying across it?"

"Maybe." I wasn't sure. That was before coffee *and* a shower.

"After that I'm guessing the grease trap in the vent caught fire," said Jeremy. "When was the last time you'd cleaned it?"

"A while back," I said, fidgeting. Boy, that Astroturf was tickly.

"Well, the rest is history," said Jeremy. "And so is your kitchen."

"Really?" I hadn't thought it was that serious.

My phone chimed again: "ETA?"

"And you've got a lot of smoke damage to the rest of the place," Jeremy continued. "Have you called your land—"

He didn't need to finish. Mae the manager stormed up the stairs dragging her little poodle on a leash behind her.

"Olive, what the hell? I take Sugar out for a walk and when I come back you've burned the place down. This is the last straw."

To be honest, there had been a few other straws. Like the time I overfilled the communal washing machine with detergent. Who knew it could make so many bubbles?

"You're out," said Mae, her gray head bobbing with each word. "Your lease is terminated as of now."

"I believe that's illegal," said Jeremy.

Mae finally noticed the large, handsome fireman right next to me. "Oh. Right. Just kidding." She waved the air around her like it could blow away her words.

Another text from my uncle: "Olive?"

"Also," continued Jeremy, "although we're not sure what started the fire," he slid a glance at me, "we did notice that the wiring in the apartment isn't up to code."

Mae had an ear cocked toward Jeremy, but she was glaring at me. "Really," she said as she turned and stomped down the stairs, pulling Sugar along like a wheelie toy. "Send me the report." She stalked into her apartment at the bottom of the stairs and slammed the door.

"Thanks," I said to Jeremy. "I'm not crazy about Mae, but I do love my apartment."

It was just off Central Avenue, cheap and cute in a kitschy way. Built in the 1940s, the two-story complex had the same layout as the motels we used to stay in on road trips, U-shaped with a swimming pool in the middle. The pool deck was covered in the same patchy green Astroturf as the stairs, and all of it harbored an icky drought-proof mold.

Uh-oh. A thought was beginning to percolate in my coffee-less brain. Astroturf...mold...

"You okay?" said Jeremy.

"Sure," I said. "Thanks again for the Gatorade."

Astroturf...mold...tickling...why was the Astroturf tickling me if I was sitting on my towel? Yikes! My bare ass was sitting on the skuzzy fake grass. I jumped up, trying to grab the railing while holding my towel in one hand and my Gatorade in the other. One of them had to go. I instinctively tossed the drink to Jeremy. The cap-less drink.

"Dang," I said to the now sticky-wet fireman. "I'm so sorry, I was trying to..."

I trailed off, not wanting to explain about the ass-troturf.

"It's okay," he said, standing up and wringing out the hem of his t-shirt. "Somebody threw up on me yesterday." He grinned at me and my heart thumped under my bath sheet.

"Can I get you a paper towel? I've got some..." I wrinkled my nose at the thought of my burned-out kitchen. "I think my paper towels may be, um, gone."

"How about dinner tonight instead?"

Wow. I should wear a towel more often. Not only was Jeremy the best-looking guy I'd ever seen, but he seemed like the poster boy for the Phoenix Fire Department. Definitely nice.

"I'd love to, but I've got rehearsal out in Surprise." The most startling thing about the westside suburb of Surprise was how long it took to drive there from central Phoenix. "I'm in *The Sound of Cabaret*." Jeremy gave me a blank look. "It's a world premiere, a combination of *The Sound of Music* and *Cabaret*. I'm an actor," I said helpfully.

"How about another night?"

I hesitated. We were ten days from opening our show, and all of us non-union actors were rehearsing every night until then.

"Never mind."

The really nice, best-looking guy I'd ever seen shrugged and started down the stairs.

My phone chimed again: "Client left."

"Jeremy, wait."

He turned and gave me a small smile. Phew, I hadn't blown it. "Let me make a quick call." I called my uncle. "Wasn't the meeting supposed to *start* in five minutes?"

"Yeah. But it was..." My uncle blew a breath into the phone, a horse-type noise. "Let's just say it wasn't important after all."

"So I can come in late?"

"Late-er," Uncle Bob said. "Yeah, okay." He hung up.

"Maybe we could grab a bite right now?" I asked Jeremy. "I haven't had anything to eat, and I could really use a cup of coffee."

He looked at his watch.

"I could do that," he said, showing me his dimples again, "as long as you don't mind a slightly funky-smelling fireman."

"Give me a few minutes to figure out my no-clothes dilemma." I scooted up the stairs to my neighbor's apartment. Tiffany was already at work, but I knew where she kept a key. She was about my size and I was sure she wouldn't mind if I borrowed some clothes, given the situation. As I padded in my bare feet to her apartment, I thought again about sitting on old moldy fake grass sans underwear. I felt all creepy-crawly, like when you see a spider and your skin crawls with imagined bugs.

If I hadn't been thinking about Astroturf and spiders and dimples, I might have given more thought to the meeting I'd missed. The meeting my uncle misdiagnosed as unimportant. The meeting that could have saved a man's life.

CHAPTER 2

I had that sort of euphoria you get from a narrow escape, plus a nice breakfast with a *very* nice fireman (eggs and pancakes with a side of dimples). So I was caffeinated and sated and generally happy when I finally made it to my uncle's office downtown. It wasn't noon yet, but I could tell Uncle Bob had eaten his lunch because the smell of liverwurst and onions hung in the air like a bad belch. Something else was in the air too.

"What the hell?" My typically easygoing uncle slapped his big hands down on his metal desk. "Thank God you missed that meeting, or I would have had to explain that...what you're..." His words tangled up with his anger, he nodded at my chest.

I'd rummaged through my neighbor Tiffany's drawers and found just one clean pair of jeans and one t-shirt. Both black. The shirt was emblazoned with a skull that shone like it was wet. Snakes (or worms?) writhed out of its eyeholes. Its open mouth said, "Suicide Rocks!" Tiff was in a Goth phase.

Uncle Bob stood up from behind his desk. "What in the Sam Hill were you thinking?"

"This was the only..."

"Olive!" Uncle Bob was never this cranky. Maybe his liverwurst had turned. He poked the air with a finger. "Go. Change. Now."

"Into what? My clothes all smell like smoke and chemicals."

"So do you," he mumbled, turning away.

I went to him, squeezing behind his desk so I could see him face to face. "Listen, I'm sorry about the meeting. I tried to make it, but..." I stopped. Uncle Bob's face matched his fuchsia Hawaiian shirt and his lips were pressed tightly together, like he was holding something in. He caught my eyes for a moment, turned away again and cleared his throat. I sat down in his wheelie chair and reached for his hand. "Is something wrong?"

"Other than the fact that I'm pissed as hell at my niece whose stupidity nearly got herself killed today? Nope. Nothin' wrong."

"But you weren't mad when I talked to you this morn..." I stopped. Maybe he'd been hiding his anger earlier. Maybe he'd been in shock. Maybe he'd had time to understand what almost happened. It didn't matter. I held his hand tighter. I wanted to say, "I love you. I love you for worrying about me, and even for getting mad when you're scared." But we don't say that in our family. What I said instead was, "I'm sorry."

"It was stupid, Olive. All because you couldn't wait for a goddamn cup of coffee."

"I know. I wasn't thinking."

"And from now on?" he said, his voice slightly calmer.

"I'll think, I promise. Scout's honor." I held up three fingers. "Even in the morning."

"Okay," he said, blowing out a pent-up breath. "Now, go change."

My cellphone rang. Tiffany. Perfect timing. Maybe she had a clean shirt hidden somewhere. I hopped out of Uncle Bob's wheelie chair, and walked to the corner of the office to take the call. It was more a matter of courtesy than privacy, since the office was only about ninety square feet.

"Hi Tiff," I said. "I was just going to call—"

"Omigod, Ivy, there was a fire!"

"I know."

"And I think it was arson."

"What?" Tiffany's pronouncement didn't worry me. I may have been the actress, but she was the drama queen. Still, I wanted to make sure there wasn't something to her theory. "Why do you think that?"

"Because someone broke into my apartment. I think they set the fire as cover. I called the police, and they're coming over and—"

"Whoa. Tiff—"

"They stole some of my clothes, and even went through my underwear drawer. Pervs."

"Uh, Tiff," I said, "that was me." I had gone through her underwear drawer, but didn't take anything. All she had were thongs. They tickle my butt, and I'd had enough of that for one day.

"You took my Suicide Rocks concert shirt!"

"I really needed some clothes. All my stuff is in my apartment, and I can't get—"

"I need that shirt *now*. Damien's picking me up in a half an hour."

"Do you have something else I can—"

"And bring my black jeans too!" She hung up.

Dang. I had planned to offer to do her laundry in exchange for a clean outfit. And I'd hoped to sleep on her couch for a day or two.

My uncle, the eavesdropping PI, said, "Sheesh. Don't think you got to finish one sentence. Reminds me of that interrupting cow joke."

"What?"

"Your phone conversation. Reminds me of that joke. You know, knock knock..."

I did know, but I played along, glad Uncle Bob was in a better mood. "Who's there?"

"Interrupting cow."

"Interrupting cow wh—"

"Moo!" Uncle Bob laughed at his own joke, then tossed me his keys. "Go to my house, and see if you can find something that'll fit you."

That's how I (five foot four and about a hundred and twenty-five pounds) ended up at rehearsal that night in a pair of rolled-up drawstring sweats that typically fit a six foot two, two-hundred-

and-fifty-pound guy. I also sported an extra-large t-shirt from Oregano's Pizza that said, "Legalize Marinara."

"Should you be advocating the use of that drug quite so publicly, dear?" asked Bitsy as I walked in the stage door at Desert Magic Dinner Theater. The sixty-something actress looked at me like she'd just spotted a large sewer roach. I didn't know if it was the thought of pot that put the look on her face or my lack of fashion sense. Bitsy was resplendent in a pink pantsuit with embroidered daisies, her white hair teased to perfection, and her real face hidden behind an entire counter's worth of Estée Lauder. Her lipstick matched her outfit perfectly. Perfectly.

"Marinara is actually a red sauce, you know, for pasta and..." Bitsy walked away before I could explain. Oh well. I trotted down the hall to the greenroom (the actors' break room) to wait for rehearsal to begin. I'd just joined the rest of the cast when my cell rang. I started to turn it off when I recognized the number.

I picked up. "Hi, Mae."

"Thought you oughta know that fireman was right. I can't evict you."

"Great. Thanks."

"But you can't come back until we've cleaned up."

"Okay." I wondered if they'd mop the floors. Maybe even clean the bathtub.

"And then of course we have to tear out the asbestos your little fire uncovered."

"Asbestos?" I said, a bit too loudly. Several cast members looked at the ceiling of the greenroom when I said that. I did too. It was a possibility.

"And renovate your entire apartment to the tune of a hell of a lot of money. Nice, huh? You burn down your place and we have to pay."

I was about to say something about the benefits and responsibilities of ownership but wisely held my own counsel.

"So how long before I can move back?"

"At least two months."

"Two months?"

"That's right. And your rent is due on the first. Of next month."

"But..."

"Do you want to keep the apartment or not?"

"Yes."

"Rent check to me by the first." She hung up.

Two whole months paying rent on an apartment I couldn't live in. I wondered if Mae's scheme was legal but didn't have time to deal with that right now. Right now I had to find a place to live.

I wondered briefly if I could stay at the theater. There was a couch, a kitchen, and a bathroom. Even more, it felt like home. Every theater I'd been in did. It was funny, but I was most comfortable in my own skin in a place where I pretended to be someone else. I'm sure a therapist would have a ball with that, but I felt lucky I'd found my tribe.

I was seriously considering the stowaway possibilities when Candy MoonPie skidded into the greenroom, brown curls bouncing. Everything else too. Candy was the most voluptuous woman I'd ever seen in real life.

"Nearly didn't make it in time." She was still in scrubs from her care center job. "The new aide they hired is useless as tits on a boar." Originally from Louisiana, Candy loved to southern it up around us westerners. She also loved MoonPies, hence the nickname. She gave me the once-over. "Hon, you ever seen 'What Not to Wear?'"

"Had to borrow Uncle Bob's clothes."

"Ah," said Bitsy, who hovered nearby.

"Is your washer broken again?" Candy was really asking if I'd overfilled it with detergent.

"No," I said. "My apartment caught on fire." That was what I was going to tell people about my latest fiasco. Sounded like it was the apartment's fault.

"What, like spontaneous combustion?" asked Candy. Hmmm. Maybe I could use that. "Maybe Marge has an extra tracksuit." She glanced to the corner of the greenroom, where Marge Weiss drank coffee while talking to our producer. The busty, sixty-ish red-haired actress had a variety of tracksuits she used as rehearsal "uniforms." Tonight's was a velour number with "Juicy" embroidered across her ample bottom.

"Wonder if she has any extra underwear?" I was still sans skivvies. "Or maybe you do?"

"Clean?"

Eww. "Never mind."

"Places for Act One in fifteen minutes, please," the stage manager said over the PA system. Bitsy scooted out of the room.

"How about a place to stay?" I asked Candy. "Since my apartment burned down and everything." I tried to look pathetic. It didn't take much work.

"Hon, you do remember that I have a studio apartment?"

"I don't take up much room."

"And a boyfriend?"

Oh. Yeah. I could see where that could be a problem. Candy had been dating Matt ever since I introduced them at a performance of *Macbeth* last fall.

"Can't you stay with your uncle?"

"He's renovating." I'd seen the mess firsthand when I dropped by to pick up clothes. Uncle Bob promised he'd move the lumber off the couch so I could sleep there tonight.

Bitsy reappeared beside me and handed me a little cloth bundle—a white cotton pair of granny panties, embroidered with "Bitsy's Sunday Undies."

"You can keep them," Bitsy said. "I have a few extra pairs. I'll just wear a Tuesday on Sunday."

"Thanks," I said. "I'll go put them on." Granny panties were better than none.

Someone tapped me on the shoulder. "Did I hear you need a place to stay?" Marge bellowed. There was a reason she was known as "Arizona's Ethel Merman."

I nodded.

"Is this perfect or what?" she said to no one in particular and the room as a whole. “I got just the thing for you.” She hooked an arm around my waist. “Bernice, my neighbor here in Sunnydale, is going to New Zealand for a couple of months and her house sitter just bailed. She’s got a four-bedroom place right next door to me, real nice.”

“Wow. Great. Thanks.” Sunnydale was a retirement community just minutes from the theater.

“All you have to do is water her plants and take care of the pool.”

“Pool?” Oh no. I couldn’t breathe.

“It’s easy. You just check the chemicals and every so often jump in and untangle the hose on the pool cleaner. Hey,” Marge caught the panicked look on my face before I could hide it, “you can swim, right?”

I ignored the warning look Candy shot me and nodded.

I could do this. I really needed a place to crash, and staying near the theater in quiet, retiree-only Sunnydale sounded perfect. Besides, a swimming pool was just an innocent inanimate object that couldn’t do me any harm, right?

I didn’t believe it for a minute.

CHAPTER 3

Lord. Even Uncle Bob wasn't up this early (though he did set the Mr. Coffee timer so I'd have a fresh pot waiting for me this morning, the big sweetie).

I settled my coffee in the cup holder and crossed my fingers as I started up my latest "new" car, a yellow '64 VW Bug. Phew. It hummed to life. Guess it was in a good mood. The digital clock I'd stuck on the dashboard glowed green in the pre-dawn darkness: 4:40 a.m. Dang. Ten minutes later than I'd planned to leave. I was supposed to be at Bernice's by five thirty. Maybe the lack of traffic (and traffic cops) would allow me to make it on time. I took a big slug of hot coffee, turned the radio up loud, and set my course for Sunnydale.

Thirty-five minutes later I whizzed past the theater. According to Marge's directions, I was only a few minutes away. A couple more blocks and I turned onto a wide street flanked by golden rock walls with bronze letters. One side said, "Sunnydale!" The other said "America's Favorite 55+ Community!" I had an evil urge to steal the exclamation marks. They'd look cool in my apartment.

I beat down my criminal impulses and paid attention to where I was going. I'd never driven into Sunnydale before. Not much reason to, unless you had a grandma living here. Sunnydale wasn't your typical retirement community. It wasn't a high-rise condo, or even a collection of retiree apartments. Though unincorporated, it was basically a city, with thousands of acres, its own zip code, and around 35,000 people, at least during the winter when snowbirds came to warm their old, cold Midwestern bones in the Arizona sun.

I slowed and drove down wide, well-lit streets with citrus trees trimmed like lollipops. From what I could see so far, Sunnydale looked a lot like most other Southwestern suburbs. Houses were single-family and one level for easy living, some ranch style, others with tile roofs and mock Spanish arches, mostly painted Navajo white, with desert landscaping and gravel yards. I didn't see any grass. Guess people had enough of mowing lawns by the time they moved here. I glanced again at the address Marge had scribbled on my *Sound of Cabaret* script: 3837 S.W. Via del Toro.

There it was. The house sat on a nice wide cul-de-sac, with 3837 in big, easy-to-read numbers mounted on its stucco garage. I parked on the street in case Bernice was driving her own car to the airport.

I walked through a tiled courtyard where a gurgling fountain sang to the early birds. Fuchsia bougainvillea draped the walls, and the heavy romantic scent of an orange tree in full bloom permeated the air. Wow. And I got to stay here.

I knocked on the door. I could hear a low rumble from somewhere inside the house. Air conditioning? Nah, too cool out. Maybe it was the heater. The sixty-degree morning was pretty comfy for me, maybe not so much for the older crowd. I smoothed down the tracksuit I wore, courtesy of Marge, who kept an extra in her car. "In case I get too sweaty during rehearsal," she explained.

I knocked again. Still no answer. I glanced at my watch. Just past five thirty. Didn't Bernice want to leave for the airport really soon? I rang the bell and heard it echo inside. I put my ear to the door, but didn't hear anything except the low thrum, which my sleep-deprived brain was beginning to shape into something more recognizable.

Shit. I knew what it was. I ran to the garage and put my ear against it. Yes—shit! A car engine. Rumbling in the garage. The closed-up-tight garage.

I fumbled in my bag for my cell, yanked it out and dropped it on the concrete drive. I scrambled for it, saw the dark screen and turned it on. Or didn't. I'd forgotten to charge it.

I pulled at the garage door—no way to open it. The rumble continued. I scanned the cul-de-sac, saw a light on at a nearby house, and sprinted over. I pounded on the door. "Emergency! Call 911! Something's happened to Bernice!"

The door flew open. A woman stood open-mouthed amongst a pile of suitcases. "*I'm* Bernice."

I looked at her house number: 3738. Marge had transposed the numbers. "Then who..." I pointed at the garage, filling up with deadly fumes even as we spoke. "There's a car idling."

"Oh, God," said Bernice. "It's Charlie Small."

CHAPTER 4

A black car with "Sheriff" written on the side made a leisurely turn into the cul-de-sac. Too leisurely.

The patrol car drove slowly past me and Bernice outside Charlie's garage, then parked on the street behind us. A tall man with a silver head of hair and a mustache to match unfolded himself from within. I ran to him. "The car's idling in the garage. We've been pounding and pounding, but there's no response."

The man reached inside his car, pulled out his hat—a cowboy-ish, state trooper type—and settled it on his head.

"I don't think anyone's in the house," I said, breathing hard. "I rang and knocked, so Charlie must be in the car. In the garage."

The guy didn't move.

"In the garage that's filling up with deadly gas?" I said. Okay, shouted.

The man took a pair of mirrored sunglasses out of his pocket and put them on. It was just past five thirty. Still dark.

"Hank." Bernice had come up behind me. Her greeting sounded carefully neutral.

Hank nodded at her, streetlights glinting off his sunglasses.

I had to stop myself from grabbing Bernice's shoulders. "Isn't he going to do something?"

She shook her head. "He's just posse."

A fire truck screamed onto the street and pulled into Charlie's driveway, a couple more vehicles right behind.

"Thank God!" I ran over to the first truck. "The car," I said to the first guy who jumped down. "It's in the garage. Running."

"When did you notice it?"

The rest of the firefighters put on what looked like scuba gear.

"I got here about five thirty." It was only a few minutes since Bernice called 911, but it seemed like an eternity.

The fireman nodded at one of the already-equipped men, who sprinted to the front door, pulled a key out of a pocket, and unlocked a small silver box mounted on the wall next to the door.

"It's a key box," said Bernice, who was behind me again. "A lot of us have them so the fire department can get in if we need them."

A wailing siren as another truck rounded the corner. "I called 'Hazardous,'" said the fireman next to me, who was burly with close-cropped hair.

The guy who'd been inside ran out, took off his mask, and shouted, "No one inside, but the door to the garage is unlocked."

Several of the Hazardous guys, wearing masks and air tanks, ran into the house.

"What now?" I asked.

The fireman put a hand on my back and steered me gently into the street. "The Hazardous team will get into the garage, shut off the car, and open the garage door so the gas will dissipate. We need to stand back."

"But what about Charlie?"

"We'll do what we can." He pushed me farther into the street as the garage door rumbled open. Bernice stood with me, watching it go up. Hank stood near the fire truck, arms crossed. A few neighbors straggled into the street, awakened by the commotion.

A flurry of activity surrounded the car in the garage, then one firefighter turned to us. He shook his head. The burly fireman's shoulders slumped.

"I'm sorry," he said to me and Bernice and the small knot of neighbors.

"Oh, Charlie," Bernice said, a catch in her voice. "At least he's where he wants to be now." She must have seen a question on my face. "With Helen, his wife." Her eyes, which had been misty with unshed tears, seemed to focus in on me, and something clicked into place behind them. "Damn," she said. "I'm going to miss my flight."

CHAPTER 5

I squeezed my Bug into a parking spot on a downtown Phoenix street, jumped out, ran past the jail, into the office building, up the stairs, and into my uncle's office. Twenty minutes past nine. Twenty minutes late.

Uncle Bob didn't look up from his computer monitor. "I'm going to call *Guinness World Records*," he said. "See if they have a category for 'latest person in the world,' or maybe 'the only person in the world who can get up at four in the morning and still be late for work.'"

Then he looked up from the computer and saw my face. "Oh shit," he said, standing up. "Did you burn down something else?"

I walked over and buried my head in his chest. He hugged me awkwardly, then sat me down in the one comfy chair and brought me a cup of coffee. I told him the whole story.

"Olive, hon," he said. "People do what they want to do. You couldn't have stopped it. Besides, it sounds like this guy had a nice life, and now he was done with it. He didn't hurt anyone, and from what I hear, it's not a bad way to go." My uncle looked at me seriously. "And if you're going to be in this line of work," he swept an arm to include the office in all its PI glory, "you gotta get used to the not-so-nice side of life."

I nodded.

"Time to get to work, then."

He handed me several manila folders that had been sitting on his battered government-issue metal desk. The desk was enormous, so there wasn't room for another one in the office. When we both worked in the office at the same time I used a laptop on a wooden TV tray near the window overlooking the jail across the street.

I got up out of the chair and walked over to my "desk" underneath the noisy swamp cooler wedged into the window frame. The cooler's damp air against my skin made me shiver, and I thought again about Charlie, all alone in his car...

"Who dressed you this morning?" said Uncle Bob.

The tracksuit Marge had loaned me was baby blue velour with "Marvelous Marge" in rhinestones on the back.

"No wait, let me guess," he said. "Marge?"

I loved my uncle and the way he was trying to make things seem normal. So much so that I shook off my mood, picked up a rubber band off my desk, and shot it at him. It landed at his feet.

"Lame." Uncle Bob shook his head.

"Did you know that rubber bands keep longer when refrigerated?" I shot another one that hit the top of his shoe.

"Did you know that 41 percent of home fires start in the kitchen?" Uncle Bob loved trivia. He said he collected obscure facts so that he could use them as conversation starters, help him with his PI work. I think he was just naturally curious.

"Really?" I said, raising my voice over the swamp cooler's rattling. "You would think it'd be more. The kitchen seems like the most logical place for them to start."

"Yeah." He frowned. "I'd have you check into that, except that you need to get right to work because you're *late*. We've got three reports to get out today."

I sighed before I could stop myself, and before I could hide it from my uncle. This job drove me crazy. Not bad crazy, more like a-dog-with-a-treat-balanced-on-her-nose crazy. Like I could see the cool stuff but couldn't get to it until someone said, "Now, girl!"

"I told you PI work wasn't that exciting," my uncle said.

"That's because *you* do all the exciting stuff."

"Yep. Today I'm going to interview an accountant, do an internet search, and talk to a lawyer. Don't know if I'll be able to sleep tonight."

"I could do some of that for you. Or maybe follow someone, or take photos or something."

"So you're staying until five tonight? Working this weekend, maybe?" Uncle Bob leaned back in his chair.

"Actually I need to leave early. I've got a meeting about this house sitting gig." I hadn't had a chance to go over my duties with Bernice (who caught a later flight), so Marge was going to give me the lowdown. "I start tonight, so I won't be sleeping on your couch." I hoped this information would distract Uncle Bob and keep him from realizing I only answered half his question.

"And this weekend?"

Guess my info wasn't distracting enough. "I have tech rehearsals."

"Ah."

He didn't have to say more. Uncle Bob knew my heart belonged to the theater. He also believed this kept me from being serious about detective work. He was wrong there. I really wanted to be a detective. *And* an actor. Why should one preclude the other? "Just keep in mind, I would make a great detective. It's in the genes, you know."

A rubber band landed squarely in my lap. "Get to work, missy."

So I typed. For all my griping, I didn't really mind. Though I wasn't a big fan of writing reports, I was a big fan of my uncle. Bob was a great mix of laid-back and dedicated, like those Deadheads who used to follow the band everywhere. His daily uniform consisted of cargo shorts, a three-day beard and a Hawaiian shirt or t-shirt that said something like "Bigfoot doesn't believe in you, either." His friendliness and familiar way of talking to strangers belied a shrewd mind and a memory like a tape recorder. And below our easy banter was a devotion to me that nearly got him killed last fall. He was not only family, but what I thought family should be like. He even stood up for me to my parents, who were not what I thought family should be like.

Around one, there was a rap on the open office door.

"Hey, Hank." Uncle Bob smiled as he got up from his chair. "Glad you're here. I'm starving."

A man with a full head of silver hair, a silver mustache, and silver mirrored sunglasses stood stiffly in the doorway—the same way he stood at Charlie's death scene.

Bob ushered his friend into the office. "Hank, meet my niece Olive." Hank took off his sunglasses, revealing gray eyes that somehow reminded me of a wolf. I found the whole silver matchy-matchy effect kind of creepy. Cut it out, I told myself. It's not like he bought his mustache to match his eyes.

"We've met," I said. "Hank was the first guy who showed up at Charlie's." The guy who couldn't have cared less, I didn't say.

"I was on posse duty this morning," he said to Uncle Bob.

"Yeah, Bernice said something about a posse," I said. At the time, all I could think of were shootouts and vigilante justice. Hank looked like he could hold his own in either case.

"You've heard of volunteer fire departments?" said my uncle. "The posse is a sort of volunteer police department. Sunnydale's unincorporated, so the county enforces the law out there. They depend on the posse to keep an eye on things."

"I thought you were police," I said. Hank had certainly looked the part, with the official uniform and car and all.

"No. Anytime anything serious happens, we have to wait for the 'real' cops." Hank's lip curled, in sarcasm or bitterness, I couldn't tell.

With a sideways glance at me, Uncle Bob changed the subject. "You guys woulda met yesterday if Olive hadn't burned down her apartment." So this was the client who left early. With everything going on, I'd forgotten to ask my uncle what happened during the meeting.

"What were you doing in Sunnydale?" Hank asked me. Guess Uncle Bob's subject-changing hadn't worked.

"I'm going to be house sitting out there."

"Far away from work."

I really wanted to say "What's it to you?" but instead politely replied, "But it's close to Desert Magic Dinner Theater. I'm doing a show there."

"Thought you were learning to be a detective."

"I am." This guy was really pushing my buttons. "Acting and private investigation are complementary career paths."

Hank gave what passed for a laugh, put on his mirrored sunglasses, and turned to Uncle Bob. "Let me know how that works out."

CHAPTER 6

"What the hell was that all about?" I asked my uncle when he got back from his lunch with Creepy Silver Hank. "You're friends with that guy? Seriously?"

"Hank and I go back a long way. He just moved here from Spokane."

"But—"

Uncle Bob held up a hand. "Listen. Hank was recently *asked,*" he made finger quotes, "to retire after being on the force for almost twenty-five years. He's not himself right now. Give him a break, okay?"

"Whatever," I mumbled as I scooped up my bag and headed for the door. "You working on the house this weekend?"

"Yeah. In fact, Hank's coming over. Going to bring his skill saw."

I kissed him goodbye on his stubbly cheek. "Be careful," I said. I meant it.

I was on my way to Sunnydale when my phone buzzed. I picked up and put it on speakerphone, so I could keep my eye on traffic and see if the car ahead of me ever decided to go more than ten miles an hour.

"Hey, Ivy," said a male voice.

"Hi," I said, turning into the Sunnydale entrance. Distracted by driving, I hadn't paid enough attention to the voice to figure out who was calling, so I waited, hoping for a bit more info.

"Beautiful day, huh?"

"Gorgeous." It was. Ducklings paddled in the water hazard as I drove past a golf course. But who was I talking to? Everyone loves Arizona in the spring. I glanced down at my phone to see if I recognized the number.

Shit! I slammed on my brakes at the same time I heard the beep of the golf cart. Two men glared at me, their cart about a yard from my front bumper.

"Sorry," I yelled.

One of the men glowered so hard that the skin on his bald head wrinkled with the effort. "Next time, pay attention." He pointed at a yellow warning sign, like you see for pedestrians or even ducklings. This one had a graphic of a golf cart on it. I realized my car was stopped in a yellow striped lane, a golf cart crosswalk, as it were.

"Is this a bad time?" asked the voice on the phone, which was growing more familiar by the second.

"No, it's fine." Then to the golfers, "Sorry again. Have a nice day!"

I put the VW in gear, but slowed my pace.

"I know you have rehearsal every night—"

Jeremy. It was Jeremy!

"But what about days?" he asked, as I passed another golf cart, this one toodling down the road beside me. "I thought maybe we could get out of town, take a picnic or something."

"That'd be great," I gushed without thinking. Then my brain kicked in. It felt more like a kick to the stomach. "But..."

"But?"

Tech rehearsals would last all weekend. And I did mean all weekend. Us non-union actors were scheduled to be at the theater both days from nine a.m. until ten p.m. while the directors (including the music director and technical director) set and reset light and sound cues, made sure scenery moved in and out when it was supposed to, and basically made the magic of theater look seamless.

"But this weekend is a problem."

I expected Jeremy to hang up, but instead heard a smile in his voice when he said, "I should have said I have to work this weekend too. Didn't you say you sometimes had weekdays off? Any chance you could get away on Monday?"

"Monday. Yes, Monday!" I didn't have to rehearse until six o'clock and could do Uncle Bob's work some other time. I hoped. I also hoped my enthusiasm wasn't off-putting. My mom had always told me to play hard to get, but it just wasn't me.

We made plans for Jeremy to pick me up at Bernice's, and I hung up just as I turned into her cul-de-sac. Into Charlie Small's cul-de-sac. A cloud skittered across my sunny mood. Charlie's house looked sad and empty, as if it mourned the people who had lived and died there. I wondered about them, and about Charlie in particular. What had made him so desperately sad? I parked in Bernice's drive, rang the doorbell, and tried to shake off my funereal mood.

Marge opened the door. "Hey, that outfit looks better on you than it does on me," she said, looking me up and down. "I'd give it to you if it wasn't customized."

She ushered me into the house, enveloping me in a cloud of positive energy and Chanel No. 5. My mood lifted. Being around Marge just did that to me.

I followed her clicking heels down the hall. "Wow, Marge."

"Yeah, nice place, huh?"

I wasn't talking about the house. It was the first time I'd seen Marge in anything but a tracksuit. She may have been sixty-something (or seventy-something if the rumors were true), but she was dressed to the nines in a body-skimming red number and, I suspected, some heavy artillery undergarments that made her generous proportions look Rubenesque. Her skirt swished over red patent leather heels, and her mouth was painted crimson. Marge was a curvy gal, but she worked out and it showed: trim waist, defined arms, muscled legs. She also suntanned. The entire effect was of a great-looking mannequin made of leather.

That said, I was still in awe of Marge. She'd made it on Broadway, still filled the house for any show she chose to do, and turned acting into a good living. She was my role model (minus the tan).

"Sorry about transposing those house numbers, chickie." She led me into a white-carpeted, high-ceilinged living room. "Put you in the wrong place at the wrong time. Poor Charlie." She shook her head. "I called his daughter as soon as I heard. Thought she should hear the news from someone she knew."

"Don't worry. I just wish there was something I could've done," I said. "You look great. Big date?"

"Not really." She sat down on a peach loveseat and crossed her legs, jiggling one foot. "Arnie's taking me to some charity thing. Asked me to sing a song or two."

As a dancer in the show, I had to be at rehearsal tonight. Marge didn't. I wasn't sure if it was because she was the Mother Superior, who appeared in just a few scenes (because she was Equity, and they'd already gone over the allotted number of rehearsal hours), or because Arnie was the theater's producer (and Marge's boyfriend) and he wanted her at this charity thing.

"What songs are you going to sing?" I sat across from her in a matching loveseat. The room's furniture and art were all Southwest pastels—mint greens, soft blues, and peaches. A dark brown cuckoo clock stood out like a lone European tourist amongst the desert landscapes on the walls.

"'New York, New York,' 'There's No Business like Show Business,' and 'Everything's Coming up Roses.'"

I nodded. Marge's big brassy voice was made for those songs.

She must have read more on my face because she said, "Listen, kiddo. I know I'm miscast as the Mother Superior, even in this..." she frowned, "this...potato thing."

"Potato thing?"

"You know." She waved her hands in the air. "*Cabaret* and *The Sound of Music* mixed up. Like potatoes."

"I think you mean 'mash-up.'"

The Sound of Cabaret used the Germanic pre-World War II era settings of both the original musicals, and then combined the plots and characters. In the new show, feisty postulant Mary is sent to teach singing to the dancers at the seedy Vaughn Katt Club. Her secret agenda, of course, is to save their souls and return to the nunnery, but along the way she falls in love with the owner of the club, Captain Vaughn Katt. The captain is like a father to his ragtag troupe of dancers, and a hero: he is actually hiding them—all of them Jews—in plain sight by disguising them as performers. When the Nazis find out, the captain, Mary, and the Jewish dancers escape over the mountains in borrowed nuns' habits.

"*The Sound of Cabaret*," Marge shook her head. "When Arnie first asked me to do it, I laughed out loud. Thought it was a joke. But he was serious as a heart attack. See, the theater is in a bit of trouble, and—"

"Cuckoo!" sang the clock.

"Really, five thirty already?" Diamonds sparkled in the late afternoon sunlight as Marge turned her wrist to look at her watch. "I gotta run, sweetheart. Sorry I didn't get to give you the ten-cent tour. Just make sure to water the plants. Bernice's got 'em everywhere, even in the bathroom."

"Okay," I said, following her back down the entry hall.

"Keys to the house are on the kitchen table." Marge clicked to the door, where she picked up a gold clutch purse from a small hall table. "Instructions for the burglar alarm are in the drawer underneath the stereo."

"Burglar alarm?" I said.

"And there's a checklist for all the pool stuff there too."

"Yeah. About that—"

"Oh, I almost forgot," she said, turning to face me. "I told Charlie's daughter you were a PI. You're hired."

CHAPTER 7

"Okay, let's take a look at your PI license," Uncle Bob said. "Oh, that's right. You don't have one." It was Friday around noon, and I had told him the big news about our new case.

I stood in front of his big metal desk, like a child called before the teacher. "But—"

"Olive, you are not a private investigator."

"I didn't say I was."

"No?"

"I'm pretty sure I said I *worked* for a detective." I was pretty sure.

Uncle Bob shook his head. "Well, since you got us the case, *if* we got the case..."

I held my breath.

"You can work it."

"Woo hoo!" I did a little happy dance on the dirty brown carpet.

"This is serious, Olive." My uncle's voice sounded serious too, but his eyes sparkled at me. I think he was glad he had a protégée.

Marge had written down Charlie's daughter's name and phone number with a note saying I should call her at four thirty Eastern Standard Time. Uncle Bob helped me prep, pulling up the police report on the computer and spending the next twenty minutes going over the case with me. My case.

Then he said, "Gotta go. I got a lunch meeting with Pat Franko." The law firm of Franko, Hricko and Maionchi was my uncle's biggest client. "You think you got it?"

"Yep," I replied. "If Amy, Charlie Small's daughter, wants to hire us, I need to interview her to see why she wants to find out more about her dad's death, which will almost certainly be ruled suicide by carbon monoxide poisoning. If she's hiring us because she doesn't think he would kill himself, I need to find out more about Charlie, why she thinks it isn't suicide, and why she cares."

"Be careful with that last part," said Uncle Bob. "That's mostly for us and maybe Charlie's attorneys. Just want to make sure she's not giving us the runaround to get some extra cash from the estate."

"Got it."

My uncle waved goodbye as I moved my stuff over to his desk so I could spread out and prepare for my interview with Amy Small. I liked the idea of having hard copies for posterity, so I had printed out all the info and put it in a manila folder marked "Case #1: Charlie Small." I took out the police report. I had already read it, but I went over it again carefully.

I knew most of the facts: At 5:31 a.m. on Wednesday, April 5, Bernice Grete called 911 to report a car running in a neighbor's garage. Hank Snow of the Sunnydale posse responded at 5:35 and the fire department arrived at 5:37, at which time they gained access to the house via a key box. They determined that a Ford Taurus was idling in the closed-up garage and found Charlie, already dead, in the driver's seat of the still-running car. There were no signs to suggest anything other than suicide, and it was expected that the postmortem would confirm the cause of death as carbon monoxide poisoning.

At 1:25 Arizona time, I got out my notebook where I had questions prepared for Amy, who was vice president of sales for a nanotech company in Boston. I dialed her office at precisely four thirty Eastern Standard Time.

"Hello, Advanced Precision Technologies, can you hold please?" The woman answering the phone spoke rapidly, like she was announcing the legalities at the end of a radio commercial.

"Actually I was asked to call—"

"Thank you," said the rushed woman. After a click, a Muzak

version of the Beatles "Let It Be" filled the phone line. Soon I found myself humming along to the catchy tune. Without really thinking about it, I began singing along. "When I find myself in times of trouble, Mother Mary..."

The receptionist came back on the line and said, "You're holding for Mary? One moment please." Another click. "Cracklin' Rosie" was playing. I knew better than to sing along this time.

"Hi, this is Mary," said a weary sounding voice.

"Actually, I want to speak with Amy—"

"This is *Mary*."

"Yes, the receptionist made a mis—"

Another click and a bit more Muzak. I remembered hearing that "Cracklin' Rosie" was about drinking. I was seriously considering it.

I looked at the clock. It was now 4:40. After five more minutes, another woman picked up. "This is Amy Small," she said. "What can I do for you?"

"Hi Amy, I'm with Duda Detective Agency, and—"

Another click. No music this time, just a dial tone.

Dang. I told Uncle Bob, Bob Duda, that is, he needed another name for his business.

I dialed again. It was four forty-five.

"Hello, Advanced Precision Technologies," said the same receptionist. "Can you hold please?"

"No!" I said, too late. Muzak.

I hung up and redialed.

"Hello, this is—" said the rapid-fire receptionist.

"I have an appointment with Amy Small," I blurted out.

"Your name, please?"

"Olive Ziegwart." I knew better than to try Duda Detectives again.

"I'm sorry, I don't see that name."

"Robert Duda?"

"You'll have to call back on Monday and make an appoint—"

"Ivy Meadows?"

A pause. "Yes, Amy had you down for four thirty." Of course. Marge only knew me as Ivy. "Unfortunately, Ms. Small had another phone appointment at four forty-five. She's on the line with them now."

"I'll wait." My first stab at detecting was not going well.

After another five minutes, the Muzak was interrupted with, "Hi, this is Amy."

"Hi, Amy, this is Olive. I mean, I—"

"Hold on. From Doodoo Detectives?"

"Yes."

I heard a sigh and could just tell she was getting ready to hang up. "Dud-*a*!" I practically shouted into the phone. "Dud*a* Detective Agency. It's a Polish name that means one who plays the bagpipes badly."

"Is that supposed to make me think you're not a crank?"

"I'm not a crank, I'm a private investigator." Yeah, I was exaggerating again, but this was an extenuating circumstance. "I'm Ivy, the one Marge recommended?"

Silence.

"Hello?"

There was a noise I couldn't identify muffled by a hand or something over the mouthpiece of the phone.

"Ms. Small?"

I heard the sound clearly then. It was weeping. Oh.

Until that moment I hadn't really thought of Charlie Small as a real person, just my breakout detective job. I felt my face flush with shame.

"Ms. Small? I'm so sorry about your father."

"Thank you," she said, snuffling. "I'm sorry. It just hit me again. I can't believe he's gone."

"Why don't you tell me about him?" I asked as gently as I could.

From Amy, who wept off and on throughout the interview, I learned that Charlie Small was seventy-eight years old. He'd been married to his wife, Helen ("his bride," he always called her) for nearly fifty years until she died of lung cancer last fall. He'd been a loving father who sacrificed his dream of owning his own business in order to send Amy to MIT. He'd worked as an accountant with a midsized firm in Omaha until he retired at sixty-five and moved with Helen to Sunnydale.

"I only saw him once since Mom's funeral," said Amy quietly, all done with crying for now. "Just once. I was so busy with work and..." She trailed off.

"I'm sure he understood. I'm sure he was proud of the job you're doing." I don't know why I said those things, but I did feel sure, somehow.

"I hope so."

"And why..." I took a deep breath. "Why do you want us to look into his death?"

"My father would never kill himself."

I waited. I'd learned from Uncle Bob not to fill the silences. He taught me that the best information came from letting other people talk. This aspect of detecting did not come naturally to me.

"My father was a strong Christian. He believed that only God had the right to end a life. And now his pastor is threatening to not perform the memorial service because he doubts my dad's faith." Amy's voice grew hard as she imitated the pompous-sounding pastor. "He said that he 'rejected the lordship of Jesus Christ by taking his life into his own hands rather than submitting to God's will.' But my dad didn't. He wouldn't. He believed in releasing all his troubles to God." Amy began crying again. "My father's faith was the most important thing in his life, even more than my mom and me. Did you know his Bible was found on the seat next to him?"

"No, I didn't." That seemed like the type of thing you might want to read right before dying, but I didn't say anything. Instead I flipped through the police report to see if they mentioned the Bible.

"I should have been there for him," Amy said. "I should have watched over him. None of this would have happened if I'd taken care of him."

I stopped flipping. Those words, Amy's words, struck my chest and lay heavy in my heart.

That night after rehearsal, I stood outside Bernice's house and stared at the pool, its black water sliced by a jagged silver shard of moonlight.

"I should have been there for him, I should have watched over him. None of this would have happened if I'd taken care of him." Amy's words beat at my ribcage, matching the hammering of my heart. It wasn't just sympathy. I knew exactly how she felt.

CHAPTER 8

An unusual silence filled the theater. No music played. All action onstage had stopped. Marge, in full nun regalia, stood in the middle of the stage looking worried, her mouth a tight line, eyebrows drawn nearly together. Mary, the Captain, and all of us Vaughn Katt Club dancers were gathered around her in a half circle. We all looked worried too.

Truth be told, we were supposed to look that way. After all, we'd just found out that the Nazis had realized we dancers were Jewish. But the real reason behind all of the creased brows was Marge's lines, or rather, the lack of them.

"Marge?" called Levin, our director, from the house. "Can we try this again?" His voice sounded tight. Mine would too, if my star performer couldn't remember her lines less than a week before opening.

To make it worse, a new show like *The Sound of Cabaret* was a big gamble for the theater, which typically produced crowd-pleasers aimed at Sunnydale's retirees. "Arizona's Ethel Merman" was the main reason the show was selling.

She nodded at Levin.

"Okay," he said. "Let's start with the Captain's line."

Roger/Captain Vaughn Katt, a broad-shouldered guy with a full head of steel gray hair, nodded at Levin, then turned to Marge/Mother Superior. "We've got to get them out of here!"

"Could we hide them at the convent?" said Hailey, the petite blonde playing Mary.

The Captain shook his head. "First place they'd look."

"Besides," I said, "we don't look like we belong anywhere near a church."

Silence.

I silently willed Marge to remember her line.

Still silence.

I tried ESP.

No dice.

Finally from the wings, we heard a loud whisper. "That's it! We'll disguise you as nuns!"

"That's it!" Marge said to us dancers. "We'll disguise you as nuns!" A pause.

"But you have to promise me one thing," Bitsy whispered from where she watched in the wings. As Marge's understudy, she knew all her lines.

Marge shook her head slightly and glanced toward the sound of Bitsy's voice.

"But you have to promise me one thing," Bitsy said louder.

"But you have to promise me one thing," Marge said. On cue, the rehearsal pianist started playing behind her. All Marge's worry wrinkles fell away and she continued, "You'll change your ways. Once you put on the habit, you'll have to respect the idea behind it."

"But we're Jewish!" said another Vaughn Katt dancer. "If we were willing to convert, don't you think we'd have done it by now?"

"That's not what I mean," said Marge, the piano building behind her. That was one long intro. "I mean no more dancing in cabarets. I mean clean up your life. I mean..." The familiar tune from *The Sound of Music* swelled as Marge opened her mouth and sang the new words in her gigantic Ethel Merman voice, "CLIMB...OUT OF THE GUTTER..."

She had it now. The rest of the song poured out of her. One by one, we sank to our knees beside her, as choreographed. She launched into the final refrain: "CLIMB out of the gutter, wipe off your blush, Nazis are behind you. You'll make it...IF YOU...RUSH!"

She delivered the last line with enormous gusto. If the theater had timbers, they would have shook. Out of the corner of my eye, I saw Bitsy offstage, shaking her head. I wondered if she didn't like the lyric change or Marge's rendition, which was more madam than Mother. Or maybe just the fact that our headliner couldn't get through a scene without help.

We broke for lunch right afterward. As I opened the door to the greenroom, something whizzed past my head.

"Flying monkey alert!" yelled Zeb. A dishwasher who was always hanging out at the theater, Zeb was barely sixteen years old and the biggest science geek I'd ever met. He retrieved the small plastic monkey that had just missed my head and jotted something down in a small black notebook. "I'm finding out how far each monkey can go depending on how far I stretch the rubber band that launches them."

He had a green tinge below one eye.

"Where'd you get the shiner?" I asked.

"On the ropes in gym class. Some guy kicked me."

"Probably because Zeb shot him with a monkey," Candy whispered.

"I've never worked in a theater where the kitchen help fraternized with the talent," Bitsy said loudly, looking directly at Zeb.

"I've never worked in a theater where old ladies carried around spare underwear," said Candy.

Bitsy pursed her lip in a pout. Not sure if she was miffed because Candy mentioned her unmentionables or because she called her "old."

"Give the kid a break," Marge said to Bitsy. "Everybody needs a place to go."

I wondered what she meant, but was distracted by the wonderful aroma emanating from the small cardboard containers that lined a long table.

"It's Yummy Lunch," crowed Arnie, waving an unlit cigar at the boxes adorned with the logo of the nearby "Yummy Food" Chinese restaurant. His bald head and big glasses gleamed under the greenroom lights, which also spotlighted his enormous ears.

"Don't get it on your clothes," said Terri, the costume designer. "I'm not doing wash before opening night."

Though it wasn't the official dress rehearsal, a lot of the cast members (and all of the nuns) wore their costumes to get used to the way they moved in them. Bitsy, who daintily filled up her plate with mostly vegetables, looked like the poster nun for a convent, her round, strangely unlined face peeking out of her wimple and veil. Marge, who was headed back to her dressing room, looked like a drag queen's idea of a nun.

Arnie made a beeline after her, and I followed, not because I was nosy (though I was), but because I needed to get my cellphone out of my dressing room.

"Babe," he said, still waving his cigar. "You feelin' okay?"

"It's this damn costume," said Marge. "I can't hear a goddamn thing." She pushed back her veil to show the white wimple that covered her head and, yes, her ears.

"Terri!" shouted Arnie. The costumer was only a few feet away so he didn't need to shout, but he was a naturally loud guy. He and Marge made the perfect couple. "Can we do something here? So Marge can hear better?"

"Of course," said Terri. "I'm a genius."

"That's why we pay you the big bucks," Arnie said, slapping her on the back.

The three of them went into Marge's dressing room. I grabbed my phone and went back to the greenroom, where I filled a paper plate with an assortment of noodle dishes and made my way toward the long folding table where the rest of the cast sat. I plopped down next to Candy, my paper plate dangerously full of greasy Chinese food.

"Keep away from my costume," she said, scooting away from me. "No noodles for this nun." Then her eyes lit up. "Hey, was Matt ever Catholic?"

"Not sure. Why?"

"I was thinking of taking the costume home with me, maybe play 'naughty nun.'"

"Too much information." I clapped my hands over my ears. "La la la la la..."

Zeb bounded up to us like a horny Labrador. "How do you play naughty nun?" The only thing that interested Zeb more than science was sex. "Can you teach me?" he asked Candy, the hormones practically zinging their way out of the few hairs he proudly displayed on his chin.

"No, but I might hit you with a ruler." Zeb's eyes gleamed.

"Don't even go there," Candy warned. He grinned and went back to the food table, where he grabbed a handful of fortune cookies.

Bitsy harrumphed and rolled her eyes.

"You know, now that I think of it," Candy smiled sweetly at her across the table, "my granny did carry a spare pair of undies with her. Not sure if it was an incontinence thing or just because she was a woman of loose morals."

Bitsy opened her mouth, then shut it again, like a goldfish. Candy gave her a "butter wouldn't melt in my mouth" smile.

I took a big slurpy bite of noodles and looked at the time on my cellphone—7:12 p.m. here in Arizona meant it was 3:12 p.m. (the next day) in New Zealand. I dialed Bernice's number.

"Gotta do some work on this case," I said to Candy.

Roger sat down next to me. "Case?"

I scooted over, ostensibly to give Roger room, but really because he was one of those guys who stood or sat just a little too close to any female under thirty.

"She's investigating some suicide." Candy took a bite of Kung Pao chicken.

"I didn't know Ivy was an investigator," Bitsy said.

"She's an investigator trying to make a long-distance call in spite of her noisy castmates," I said. I tried to say it with authority, but was stymied by a mouthful of noodles.

"Swallow, hon," Candy said, just as Bernice picked up.

"Hello? Ivy? Is everything okay?"

"Yeah, hi, Bernice. Don't worry, everything's fine. I was just wondering: Did you hear or see anything the morning of Charlie's death?"

"Just you. And the landscaper, of course."

"The landscaper?" I asked.

"Yeah. Charlie must have had a yard guy. They work real early, you know."

They did. For half the year (May through October), any outdoor work in the Valley had to be done before the day got beastly hot. I guessed landscapers kept to this schedule the rest of the year for continuity's sake.

"I mostly heard him. Had one of those annoying leaf blowers."

"Did you get a good look at him? Or her?"

"Not really. Whoever it was wore one of those jumpsuit things."

"Jumpsuit?"

"Probably a coverall," said Candy, who'd been listening along with the rest of the table.

"And a hat. Maybe even glasses. I really can't remember."

"No, that's great information, Bernice. Thanks. Bye now."

"Ta da." Arnie re-entered the greenroom with Marge and Terri in tow. "Terri, costumer extraordinaire, has saved the day. Show 'em, babe."

Marge pulled back her black veil. Her white wimple still surrounded her head and neck, but her ears stuck out of the holes Terri had cut on either side of the wimple. "The better to hear you with, my dear," Marge said.

"Fantastic, right?" said Arnie. "Now she can hear just fine. Take a bow, Terri."

Terri bowed, to the accompaniment of applause from Arnie and the cast. I wondered if anyone else noticed that Marge was not clapping.

CHAPTER 9

"Can you let them know I'll be a little late?" I asked Candy via cellphone the next morning. "My car caught on fire."

"Again?"

I have to confess. When Uncle Bob asked if I'd burned down something else, there was a bit of seriousness to his question. This past winter I'd traded in my little green Aspire for a yellow vintage VW Bug. No one had told me it caught on fire at the most inconvenient times. My mechanic said it was probably something to do with fuel escaping into the engine compartment, but he couldn't tell for sure. He didn't think it was a life-threatening problem, and I couldn't afford to have the engine taken apart to confirm his diagnosis, so I kept an eye out for any telltale smoke.

I put my fire extinguisher down on the asphalt of the parking lot I'd pulled into and peered through the stinky black smoke at the engine, which was at the rear of the car. "Nothing looks too melted." I'd learned to repair most damage by myself, with spare belts I kept on hand and...

"Got your duct tape?" asked Candy.

"Always." I kept a roll in my duffle bag, so I could wrap any hoses that looked melted. Plus it was great for repairing flip-flops and making strapless bras. "Need to let the engine cool down a bit, but I should be there in about fifteen minutes."

And I thought that was going to be the low point of my day.

"Hold it. Stop!" Levin shouted from his seat in the audience.

We had just finished my big duet, "Sixteen Going on Twenty-

One," where Wolf, a regular customer from the cabaret, tries to convince my character, Teasel, a yet-to-be-deflowered Vaughn Katt Club dancer, that she is old enough to, well, you know. It was our first rehearsal with the orchestra and I was onstage with Timothy, who played Wolf. We were working on sound levels, just standing in place singing. Or in my case, making noises like a barfing cat.

"Ivy," Levin said. "What's the problem?"

"I don't know," I said miserably.

But I did know. Sitting in the audience behind Levin, our director, were the Friends of the Theater. Arnie had invited the group of donors to see what a real technical rehearsal was like. Real technical rehearsals were boring, full of stops and starts as lights and microphones were adjusted. So boring in fact, that a few Friends were sleeping. That didn't matter. What did matter is that there were more than five of them.

"Let's take it again from the top," Levin said.

"Levin," Keith, the musical director, shouted from the pit, "can we move on? We only have the orchestra until noon."

Now Levin made a noise like a barfing cat. "O...kay."

Keith flipped the pages of his score. "So on to 'Don't Tell Mother.'" Mary sang this particular song to a group of nuns who had discovered her in a rather immodest dancer costume.

Saved by an overly long rehearsal. I quickly slipped offstage and into my dressing room.

The frustrating thing was, I actually had a nice voice. Not great, but pretty. Kind of like the rest of me. I thought of myself as good-looking but not a striking beauty, except for my legs, which were long and shapely. Whenever I'd been cast in a musical before, it was for my dancing ability—and my legs—not my singing.

"Hon," said Candy MoonPie's voice from outside the door. "Can I come in?"

"Of course," I said. It was her dressing room too, after all.

She came in, dressed in her nun costume, and sat down next to me at the dressing room counter. "Tell me, my child," she said in a solemn voice, "was it the Old FOTs?"

I nodded. Everyone knew Candy's name for the Friends of the Theater.

"Is there anything I can do?" asked Candy

"Kill me now?" I was only half-joking. I'd been lucky so far in my fledgling acting career. Decent reviews, good word-of-mouth. And now I was poised to torpedo my own boat. I couldn't sing in public. More than five people in the audience put me over the edge and my sense of pitch somewhere far, far away.

"Maybe if you concentrate on the times you sounded good? You've been great in rehearsal."

I had been—there were never more than a few people in the audience. I nailed the audition too, since Levin and Keith were the only ones listening. I did so well, in fact, that I really thought I was over my little problem. That's what I got for being cocky.

"Hey, dolls." Arnie walked through our open dressing room door flourishing a white plastic contraption that looked a bit like a fancy pair of pliers. "Look what I just got in the mail." He wore a blue sports coat with brass buttons, presumably for the FOTs, and talked through the unlit cigar that nearly always hung from his mouth.

"Let me guess." Candy squeezed the handle of the doohickey, which pressed down a lever. "A real big garlic press?"

Arnie shook his head happily. He looked like a bald five-year-old with a new toy.

"A mousetrap?" I asked. That was more of a hint than a real guess. We'd seen a few of the little critters running around in the dressing room area late at night.

"An EZ Cracker!" said Arnie, the words bursting out of him like Bazooka bubbles. "Watch this!" He grabbed a ceramic coffee cup from a shelf (coffee and its accouterments are essential theater tools) and cleared a spot on the dressing room counter. He carefully took an egg from his jacket pocket.

"You been carryin' eggs around all day?" asked Candy.

Arnie shushed her and set down his new prize. "You watchin', ladies?" He placed an egg in the cracker, humming as he worked.

He squeezed the handle, the eggshell split perfectly in half, and the egg plopped in the coffee cup. "Ta da! A perfectly cracked egg. No shell, no mess! Neat, huh?" Arnie grinned, big ears glowing pink in the dressing room lights.

"Very cool," I said.

"You ever want to see the latest and greatest gizmo, you just ask me," said Arnie. "I got 'em all." He picked up the cup with the egg in it, put the EZ Cracker under his arm, and chucked me on the shoulder. "Gotta go. Do me proud, ladies." He waved his cigar at us as he left. I got up and closed the dressing room door.

"Wonder what he's gonna do with that egg?" said Candy. "I didn't have breakfast."

"What was that all about?" I asked.

"I think he was tryin' to cheer you up. Either that or make an omelet."

Of course. Five days 'til opening and two of his cast members sucked. Poor Arnie.

Another knock on the door. "Hello?" Roger, a.k.a. Captain Vaughn Katt, poked his head in. "You okay, Ivy?"

Wow. Had I really been that bad?

"I'm gonna follow up on that egg," said Candy. "I could microwave it, you know." She winked at me in the mirror. I'm sure Roger saw her. I sighed. Candy was always trying to fix me up. She loved double dates. I'd told her about my lunch date with Jeremy and the upcoming picnic, but it must not have sunk in.

Roger, though a nice guy, was not my cup of tea. Too old to begin with (probably in his early sixties) and too...something. He worked out a lot and often walked around the greenroom shirtless, while the older actresses who played nuns batted their eyes at him and he pretended not to notice.

"Just checking in," he said, sitting down next to me with a fatherly smile. A big lump of self-reproach swelled up in my throat and I swallowed it, along with all of my unkind thoughts. "Seems like there's something bothering you," said Roger, watching my eyes in the mirror.

There was more than one thing.

Number One: I couldn't sing in public.

Number Two: I was way behind on my detective work. Except for the call to Bernice, I hadn't done anything.

Number Three: I hadn't figured out what to do about Bernice's pool.

I picked Number Three. "I'm worried about my house sitting gig."

"Really?"

"I'm supposed to take care of the pool, and...I have a phobia about water." This was also true, though again, not the entire truth.

"Easily remedied," said Roger. "How often do you need to address pool maintenance?"

"Bernice's instructions said twice a week."

"Perfect. Twice a week, I'll take care of your pool chores in exchange for a home-cooked meal."

"Oh! Well..."

"I'm a horrible cook," he said, smiling over my head in the mirror. "I'm sure whatever you make will be better than the frozen dinner I usually eat."

Oh, what the heck. "Great." I stood to face him and held out my hand to seal the deal.

"Shall we start tomorrow? I could come over during the day."

"Can't. I have a—" I was about to say "date" when Roger interrupted.

"Tuesday then." He took my hand, but instead of shaking it, he kissed it. "Until then," he said.

Uh-oh.

CHAPTER 10

The next morning, I sat in the cab of Jeremy's pickup, trying hard to breathe normally. A careful driver, Jeremy was watching the twisting two-lane road, so he didn't notice my discomfort. I turned to face the open window, just in case he looked at me. Warm air caressed my skin. Saguaro cactus flashed by, fat with water from the recent spring rains. Brittlebush bloomed yellow and a few hedgehog cactus boasted fuchsia flowers. It was a beautiful spring day. A gorgeous guy sat next to me. And I was going to ruin it all.

As we drove around a curve, a sign said, "Lake Pleasant—five miles."

"Almost there!" said Jeremy, grinning. He wore a t-shirt from Four Peaks Brewery, a pair of board shorts, and a smile that made my insides turn to goo.

A flash of blue appeared around a curve.

"Yes!" Jeremy said.

There is something about water in the desert. Maybe it's the unexpectedness of it. Maybe it's the reflection of blue sky amongst so much dusty brown. Maybe it's something more primal, the lifesaving oasis. Whatever it is, even I can't deny the nearly magical effect it has.

But there was no way this was going to work. I was trying. I really was. I had smiled when Jeremy picked me up, Jet Skis in tow behind his truck. I made happy noises when he told me about borrowing them from one of his fireman buddies. And when we arrived at Lake Pleasant, I even jumped out of the truck and waved

Jeremy down the boat ramp, so he could back the trailer into the lake.

But then I stopped, my feet glued to dry land.

"Okay!" Jeremy yelled from the cab of his truck. "Now just wade out and unhook one of the Jet Skis from the trailer."

I managed to get pretty close, maybe five feet. Then I froze.

"It's easy," Jeremy shouted. "You just wade in and...hey, are you hyperventilating?"

I was. I was bent over, hands on my knees. I hoped he couldn't tell, but then again, he was a trained professional. And a kind one. He hopped out of the truck and ran over to me. "Here." He handed me a crumpled paper bag. "Breathe into this."

After I calmed down, Jeremy helped me back into the truck and we found a picnic spot on a deserted stretch of rocky beach. A few minutes later, we were settled on a Mexican blanket a nice safe distance from the water. I could just barely hear the waves lapping against the shore.

I hadn't said much since my little freak-out. I'd blown it. I was sure I seemed hysterical, maybe reminded Jeremy of some victim. Not exactly how I wanted him to think of me.

Jeremy didn't seem upset, just plopped down on the blanket next to me. "Hi," he said.

"Hi."

He smiled back, but didn't offer any more conversation.

"Do you always carry paper bags with you?" It was the only thing I could think to say.

"Not only am I a firefighter, but I used to be a Boy Scout. I'm always prepared. Paper bags, first aid kits, and," he sat up and rummaged in the cooler behind us, "beer."

He handed me a cold bottle of Kilt Lifter ale. My mind presented me with a brief flash of Jeremy's strong tanned legs in a kilt. I thought about lifting that kilt and smiled.

"Beer makes me happy too," Jeremy said, popping the top on mine and grabbing a bottle for himself. He settled himself against the cooler. "So you're scared of water?"

Wow. Way to head right into the issue. He sure wasn't from my family.

I took a big swig of cold beer and nodded.

"Just big bodies of water?"

I shook my head. "I don't even like baths."

"Really?"

"People have drowned in the bathtub, you know," I said, more sharply than intended.

"I know." Jeremy's eyes softened and I realized that he had seen a lot of things I didn't want to imagine.

"It's a long story."

Jeremy eyes, still soft, met mine. "We have all afternoon."

So I told him. About long ago when we lived in Spokane, Washington. About one winter when I was eleven and didn't want to take my little brother Cody with me when I went ice-skating with my girlfriends. About ignoring him after my mother insisted he go with us to the park. About the crack of the ice and the sight of Cody's yellow hair floating beneath the surface of the pond.

"He died?"

"No. He lives in Phoenix now too. In a group home."

"Oh." Jeremy was probably familiar enough with bodily functions to understand that the icy cold pond water had kept my brother alive. And that the lack of oxygen had damaged Cody's brain.

"It's a nice place." I said it partly to get the conversation back on a happier note, and partly because the group home was a nice place, a bungalow that housed several guys with cognitive disabilities and was staffed with some really good people, especially Matt, Candy's boyfriend. Matt had a calm presence, a great sense of humor, and a real love for the guys, like a wise older cousin.

Jeremy put down his beer. "Ivy, I'm so sorry."

"About Cody?" I said, too quickly, too harshly. I did not want pity for me or my brother.

"That the accident happened." He put an arm around me.

"Thanks." Maybe he could understand.

I leaned my head on his shoulder and watched the sun fracture into skittering diamonds on the surface of Lake Pleasant. Jeremy shifted next to me, and I turned my head to see those golden eyes watching me. He bent his head toward mine and...

A stinky spray of water hit us smack in the kissers.

"What the hell!"

Jeremy jumped up. A gray-speckled dog shook itself in front of us, dirty water flying everywhere. I ducked my head into my knees to get my face out of range of the doggy-smelling shower.

The dog, some sort of wiry-haired hound mix, stopped shaking and stared at us, panting, his tongue lolling out the side of his mouth.

"Good dog," I said. "Go away now, so I can kiss Jeremy."

Jeremy laughed and turned to me, so he didn't see the dog run between his legs until he wound up ass-over-teakettle on the pebbly sand. "Hey!" He stood up, reaching a cautious hand toward the mutt. "What'd you do that for?"

I swear the dog looked like he wanted to reply. Instead, he bumped Jeremy with his nose, wet sandy whiskers trembling.

Putting my empty beer bottle down, I scanned the shoreline. "Where's his owner?" I didn't see anything except a small aluminum boat sitting at the edge of the lake, maybe a quarter mile away.

"No collar," said Jeremy. "Maybe he's a stray."

The dog whimpered and bumped him again. "Are you hungry, boy?" Jeremy stood up and stepped toward the cooler when the dog nipped his ankle. "Hey!"

The dog ran a few feet toward the boat, then stopped and looked back at us. When we didn't move, he ran back. It looked like he was going for my ankle this time, but I jumped up before he could get me.

"Ha!" I said. "I'm smarter than you, dog."

The dog tilted his head, looked back at the boat, and then at me again. I reassessed his intelligence. He seemed pretty smart, like those animal heroes in the movies.

"Want to take a walk?" I said to Jeremy, gesturing toward the boat.

"Nah." He brushed the sand off his shorts. "But I'll race you!" He took off like a shot. The dog caught up and then passed him, zooming up ahead. I, no runner, took off at a decent trot, and enjoyed the view from behind, if you know what I mean. Jeremy turned around once, jogging backward to make sure I was following. I could see him smile. I waved and kept trotting, hoping he didn't prefer athletic women.

The dog got to the boat first and clambered in. Jeremy approached, then turned, and waved his arms at me. "Call 911!"

Wow, it really was like those animal hero movies. I grabbed my cellphone out of my back pocket and dialed. Nothing. I looked at the signal strength.

"No reception!" I shouted.

I couldn't be sure Jeremy heard me, because he had disappeared into the boat, which was grounded on the rocky beach. I ran the rest of the way.

"Couldn't call," I panted, when I was near enough that he could hear me. I stood a few feet from the bow of the boat and a safe distance from the lake.

"It's okay," said Jeremy, kneeling in the boat. "I think he's coming around."

"He" was a guy in his sixties with a mustache, closed eyes, and a sunburnt face that looked a little familiar. He wore jeans and a Western shirt and lay in the bottom of the boat amidst fishing gear, bags of Cheetos, and Coke and Budweiser cans. The dog, also in the boat, seemed satisfied that help had arrived and busied himself trying to open a pack of Twinkies.

An alarm sounded faintly in my mind, caused by something more than the water or even the unconscious man. "Is he asleep?" I whispered.

"No need to whisper. We want him to wake up. Sir," Jeremy addressed the man in the boat in a loud voice. "Can you hear me?"

The man just breathed noisily.

My mental alarm chimed louder. "Can't we just let him sleep it off?"

"Not out here," said Jeremy. "Between sun exposure and dehydration, he could be in trouble. Sir?" he said again, loudly.

The man's eyes twitched open. They were silvery gray and matched his mustache.

"Hank!" I said.

Hank blinked a few times at me, his bloodshot eyes trying to focus.

Though my alarm was ringing full blast, I put on a friendly face. "It's Olive. I didn't recognize you out of uniform."

Hank didn't look like he recognized me at all. "He knows my uncle," I said to Jeremy, loud enough so Hank could hear too.

The mutt came over and licked his face. Hank shook his head and sat up.

"That's a good dog you have there, sir," said Jeremy. "He came and told us you were in trouble."

Hank patted the mutt on its wiry head. "Yeah," he said slowly.

"You okay?" I said.

He looked around. "Must have fallen asleep."

"Do you have any water with you?" asked Jeremy.

Hank gestured behind him. "Whole lake full."

"Drinking water, sir?" Jeremy asked. I was beginning to get an idea of what he dealt with on a regular basis.

Hank fumbled around the bottom of the boat and came up with an old-fashioned metal canteen.

"Why don't you sip some water slowly," said Jeremy.

Hank took a long drink from the canteen instead. "I'm fine," he said. "Must've run aground when I fell asleep."

"Sir..."

Hank reached for a Vietnam Vet cap that lay in a puddle of water in the bottom of the boat. He tugged it on and leveled a stare at Jeremy. "Now if you'll get out of my boat, I'll be off."

This was Uncle Bob's friend?

"Sure thing." Jeremy climbed out of the boat. "Just making

sure everything's okay." He held his hands up—no foul. "Your dog seemed worried."

Hank looked at the mutt for a long second. "He's a good dog." Hank got out of the boat, pushed it back into the lake and jumped in. He jerked the cord to the outboard motor and it roared to life. The dog ran to the bow and stood facing front, like a canine figurehead. Without looking at us again, Hank took off, the wake foaming white behind him.

The alarm in my head quieted as I watched Hank's boat grow smaller and smaller. Something bothered me about him, something more than just his incredible rudeness. "I know you're used to dealing with things like that," I said to Jeremy, "but didn't that seem a bit weird?"

"Did you say you didn't recognize him out of uniform?" Jeremy's eyes kept track of the boat as it got smaller and smaller.

"Yeah, he's on the Sunnydale posse."

"Then yeah, it does seem weird," Jeremy said. "'Cause I could swear he was high."

CHAPTER 11

I strolled into the theater after my day at the lake with Jeremy. My shoulders felt sunburned, my head a bit buzzed from the Kilt Lifter, and my stomach aflutter with the promise of romance. Somehow it all added up to a glorious feeling.

As I walked through the greenroom, I blew a kiss to Arnie, tugged on Candy's veil, and even smiled at Zeb, who was writing in his black notebook, presumably making notes about a bubbling concoction that sat in front of him. He looked around to see who my smile was aimed at, realized it was him, and preened a bit, stroking the few hairs on his chin. My cellphone rang just as I opened the dressing room door—my uncle's ringtone.

"And how are you this fine evening?" I plopped down in my chair.

"Someone's in a good mood," said Uncle Bob. He sounded like he was in a pretty good mood himself.

"Why yes, I am," I said. "I just spent the day at the lake." I put my cellphone on speaker and pulled my makeup case across the counter toward me.

"At the lake?" My uncle was well aware of my water phobia. In fact, he'd been after me to go to counseling for a while.

"I was in the company of a very fit fireman." And because I had learned to always tell my uncle the truth, I added, "And I didn't go near the water. Oh! I saw Hank."

"Out fishing?"

"I think so," I said carefully, wishing I hadn't brought up the subject. "We didn't talk much." I began putting on my makeup.

"Hank's a man of few words," Uncle Bob said.

And a few too many beers. Or something else if Jeremy was right.

"So," said my uncle, "I'm still knee deep in building materials, but I wanted to see how the investigation was going."

"Good." Foundation finished, I moved on to eye makeup. "I had a nice conversation with Charlie's daughter on Friday."

My uncle didn't say anything. I figured he was doing that "wait and get them to say something" ploy, so I kept silent. Finally he said, "And?"

"And I talked to Bernice and made a few other calls over the weekend." I had made a few other calls. No one had answered, but I did call.

"And?" my uncle said again.

Uh-oh. "And?"

"The neighborhood investigation?"

Phew. Though Uncle Bob and I hadn't talked since Friday, he'd left me a voicemail asking me to canvas Charlie Small's neighborhood, just to see if anyone saw anything fishy around the time he died. I had it all planned out.

"Yep," I said. "Going to do that tomorrow."

Another silence. Again I waited, though I also took the time to put the finishing touches on my eye makeup.

"Olive," said my uncle, who did not sound in a good mood any longer. "What's the first rule of a criminal investigation?"

"Do it as quickly after the incident as possible."

"And Charlie died when?"

"But this isn't a criminal investigation."

"What sort of investigation is it?"

"We're just trying to make sure that Charlie really did commit suicide."

"And if he didn't?'

"Then it was either an accident, or..." I stopped, having dug my own hole.

"Go on."

"Or foul play, which would mean this is a criminal investigation," I said, feeling like a seven-year-old who forgot to feed the fish again. "But come on. Who's going to murder a seventy-eight-year-old by putting him in his car with the engine running?"

"Olive."

"I was at the theater all weekend. All weekend from morning to late night." And with Jeremy today, I thought, swallowing a lump of guilt.

A noise on the other end of the line sounded a bit like teeth grinding. "Olive, do you want to be an actor or a detective?"

Aye, there's the rub. I really did want to be a detective. I also desperately wanted to be an actor, had ever since I was little. I felt like I was in love with two demanding men at the same time.

"Can't I be both?" I asked.

"I don't know. Can you?"

I could. I wanted both things so badly that I would find a way. "I can. I'm sorry. I'll get to it first thing tomorrow. I'll even get up early."

Another silence.

"Really. I'll hit the street by eight o'clock at the latest."

"I should be in the office tomorrow afternoon," said Uncle Bob. "Call me then and fill me in." He hung up without saying goodbye.

CHAPTER 12

My sunburned shoulders now felt hot and tender, my head a bit achy, and my stomach aflutter with something other than romance. There were few people in the world I wanted to please as much as my uncle. I just hadn't thought things all the way through, both in terms of what I needed to do for this investigation, and what it might mean to be a PI while pursuing an acting career. This not-thinking-things-through was an unfortunate habit of mine, as evidenced by my burned-up apartment.

But right now it was dress rehearsal, and I had to buck up and get into costume. I pulled on my first Teasel outfit, a tarted-up sailor suit with a pleated micro-miniskirt and a low-cut top that tied at the midriff.

I stared at myself in the mirror. The ridiculous and somehow sexy costume flattered me, as long I kept doing my morning sit-ups. But my face...Sixteen years old seemed a stretch. I figured that the distance onstage helped, but just in case, I put extra blush on the apples of my cheeks, hoping for a youthful glow.

Candy opened the door and glanced at me in the mirror. "You got a fever, hon?" She laid a hand on my forehead.

I wiped off the extra blush with a Kleenex. Strike that idea. "Just worried about looking young enough onstage," I said.

"That's the magic of theater," said Candy. "You say you're sixteen, the audience believes it."

I noticed that she didn't actually say anything about me looking young enough.

"I mean look at Liesl in *The Sound of Music* movie." Candy

whizzed around the dressing room, grabbing her nun costume and veil off a hanger. "She looked twenty-five, but we believed she was sixteen."

"Actually it sounds like you thought she was twenty-five."

"Huh." That stopped her. "Yeah. I guess so."

Oh well. I decided to believe in the magic of theater and finished getting ready. Once done, I took my place in the greenroom to wait with the rest of the cast and eat the homemade cookies supplied by one of the nun actresses.

"Hey," Arnie said to me. "What happened to that big smile we saw earlier?"

"She's worried about looking sixteen," said Candy.

"Oh, dear," said Bitsy. She didn't say anything else, but she did look pointedly at the calorie-laden cookie in my hand. I took a big bite, just for spite and because it was delicious.

"No," I said, as much to myself as anyone else. "I'm mad at myself. I need to do a neighborhood investigation and I really should have done it earlier."

"Neighborhood investigation?" said Bitsy.

"Yeah, for that case I'm on. I need to go interview Charlie's neighbors."

"I told Amy about Ivy. Got her the job." Marge poured a cup of coffee from the thermos she always brought.

"Amy?" Arnie said. "Are we talking about Charlie Small?"

"Yeah, I'm investigating his death." I heard several intakes of breath. A clue? Nah. These were naturally dramatic folks.

"I thought he committed suicide," Arnie said.

"You knew him?" I said.

"Sure." Arnie helped himself to a cookie. "He was on our board."

"And in my karaoke club," said Bitsy.

"Everybody knew Charlie," said Marge. "He was a sweetie."

"So what's a neighborhood investigation?" said Roger.

"Oh, I interview the neighbors, scout the area for clues, that sort of thing."

"Do you want to use my spy sunglasses?" asked Arnie. "They look like regular sunglasses, but they have little mirrors inside them so you can see behind you."

"I'd love to." I couldn't figure out how they'd help me interview neighbors, but I did want to try them out.

"You need other spy stuff, you just ask," said Arnie. "I got everything."

Before I could even ask why, Marge said, "Him and his gadgets. Nearly cost us our vacation last winter."

"Airports are so big," Arnie brushed the cookie crumbs off his hands, "that I take a cane in case my hip starts bugging me. Last time I took the wrong cane."

"It has a sword hidden inside," said Marge. "They thought we were pirates."

The speaker in the greenroom crackled to life: "Places for top of the show." The nuns scuttled off for their first scene. I did too. I wanted to watch from the wings to see how the show was shaping up—and, I admit, to see if Marge remembered her lines.

The lights came up on Bitsy and three other nuns in a huddle onstage. "It's a disgrace!" said Bitsy.

"A temptation for our young people," agreed a tall nun.

"Is the music any good?" asked a short one.

Marge/the Mother Superior entered with the elfin-looking Hailey/Mary.

"What is it you're discussing?" Marge asked the gaggle of nuns. Phew, first line down. A tune that sounded a lot like *The Sound of Music*'s "Problem Like Maria" began to play, and Bitsy opened her mouth and sang, "How do you solve a problem like a nightclub?"

"Can't we get the law to shut it down?" sang the tall nun.

Marge/Mother Superior shook her head.

"Who do you send to shutter up a nightclub?" sang the short sister.

Bitsy and the two nuns sang in turn:

"A politician?"

"A monsignor?"

"A clown?"

"Many a time I've thought we could save souls there," sang a chubby nun.

"Many a time *I've* thought they're damned to hell," Bitsy replied in song.

"It's so full of sin," sang the tall nun.

"And lots and lots of men," sang the short one, with a wistful smile.

"What can we do to break the nightclub's spell?" sang the chubby one.

All of them chimed in, "Oh, how do you solve a problem like a nightclub?"

"WHAT DO THEY WANT THAT WE HAVE GOT TO SELL?" Right on cue, Marge sang perfectly. Loudly, brashly, but perfectly.

I sang beautifully during my scene too (sure, there was no one in the audience, but still). In fact, the whole dress rehearsal went smoothly, except for one of my changes in the wings, where my dresser somehow guided my arm through the neck hole of my dress.

I was just leaving the theater when Hailey slid up to me. "Walk me to my car?" she said.

"Sure." I couldn't imagine why. This part of town was not scary at night. Most people went to bed around eight.

The cool night was quiet, the silence broken only by a jet far overhead. "You're house sitting for Marge's neighbor, right?" Hailey's pale blonde hair shone silver under the parking lot lights.

I nodded.

"So do you see Marge outside of the theater?"

"Not really."

Hailey tugged on a lock of her hair, a gesture I recognized from fraught rehearsals.

"I guess I could," I said. "Why?"

She leaned closer to me. "I think someone should keep an eye on her. I'm really worried about her. I think she's...not okay."

Marge had looked as fit as ever.

"You mean her mind? But she did really well tonight."

Hailey shook her head. "I fed her lines all night. She couldn't remember anything."

CHAPTER 13

I knocked on the carved wooden door, the first door in my neighborhood investigation. I was going to be a great detective. I just knew it.

The house was unlike any other I had seen in Sunnydale—stucco and a tile roof, yes, but newer, two-story, and oversized, barely squeezed onto the lot. As I was wondering how the neighbors felt about this monstrosity looming over them, the door opened. The blonde woman who stood there wore yoga pants and a cropped top that showed her pierced belly button. She was beautiful, and way too young to be living in fifty-five-plus Sunnydale. The homeowner's daughter, maybe? Granddaughter? I decided to figure that out later. Instead I said, "I'm from Duda Detective Ag—"

Slam. Dang Uncle Bob Duda's pride. I knocked again. The woman opened the door a crack. "Let me explain. I'm Ivy Meadows—"

It's pretty hard to slam a door that's open just a few inches, but somehow she managed it.

I took a deep breath and knocked again. No answer, not that I expected one. I took one of Uncle Bob's business cards out of my messenger bag and wrote my name on it above Uncle Bob's. I drew an arrow indicating that the card should be turned over. On the back I wrote, "re: Charlie Small's death." I stuck my business card in the crack between the door and the frame, and walked down the concrete path that cut through the gravel lawn. The tiny rocks reflected the heat, even on a spring morning. No wonder half of Sunnydale took off for the summer. Their lawns would bake them.

Nobody was home at the next several houses I tried. It was eight thirty on a beautiful spring morning. Most people hadn't gone north for the summer yet. Where was everyone?

I decided to widen my search. I got in my Bug and drove around until I found the cul-de-sac that backed up against Charlie and Bernice's cul-de-sac. Though it took several minutes to drive the winding streets, the houses' backyards on this street faced the ones on Charlie and Bernice's. Only a gravelly sagebrush-lined wash separated the houses' yards. Maybe someone over here saw or heard something.

More empty houses. Wait, was that movement? I paused in front of a rambling ranch-style house with a green gravel lawn. A shadow passed by the picture window. Yes!

I strode up the walk, past a brightly painted concrete mule pulling a wagon full of fake flowers. I pressed the doorbell and Beethoven's Fifth played loudly on chimes. This time I'd skip the introduction to me or my uncle's detective agency, hoping to get past any slammed doors.

The lady who opened the door had gray hair that was squashed on one side, like she'd been sleeping on it, and enormous sunglasses. I whipped mine off, hoping to make a better impression. I had dressed to impress this morning, in a conservative white blouse and navy polyester skirt.

"Good morning, ma'am. I'm investigating the death of Charlie Small and wondered if I might ask you a few questions."

"Goodness me," she said in a trembling voice. "Am I a suspect?"

"Oh, no." Nice job, Ivy, scaring an old lady. "I'm just doing a neighborhood investigation, finding out if anyone saw or heard anything that might help us."

"Well, I'll certainly tell you what I can," said the woman, turning away from the door. "I'm Fran Bloom." She walked toward the back of the house. "I just made some coffee. Come sit and have a cup." Her voice still quavered. Maybe she was nervous. Maybe she did know something.

I followed Fran into a dark kitchen redolent with the smell of fresh-brewed coffee. She opened a cupboard door and took down two large plastic mugs. Her hands shook as she poured coffee into them.

As she worked in the kitchen, I sat at her table and reviewed what I knew about investigating witnesses. Uncle Bob had counseled me to begin with questions they could answer truthfully, so I could see which direction they looked when they were telling the truth. Then I should ask a question that caused them to use their imagination and watch where their eyes went. Then start in on the real questions. If their eyes drifted to the imagination place, said Uncle Bob, they were usually lying.

"How do you take your coffee?" asked Fran. She set down a silver tray. A dainty creamer and small sugar bowl, both beautifully wrought in silver, looked incongruous beside the white plastic mugs filled with coffee.

"With cream," I replied. "You?" My first question.

"Oh, I like lots of sugar," she said. I counted the spoonfuls she sprinkled into her coffee. Three. Good. She was telling the truth. But she was also still wearing her sunglasses, so I couldn't see her eyes. This was going to be harder than I thought.

"I didn't get your name, dear," Fran said.

"Oh, I'm sorry." I decided to use my family name for detecting. "I'm Olive Ziegwart with Duda Detective Agency."

"Pardon?"

"Du–*da*." I pulled a business card out of my bag. "It's a Polish name. It means 'one who plays the bagpipes badly.'"

"I didn't know Polish people played the bagpipes." Fran took the card and peered at it, or so I thought. I couldn't see her eyes behind those enormous sunglasses. "Your name's not on here."

"I'm new with the agency," I said quickly. "It's a family business."

"But your name isn't 'one who plays the bagpipes badly' is it? Didn't you say Zieg..."

"Wart. Olive Ziegwart." I really needed to get my own business cards. And lest she ask me what Ziegwart meant ("victory nipple," my dad always said), I turned the conversation back to my original purpose. "So, Fran," I said, sipping my coffee. "Mr. Small died early Thursday morning. I'm trying to find out if anyone saw or heard anything out of the ordinary."

Fran laughed. "I can tell you're new at detective work. See these?" She pointed with both fingers at the sides of her head. Two tiny hearing aids were tucked inside the whorls of both ears. "I can hardly hear you, much less anything outside the house."

"Oh," I said. "And your vision?"

"I have photophobia."

I was about to tell her that I didn't like having my picture taken either, but kept my mouth shut for a change.

"That's why I wear the sunglasses," said Fran. "It's another 'Parkinson's perk,' as I like to call them."

Parkinson's. Of course, that explained the trembling. She was right. I was really new at this.

"Since the light hurts my eyes, I stay indoors a lot." Fran sipped from the plastic mug, which I realized was light and unbreakable. I was pretty good at discovering this stuff after the fact.

"But you did know Charlie?" I asked.

"Oh, yes. He was a lovely man. And his wife, Helen, such a lady. We were all so upset when we heard about it." She shook her head. "And then that business with Pastor Scranton..." Fran's mouth puckered with distaste. "I think he was grandstanding. Talking openly about denying Charlie a funeral."

"Because suicide's a sin?"

"Because he was trying to make a point." Her voice became strong and clear. I sat up. "Pastor Scranton felt like people were being unduly influenced by the suicides. Wanted to put the fear of God—or hell—in us, I suppose. Imagine, believing that someone would kill himself just because someone else did. Ridiculous!"

"Did you say suicides? Plural?"

"I did," said Fran, her voice quavering again. She took off her glasses and rubbed her eyes. “If you include Charlie, three people committed suicide in the past two months.”

“Three? That does seem like a lot for one town.”

“Oh no, that was just people in our congregation. In Sunnydale, we’ve had...” She counted on her fingers, her lips moving slightly. “Eight.”

CHAPTER 14

As I made my way back to Bernice's house, I rounded a corner, nearly rear-ended a slow-moving golf cart, and solved a small mystery. I knew why the streets of Sunnydale were empty. Everyone was at the annual Spring Craft Sale.

Banners announced the sale in the main rec center parking lot: "Stock Up on Gifts! Support the Sunnydale Elks Club!" As I drove past the pancake booth, the smell of bacon wafted in my open car window and I had to stop. I had to. Bacon somehow overpowers every impulse in my body, especially if I've only had a banana for breakfast.

The Elks Club pancake booth sat at the far end of the rec center parking lot, surrounded by long folding tables full of happy bacon-eating people. I pulled in, paid my five-dollar donation, and ate too many pancakes and way too much bacon. I did think about my midriff-baring costume at one point as I dipped an especially crispy slice of bacon into a pool of maple syrup, but decided that eating for a good cause karmically canceled calories.

When I couldn't eat one more bite, I sat back and enjoyed the sun. Its warmth felt good on my shoulders, but its reflection off the asphalt was near blinding. I dug around in my bag for sunglasses, and pulled out Arnie's spy shades. I put them on. Wow. They really were cool. I could see everything behind me: the whole craft sale with tables full of handmade quilts, wooden toys, and stained glass sun catchers.

What the heck, I had a few minutes to spare. I pushed me and my full belly out of my chair, and started down one of the long aisles. I was just checking out some beaded earrings when I heard a familiar voice say, "My grandkids love these mittens." I used Arnie's sunglasses to look behind me. Yep. It was Bitsy, standing behind a table and holding out a pair of lumpy striped mittens to a mustachioed man who had stopped at her booth. Some instinct kept me from turning around.

"You are *not* old enough to have grandkids," the man said.

Oh, please.

Bitsy—white-haired and obviously grandma-aged despite whatever work she'd had done—gave a tinkling, flirtatious laugh. "I do, but they're *very* young."

"Your grandkids live here in town?" The guy, buff in a fitted gray t-shirt and athletic shorts, looked to be late fifties.

"I can do custom work if you like those, dear," said the woman behind the beaded earring booth. I ignored her. I wanted to hear what Bitsy said, especially since she had never mentioned grandkids even once. Come to think of it, I hadn't heard her mention family at all.

"In Nebraska," replied Bitsy. "That's why the mittens come in handy. So to speak." She laughed at her own joke.

"You and your husband from Nebraska?"

"My husband passed away a few years ago. Do you know Nebraska?"

"No, ma'am. I just know it's cold," the guy said with a little chuckle. "I'm from the south, originally." He stuck out a hand. "Colonel Carl Marks."

Even from my vantage point, I could see a shadow flit over Bitsy's face. "Karl Mar..."

"Not the communist," the guy said, grinning. "Just a man who fought communists."

"I also have some with peacock feathers," the earring lady said to me. I nodded, hoping the gesture would keep her quiet for a moment.

Carl Marks picked up a blue dog sweater with pink felt hearts.

"This is great." He looked it over. "But it's too big for my dog. Too bad," he said. "You're very talented, ma'am."

She wasn't. I'd seen some of the things she had knitted during breaks in rehearsals.

"I can knit one to order," said Bitsy. "And I have many talents." She dipped her chin and looked at him from under her eyelashes.

"I see," said Carl in a slow drawl. "Maybe I could bring the dog in question over to your house. Just to get his measurement for the sweater, of course. Maybe around the cocktail hour?"

This was getting weird. Bitsy was probably nearing seventy, a good fifteen years older than the buff Colonel Marks.

The earring lady handed me a little square of tissue paper with her business card taped to it. I guess she had taken my nod for a buy signal. "Ten dollars, dear."

In Arnie's glasses, I could see Carl and Bitsy exchange business cards. I took a twenty out of my wallet and paid the earring lady.

"Thank you, dear," she said. "Those peacock feathers will look lovely against your blonde hair." She opened a metal box. Inside were neatly stacked bills, some quarters, and a business card that said, "Colonel Carl Marks."

"Unusual name," I said, pointing at the card. "Carl Marks."

"I know. What were his parents thinking? Nice man, though. Or at least I hope so, since he'll be coming by my house tomorrow," said the earring vendor. "He just ordered some custom work from me."

CHAPTER 15

I was working on my laptop at Bernice's glass-topped kitchen table, finishing up an insurance report for Uncle Bob, when my cellphone rang. I didn't recognize the number. I had left my number on Duda Detective Agency business cards at a lot of houses that morning, so I answered with my professional voice: "Good afternoon, this is Olive."

"This is Colonel Carl Marks."

I felt a stab of something like fear. Had he seen me watching him and Bitsy? I shook it off. So what if he did?

He continued: "You left your business card at my house."

Ah, just a coincidence. Right?

"Yes," I said. "I'm investigating the death of Charlie Small."

A pause, a bit longer than felt comfortable. Then he said, "I'm afraid I don't have anything to tell you, ma'am." Chewing noises followed. Was he eating lunch?

"Did you know Mr. Small? "

"Yes, but—"

"I'd love to have just five minutes of your time," I said.

"Okay," he said, finally. "Go ahead." More chewing.

"Would it be okay if I came over?" My uncle had taught me it was always best to question people in person, so you could see their eyes and read their body language. Of course, I couldn't say that. "This connection isn't great." I crumpled some paper next to the phone and made little crackly noises with my voice.

"Well..."

"Great, thanks!" I said, making more crinkling crackling

noises. I got Carl's address, told him I'd be there in fifteen minutes, and hung up, hoping he didn't wonder how I heard his address through my "bad connection."

I sat for a minute, mentally prepping for the upcoming interview. The man made me nervous, but I was glad I was going to get to question him. Something was up with Colonel Carl Marks, and I wanted to know what.

Fourteen minutes later, I knocked on the door of the first house I'd visited that morning, the oversized behemoth just a few blocks from Charlie's. The same belly-ringed woman opened the door. "Carl!" she shouted as she turned away and walked into the interior, her blonde ponytail swinging above tight yoga pants. "Honey? It's that detective."

So the guy who was flirting with Bitsy had a trophy wife. Hmmm.

Carl Marks entered the hallway from somewhere. He'd put on jeans and exchanged the gray t-shirt he wore at the craft fair for a U.S. Marine's tee that said, "Mess with the Best, Die Like the Rest." I wondered if he'd chosen it on purpose.

Then I saw him really see me. His eyes gleamed, just for a second. I recognized the look. I'd been getting it all my life. It was the "no one to seriously contend with" look. I was female, cute, and not particularly serious-looking (or serious-acting, I had to admit): thus, the dismissive look. It used to piss me off royally—until I learned to use it.

"I'm Olive Ziegwart with Duda Detectives," I said, making my voice higher and softer than usual. I held out a delicate hand.

"Colonel Carl Marks at your service, ma'am," he said, taking my hand. I made sure to keep it limp as he shook it.

I dug in my purse for the black notebook I used for work, then decided to switch to a sparkly one I'd picked up at the dollar store. "Colonel..." I said, pen in hand, eyes wide with a question.

"Carl with a C," he said. "And Marks is spelled M-A-R-K-S."

"Interesting name." I wondered if the bimbo I was role-playing would know the father of communism, but couldn't help myself.

"Yours too," he said. "Olive Ziegwart with Doodoo Detectives." He gave me the same grin he'd given to Bitsy a few hours earlier, his trim mustache spreading like a caterpillar going for a walk.

"Duda," I said. "My Uncle Bob's last name. I help him out from time to time."

"I see." Carl didn't even try to hide the patronizing look on his face. "Come on in." He led me down the tile hallway. "Can I get you a cup of coffee? Or a smoothie?"

I made the more bimbo-y choice. "A smoothie would be fabulous." I slipped the notebook back into my purse, stuck my pen behind my ear and followed him into the living room, where I stopped dead.

"Wow," I said in my real voice.

Carl didn't notice the change. "Yeah, people usually say that when they see this room."

I bet they did. A black leather sofa and chairs sat upon a black slate floor surrounded by black walls and topped off with, yep, a black ceiling. Giant mirrors took the place of artwork and the biggest flat screen I had ever seen took up almost an entire wall. An ocean scene played on the screen: small silvery fish darted amongst coral while a shark swam lazy circles around them.

"Cheri?" Carl shouted in the direction of the open kitchen where I could see Ms. Yoga Pants opening the fridge. "Would you make an extra smoothie for Ms. Ziegwart here?"

"Sure," she said. Then to me, "Hemp milk okay?"

"Great," I replied, even though I wasn't crazy about the stuff.

"Hey!" she shouted over the whir of the blender. "I have a question for you, since you're a detective and all."

"Okay."

Carl waved me toward a chair that faced the back of the house, where big windows framed a patio and pool.

"Hemp. That's pot, right?" Cheri said as she poured the brown sludgy liquid into glasses.

"Hon, we've been over this," said Carl.

"But it's the same plant, right? Right?" She aimed the last "right" at me as she walked toward us, a tall glass in her hand.

"Umm..." I said, trying to figure out if I was being put on.

"So why isn't hemp milk illegal?" She set the smoothie down on the black glass coffee table in front of us.

"What a kidder!" said Carl, swatting Cheri on the ass. She shook her head at him, and padded back to the kitchen to get her smoothie. Carl reached into a jeans pocket, pulled out a piece of gum, and popped it in his mouth. Ah, the chewing noise over the phone.

I leaned forward to get my drink, dipping my head just enough that my pen flew out from its place behind my ear. "Dang. Did you see where my pen flew to?" I bent over the edge of the couch, and peered at the floor by Carl's feet, pursuing my own little investigative theory.

"Here you go," said Carl, handing the pen back to me.

"Thanks," I said, facing him now and meeting his eyes. "So why all black?"

"It's Cheri's favorite color." He smiled and chewed his gum at the same time.

"Is not," said Cheri, who now carried her smoothie in one hand and a shivering Chihuahua in the other. She nodded at Carl. "*He's* the one who likes black." She and the dog headed out the sliding glass door to the pool.

"Me too," I said to Carl. "It's slimming." I sipped my smoothie, which was cool and chocolaty, but still not exactly delicious. "Thanks for calling me back."

"Anything I can do to help, ma'am," he said. "You're looking into Charlie's death?"

"That's right." I set down my smoothie and took my sparkly notebook out of my bag again. Outside, I saw Cheri slip out of her clothes. She ambled, buck naked, toward the diving board. Two thoughts wrestled for control of my mind:

1: This was one strange household.

2: I would drink hemp milkshakes for breakfast, lunch, and dinner if I could be guaranteed a figure like that.

The colonel followed my gaze. “Oh.” He grinned and snapped his gum appreciatively as he watched Cheri dive into the pool. “We’re ‘clothing optional’ at home. Hope you don’t mind.”

I shook my head. Thanks to shared dressing rooms and quick changes backstage, the sight of unclothed people didn’t bother me. I took another sip of my smoothie. Though it was growing on me, I decided against a diet of hemp milkshakes. I’d miss bacon.

“So, Charlie’s death...” said Carl. Was he chewing his gum a little faster?

“Yes.” I gave him a bimbo-like smile to cover the fact that I was employing Uncle Bob’s waiting game.

He didn’t bite. “What would you like to know?”

“What can you tell me?” I said, trying the answer-a-question-with-a-question game.

“Not much. Sad situation. Killed himself, despondent over the death of his wife, I guess. I saw the police and fire trucks at his house that morning, but nothing else.”

“About what time was that?”

“Maybe oh-six-hundred hours.”

“Did you see or hear anything else that morning, or the evening before?”

“No, nothing unusual.”

I was afraid I was beginning to sound like a real detective so I mixed it up. “This house, it’s not like the rest of Sunnydale.” I made my voice go up at the end of the statement so it sounded like a question.

“No.” Carl sat up straight with misplaced pride. “None of that old-fogey stuff for us. We wouldn’t have moved here if we couldn’t have something new. There are just a few of these beauties around. This was the first of them. We snapped it up as soon as it came on the market.”

“When was that?”

“About a year ago.”

"It's beautiful." I gazed around the scary black room with a rapt look on my face. Being an actor *was* handy when it came to detecting. I made a mental note to tell Uncle Bob. I brought my eyes back to Carl's face. "How did you know Mr. Small?"

"He was my neighbor, obviously. And I used to be his insurance agent."

"Used to be?"

"I'm retired." He looked at me with flat, dark brown eyes.

"So you knew him before you moved here a year ago?"

"...No. Met him right before I retired." I caught a faint flicker in those guarded eyes.

I looked directly at Carl, intentionally letting the bimbo mask slip. "Did Charlie have any policies with you?"

"You know, I think he did." He definitely sped up his chewing gum tempo.

I stared at Carl until he fidgeted. "What type of insurance?" I said in my real voice.

"I can't remember exactly." He tugged the collar of his t-shirt. This guy really needed acting lessons.

"I see. Well, I'm sure I'll be able to find the policies." I rose, enjoying the "what the hell just happened" look on his face. Carl stood.

"I'll let myself out." I walked down the hall. "Thank you for your time, Mr. Marks."

"It's Colonel."

I knew that.

CHAPTER 16

I did not like Colonel Carl Marks. It had nothing to do with the fact that I distrusted men with mustaches. It wasn't his too-young wife with the perfect body and belly ring. It wasn't even the fact that he'd painted an entire room black. It was his eyes.

Carl's eyes weren't windows to his soul. They were locked doors and I wasn't sure I wanted to know what occupied the rooms beyond. I'd watched his eyes as he talked, to look for the lies. If Uncle Bob's theory held water, Carl looked me in the eye when he lied. Cheri had outed the first one, about black being her favorite color. I couldn't figure out why he lied about it. Habit, maybe? And Carl looked directly at me two more times: once when he said he was retired, and again when he said he didn't know which policies Charlie had with him. Plus he chewed his gum faster and played with his clothes. Yep, pretty sure he was lying both times.

Why? As I pondered this on my walk back to Bernice's house, I got a prickly feeling on the back of my neck. Something wasn't right. I slowed my pace and concentrated on my surroundings: wide streets, cactus gardens, and...a flash of red in Arnie's spy sunglass mirrors. A red convertible about a block behind me, going way too slow. Following me.

The prickly feeling invaded the rest of my body, while my mind flipped through options. I could call someone. I could knock on someone's door. I could run back to Bernice's house. Or...

I turned and waved at the car. "Hi!" I shouted. "What's the matter? Doesn't your car go any faster?"

The Ferrari convertible revved its engine and zoomed past me,

Carl at the wheel. I fumbled around in my purse for a pen to write down the license plate number. Dang. Must have left it at the colonel's house. Bernice's pen-filled house was still a few blocks away

"D...OD...one five six eight." I sang to the tune of "Do Re Mi." Why was Carl following me? It must be something to do with Charlie. His insurance policy?

"D...OD...one five six eight," I sang the license plate number again. I learned this musical memorization trick in high school, when I had to learn the table of periodic elements while I was also in a production of *Oklahoma!* My science teacher was so impressed with my method that he used it himself. I'm very proud of the fact that students all over Arizona now sing the elements to the tune of "The Surrey with the Fringe on the Top."

"D...OD...one five six eight."

"Or 'Dough, the bucks, the rent I owe,'" sang a voice behind me. I turned to see Roger in a t-shirt and shorts that showed off his muscled legs. "Your turn," he said.

"Ray, the landlord that I hate," I joined in, keeping one eye out for that red Ferrari.

"Me, the one who foots the bills," Roger chimed back in. In *The Sound of Cabaret,* this song was all about us Vaughn Katt Dancers being down on our luck.

"Fa, a—"

"I think you have the words wrong," said a gray-haired lady who was walking her schnauzer.

"No, it's *The Sound of Cabaret*, a brand new musical." Roger took the opportunity to put his arm around me. "Captain Vaughn Katt and Teasel the dancer at your service. Come see the show at Desert Dinner Theatre. It opens on Friday."

The lady waved over her shoulder as her determined dog pulled her away. "Sounds nice."

"Maybe she'll bring her bridge club," Roger said to me, his arm still draped around my shoulder.

"If her dog lets her." The lady's schnauzer charged ahead of her, like a mustachioed general on a mission. “What are you doing in this neck of the woods?” I spoke metaphorically, since there was not a tree to be seen unless you counted palm trees. Which I did not.

“Just out for a run.” Roger released me, thank heavens, then stood on one leg, bent his other behind him and grabbed it, as if to punctuate his point. “The theater puts me up in a nice little townhouse over on Lee Trevino Court. It’s about a mile away.” He stretched the other leg. “What were you singing?”

“A license plate.” Should I tell Roger I was being followed? No. He might hug me or something. “I better go write it down.”

“What time should I come over for pool duty and dinner?”

“We’d better do dinner tomorrow. Keith called an extra music rehearsal later this afternoon.”

“Just for you?’

“What? No.” At least I hoped not. “He said it was for all of us non-union types.” Equity rules put a cap on union actors’ hours. The theater could ask the rest of us to rehearse 24/7.

“Are you worried?”

“Nah,” I lied.

“The theater will start serving meals on Thursday,” Roger said.

“Yay. I’d forgotten about that.” Free food was one of the perks of dinner theater and was especially exciting to those of us who ate beans three times a week.

“So as far as our dinner for pool arrangements…” Oh please, God, he *had* to take carc of the pool. “Why don’t you just feed me on our nights off?” Arghh. After the show opened on Friday, we’d have just Monday and Tuesday nights off. Only two nights a week, and I wanted to keep them open for Jeremy. My discomfort must have showed, because Roger said, “I’m sure we can work something out. See you in a few hours.” He jogged away.

I watched him for a moment, legs pumping, white running shoes flashing. Something tugged at the corners of my mind. Jogging? Legs? Shoes! That was another thing that bugged me about Colonel Carl. His shoes.

Uncle Bob has his eye theory—I have a shoe theory. I believe a person's footwear provides a plethora of clues. Take me, for example. You could pretty much get an idea of my age (twenties) and income (not much) by looking at my usual footwear: Dollar Store flip-flops. You could also tell that I lived in a hot sunny place (the bottoms were slightly melted from walking on hot asphalt) and that I walked with the weight on the outside of my feet (the edges of my flip flops were smooshed more than the rest of the shoe). I had pretended to drop my pen so I could get a good look at Carl's shoes. They were white athletic shoes, pretty new, not a scuff on them. They were also made by Gucci and cost more than the theater paid me for a week. Those shoes, the enormous flat screen TV, and the Ferrari added up to more than a mid-life crisis. How much money did insurance agents make, anyway?

CHAPTER 17

"Wanna take a trip?" my brother asked over the phone.

I sat at my dressing room counter putting on makeup before rehearsal. Or *trying* to put on makeup. Those of us who had to attend the extra afternoon rehearsal had a really short dinner break before tonight's full-fledged rehearsal, so Arnie had brought in pizza. I was finding it difficult to apply lipstick over pizza-greased lips.

"Sure," I said. "As long as I—"

"Don't have rehearsal." Cody finished my sentence. He knew me all too well. "Matt says Candy doesn't. It's tomorrow."

"Where are we going?" I scrubbed off my oily lipstick and tried again.

"It's a secret. Meet us at the house at..." He stopped. "When are we going tomorrow?" Cody shouted into the phone. I pulled my cell away from my ear. I could still hear him, even holding the phone a good two feet away. "Matt says to meet us at noon."

"Okay. Later, gator."

"In a while, crocodile," said Cody.

I hung up, finished getting into costume and makeup, and crossed my fingers about tonight's rehearsal.

I should have crossed all my toes too. My singing was passable, but someone had tattled on Hailey, who was now forbidden to feed Marge lines. In her first scene, Marge walked onstage and smiled at the huddle of nuns. And smiled. And smiled. Opened her mouth, and...nada. Shut it again and smiled, tighter than before. When it became obvious Marge was not going to say her first line, Keith started up the music, the nuns skipped the beginning of the scene and Bitsy launched right into, "How do you solve a problem like a nightclub?"

Marge's performance did not get any better. The cast and crew were on pins and needles the entire night.

After rehearsal, as I passed Marge's dressing room, I heard Arnie's voice from within: "C'mon, doll, this is..."

"This is CRAP!" Marge could probably be heard in the front of the theater.

I felt sorry for everyone involved. We only had one more rehearsal without an audience. Then preview on Thursday and opening on Friday. The show wouldn't work unless Marge's memory improved overnight—or Arnie replaced her.

"I'll get them, OKAY? I'll get my EFFIN' LINES!"

I scurried out the stage door. A red convertible drove slowly past the parking lot.

"Ready?" I jumped at the voice at my elbow.

"Sorry," Roger said. "Didn't mean to scare you."

The convertible was nowhere in sight. Was it Carl? Too dark to tell.

I turned to Roger. "No worries. I'm just jumpy because it's...late." I never was good at improv.

"Let's get at that pool then."

"I thought since I couldn't cook you dinner—"

"I'll take a rain check. You can't let pools go, you know."

The health department shut down the pool at my apartment building last summer after it had turned lime Jell-O green. "Right," I said. "Follow me."

I was actually glad Roger was coming over. I kinda wanted someone with me.

When we got to Bernice's, Roger pulled his white Audi into the drive next to my VW.

"Nice car," I said as he got out.

"It's Arnie's. It's something, huh?" The car alarm tweeted as he locked it remotely.

"Arnie loaned you his car?"

"My agent negotiated it," said Roger. "Normally when I'm on the road, I just ask for travel expenses and housing—plus my wages, of course—but you really can't get around this city without a car."

Hmmm. Housing, travel expenses, and a car, plus Equity wages and free dinners on the nights we had shows. Maybe all actors didn't live on beans.

My phone rang as we walked through the front door. Jeremy! I picked up and motioned Roger to go on ahead of me.

"Hey, you done with rehearsal?" said Jeremy. "I'm over on your side of town. I know it's late, but maybe a drink?"

"Oh, sorry. It's—"

"Ivy?" Roger called from the back of the house, too loudly.

"You still at the theater?" Jeremy said.

"No. A friend came over to take care of the pool."

"At eleven o'clock at night?"

"It's the only time he had."

Silence.

"I really needed him to help me. You know how I am about water." It was a pretty pathetic shot, but true all the same.

"I understand," said wonderful, thoughtful, gorgeous Jeremy.

After telling him where to pick up his ticket for opening night, I hung up, grabbed the pool instructions from underneath the stereo, and met Roger, who stood waiting by the sliding glass door. We went onto the patio and Roger, directions in hand, flipped a switch on the stucco wall beside the doors. The dark hole that had been the pool now glowed turquoise, a calm presence in the black night. I wasn't fooled. It was still water, deep enough to drown in.

I waved at the deathtrap. "All yours." I sat down in a chair with beige-striped cushions, a good fifteen feet from the water.

"No problem." Roger found a kit mounted on the back patio wall next to some other pool implements, and brought it and the instructions to a table near me. "It'll be good practice for me. My new house is going to have a pool."

"You're buying a house? Back east?"

I only had a vague idea of where Roger lived.

"I'm building a house," he said, straightening up. "In Mexico. Cheaper there, you know."

"You speak Spanish?"

"Un poquito."

Though most of my knowledge of Spanish came from watching telenovelas, I was pretty sure that meant "a little bit."

"Are there jobs for English-speaking actors in—"

"I'm retiring," Roger said. "This is my last gig. Then I'll be off to the land of sun and cerveza." The Spanish word for beer I knew. Roger grabbed a pool skimmer from the wall. "So you're afraid of the water?"

"No. Terrified. Truly, deeply terrified."

"May I ask why?" He skated the skimmer across the surface of the pool, working around an inner tube that bobbed on its surface like an innocent toy.

"Maybe some other day." Probably not. Cody's accident was not something I talked about lightly. "Let's talk about fame and fortune instead," I said. "Tell me what I have to look forward to."

"Hard work, rejection, and poverty," said Roger, the blue light from the pool reflecting a too-serious face. Then he laughed, "Don't listen to me. It's not a bad life, if you play your cards right." He hung up the dripping skimmer and retrieved a couple of clear plastic vials from the pool kit on the table.

I waited for him to go on. Sometimes the things Uncle Bob taught me worked in real life too.

"I've done okay for myself, but just because of some lucky investments." He dipped the vials into the pool, then brought them back to the table. "I missed the boat when it came to real success."

"You don't think of yourself as successful? You travel free of charge, you make your living doing what you love, and you're building a house in Mexico. Seems like a pretty nice life to me."

Using a dropper, Roger dripped some chemicals into the clear vials. "I could have done better." A trace of bitterness crept into his voice. "I should have been on Broadway, or at least off-Broadway, but I was...unlucky. Not like some." He jerked a chin in the direction of Marge's house next door. He put down the pool test kit and stood in front of me. "You, though...you have a chance." Before I knew it, he had cupped my cheek in his hand. I gulped, not sure what to do. "You're so pretty," he went on, turning my face from one side to the other, like a cowboy checking out a new horse. He dropped his gaze to my legs. I bet cowboys do that too. "And you have the most magnificent legs I've seen in ages. Which brings me to the real reason I wanted to help you out with your pool."

He was making me nervous, but I waited, not saying anything. I was getting good at this.

"I'd like to be your..."

Please God don't let him say "sugar daddy."

"Mentor."

Phew. "What exactly do you mean? I've never had a mentor before." Of course Uncle Bob was my mentor, but he only taught me things that dealt with PI work, like patience and observation and perseverance.

"I'd like to offer you advice on your acting career, help steer you. I think you've got talent—and great legs—and with some work, I think you can have a successful career." He sat down across from me and leaned in. "And I think I can jumpstart it for you. An old New York producer friend of mine is going to fly in and see the show later this month. He heads up Mooney Productions—maybe you've heard of them? They produced *Mother Teresa, The Musical.*"

I nodded. Everyone knew *MTTM.*

"He'd like to mount *The Sound of Cabaret* with plans to take it off-Broadway, and he's looking for new talent. I'd like to introduce you."

For once, words escaped me. This could be my big break. But why me? Hailey, who played Mary, had a singing voice that sounded like clear water over rocks in a mountain stream, plus she was a true triple threat—an actor who could act, dance, and sing. I was more of a 2.5 threat.

"What do you think?" Roger asked.

"I'm...wow...It's..." I still struggled with the idea that this was a real possibility. "An amazing opportunity. I can't thank you enough."

"Good," he said. "But we have work to do. And the first order of business is to get you some voice lessons."

"Oh. I..." Lessons were expensive and my budget was stretched to its limit.

"I'll teach you. Gratis," said Roger. "We'll start tomorrow. I'll meet you at the theater a half hour before dinner. Sound good?"

It did and it didn't. Free singing lessons and an introduction to a New York producer sounded pretty great, but I had a nagging doubt about Roger's real intentions. But hey, I'd handled unwanted attention before. I could certainly handle Roger.

"You bet," I said.

CHAPTER 18

The next day, I went into Duda Detective Agency early so I could tackle my clerical backlog before meeting Cody and Matt. Uncle Bob wasn't in—had to deal with "a little plumbing issue." I knew I'd get a lot of work done without him there to distract me, but the office felt cold and gray without him. It *was* a pretty gray office. Uncle Bob had acquired the furniture secondhand from some state government department that was updating their décor, so the office was furnished with a big metal desk, a bookcase, three enormous filing cabinets and a wheelie chair with scratchy stained upholstery—all gray. On a typical day, my uncle's ubiquitous Hawaiian shirt provided the color in the office, and he supplied the warmth.

I plunked down my to-go cup full of coffee and got to work. I flew through the paperwork my uncle had left me and began typing up notes from my investigation. Soon I didn't even notice that Uncle Bob was gone. I had a lot of questions: Eight suicides in Sunnydale? What was up with the pastor? His reaction to Charlie's death seemed less than compassionate. And who was the landscaper Bernice saw that morning?

I dialed Amy. This time I got through right away. "Quick question: do you know if your dad had a landscaper? Or someone who might be blowing leaves at his house?"

"A landscaper?" She sounded puzzled. "You've seen Dad's house. The landscaping is made up of gravel and rocks and a few cacti. He doesn't even have a palm tree."

Should have caught that one.

I hung up and began working on my next area of research: Colonel Carl Marks. I found the first piece of info I wanted fairly easily. According to Bureau of Labor Statistics, the annual salary for insurance agents was $63,400. The best-paid ten percent made an average of $116,940, while the lowest-paid ten percent were paid $26,120 on average. Even if Carl was one of the highest-earning agents, Gucci shoes and a Ferrari convertible seemed a stretch.

I was trying to look up his license plate ("trying" was the operative word) when I noticed the clock on my computer: eleven forty-five. Yikes! I grabbed my things, locked up the office and ran down the stairs, out the door, and down the few blocks to my car.

Cody's group home was about ten minutes away in the somewhat gentrified Coronado neighborhood. The bungalow where he lived had a patchy lawn and a cracked concrete path, but it was tidily kept, with a clean-swept front porch, trimmed oleanders, and even a few rosebushes out front.

I parked in front of the house and had barely gotten the car door open when Cody ran to greet me. He wrapped me in a hug. "Olive-y!" It was his pet name for me, a combination of Olive and Ivy that his friend Stu had come up with. Cody had comb tracks through his damp blonde hair and smelled of soap.

"Hey, mister," I said. "You smell purty."

"Just had a shower."

Stu, a round-faced young man with Down syndrome, ran up behind Cody. "Me too," he said. "I took a shower too." He held out his arms, angling for a hug.

"Stu," said Matt, as he came up the walk. "What have we been talking about?"

Stu hung his head in mock sorrow. "Handshakes, not hugs."

"Right," said Matt.

"But Cody—" Stu began.

"Can hug Ivy because she's his sister."

"Okay." Stu stuck out his hand. "Hi Olive-y."

I shook it. "Good to see you, Stu."

As Cody, Stu, and their housemates Kerry and Chad clambered

into a white minivan, I walked a few steps behind them with Matt. "We're working on appropriate adult behavior," Matt said quietly.

"But no hugs?" I said. "C'mon, isn't that a little over the top?"

"Not so much." Matt's eyes smiled behind wire-framed glasses. "You'll notice Stu only asks good-looking women for hugs." He clambered into the driver's seat. "Follow us!" he called out the window. I couldn't ride in the van, some liability issue or something. "We're going to lunch."

I got back into my Bug and followed them, calculating how much cash I had in my wallet. Not much. I hoped we were going somewhere cheap.

After about ten minutes, they pulled into the Costco parking lot. The guys tumbled out of the van as soon as it was parked.

"Costco lunch date!" yelled Stu.

"C'mon, Olive-y," cried Cody.

As we all walked across the enormous parking lot, Matt said, "We've figured out when the samplers are working. Management doesn't mind if the guys take a little food tour. And today's tour should be kinda special. It's one reason I asked Cody to invite you."

Matt wanted me there? I studied him as he stopped at the entrance to show his Costco card. His brown hair curled over the collar of his blue shirt, which I noticed, with a start, was exactly like the one Cody wore. Duh. Cody adored Matt. I could see him buying a shirt that would make him look just like his hero.

"Okay," Matt said to the group once we were all inside. "Time to synchronize watches." The guys all looked at their watches. "I have twelve fifteen," Matt continued. "Let's all meet at the deli at twelve forty-five. Alright?"

"Alright!" yelled Stu, who was hopping from foot to foot.

"And remember, no running, anyone." Matt looked at Stu, who pretended he didn't see him.

"See you then," said Matt. Stu took off like a shot, but to his credit, he was race-walking, not running. Kerry and Chad followed him at a slower pace. Cody stuck with us. We stopped at each sampling station, trying dried cranberries, granola bars, and tasty little crackers. As we sipped chicken soup from paper cups, Cody's gaze settled on something behind us. He smiled broadly, crumpled up his paper cup, and tossed it toward a wastebasket as he strode toward the meat section. I picked up the paper cup from the floor where it had landed. Cody had ataxia, a lack of coordination resulting from his brain injury, and getting something from his hands to a wastebasket was difficult when he was distracted.

And he did seem to be distracted. Matt and I caught up with him near a young woman stirring small hotdogs in an electric skillet. She watched her hands as she worked, brow furrowed with concentration, a few ringlets of black hair escaping her paper cap. Focusing on the sausages, she said in a low, slow voice, "These cocktail weenies are all-natural, made from beef with no added hormones."

The young woman pinched a hotdog with tongs and placed it in a small paper cup. "They're fully cooked." She spoke the memorized words in her Lauren Bacall-ish voice. "And perfect for parties."

Cody picked up the paper cup and ducked his head, peeking at her from under his lashes.

I shot a look at Matt. Cody was not shy around anyone.

The young woman looked up at Cody. "Oh," she said. "I know you." A smile spread across her face.

"From the dance," said Cody.

"Last month," whispered Matt to me. "The Arc mixer." ARC was an acronym that had once stood for the Association of Retarded Citizens. Since "retarded" had become a put-down, the group had renamed itself simply "The Arc."

"You know who you look like?" said the young woman, whose name tag read "Sarah."

Cody shook his head.

"Brad Pitt," said Sarah.

"Brad Pitt?" he said to her, then turned to us. "Brad Pitt!" He had a cinematic glow I'd never seen before. Brad Pitt, indeed.

"Do you like movies?" Cody asked Sarah. She looked down at

her weenies, studying them intently. Cody shifted from one foot to another, and back again.

"I need to pick up some ice cream." Matt took my arm and led me toward the freezer section.

"Was Cody asking her out?"

"Yep," said Matt. "He's been practicing for a week, mostly on Stu. I finally took all the guys to a matinee a few days ago. It just seemed fair, after Cody had asked them to the movies over and over again."

"You would have made a good fireman." After all, "Be Nice" seemed to be part of his mission too.

"Huh?"

"Never mind."

"It's great, don't you think?" said Matt, with a nod toward Cody and Sarah. She was still looking at the hotdogs, but her smile was as wide as the sky. Cody leaned toward her, hands in his pockets. His ears were pink, like they always were when he was nervous.

Matt had pulled my attention back to Cody, where it belonged. This was a big moment in Cody's life, and I'd been focusing on Matt and firemen instead. I wondered why.

Matt grabbed a jumbo tub of chocolate ice cream from the freezer. "Would you get a tub of vanilla?"

I pulled out a vat of vanilla, its cold carton stinging my bare hands.

"C'mon," said Matt. "Let's find a rogue cart so we can put these puppies down."

"What about Cody?"

"He'll meet us by the deli."

I followed him toward the front of the store. "Sarah's great," said Matt. "I worked with her a few years ago. She's out on her own now."

"Really?"

"Well, it's supervised housing, but she's in an apartment with a roommate. I hear she's a pretty good cook too. Aha!" Matt pointed at a lonely cart down a side aisle. "Score!" When we'd put the ice cream cartons in the cart, he looked at me straight on. "What's wrong?"

"Nothing. Just stuff on my mind." What was on my mind was Sarah with an apartment. The thought of it felt like a burr in my sock. I didn't know why.

"Of course. The show opens this weekend, right?"

"She said 'yes!'" Cody bounded up to us. He caught the tip of his sneaker on the floor, and stumbled into me. He righted himself. "Sarah said yes!"

My cell rang: Jeremy. I took the call, grateful to be distracted from the itchy feeling I got when I thought about Cody and Sarah. "Hi."

"Can't talk long, and you may not be so happy when you hear why I'm calling. I can't make it Friday."

"But it's opening night."

"I know, but one of the guys is in the hospital with a burst appendix. I promise I'll make the show another night. And we're still on for Saturday afternoon, right?"

"Right." I tried not to grumble. I did realize that being available to save lives was more important than opening night at a dinner theater, but still.

After I'd hung up, Cody said, "What's wrong?"

"The guy I'm dating can't come to opening night."

"Oh! Can I come? With Sarah?" Cody turned to Matt. "That would be even better than a movie, right?"

"I only have one ticket, and we're sold out." Since Jeremy had planned to come solo, I had just made one reservation for Friday. And truth be told, I was relieved about that.

"Ivy." Matt pulled me aside. "If it's okay with you, I can give Sarah my ticket. I have a big paper due next week"—Matt was going for his Masters in social work—"and Candy already told me she doesn't care when I see the show." He didn't pull me aside quite far enough, because Cody said, "Say yes, Olive-y. Say yes."

"Sure. Of course." I nodded, then turned away to hide the

discomfort I felt. That's when I saw Arnie, strolling behind a cart. What was he doing here? Surely there was a Costco closer to Sunnydale. I waved at him. Was it my imagination, or did he not look happy to see me?

"I'll meet you guys at the deli," I said to Cody and Matt, then caught up with Arnie. Ah, I knew why he was unhappy. "Hey." I pointed at the cigar in his pocket. "Can't you chew on that in here?"

"Somebody once complained I was smoking it." He shook his head. "People."

Arnie's cart was filled with toilet paper, paper towels, coffee, and other stuff that was probably for the theater. On top of it all was a box labeled "Home Monitoring and Control Kit." It looked like it had cameras and monitors and all sorts of cool stuff. I waited for Arnie to tell me all about his latest and greatest gadget. But he didn't.

CHAPTER 19

They weren't supposed to be there. It was Wednesday night—preview wasn't until tomorrow. I shut my eyes for just a moment, trying to wish them away. But I couldn't. When I opened my eyes, all the Old FOTS were still there, sitting at the dining tables in the front of the theater, focused on me.

I'd made it through "Dough Ray Me." With all of us dancers singing, I was able to sing softly enough that no one could tell if I was off-pitch. But now, Timothy finished his intro into our number and whirled me into our dance break.

This was where I shone. My jetés were high, my pirouettes perfect. My eyes even gazed lovingly into Wolf's, but my mind had already leapt ahead to sure failure. And then it was time. I opened my mouth:

"I am sixteen going on twenty-one..." Aaaaa, a little wobble there.

"Pure as the driven snow." I tried to remember the tips Roger had given me at our singing lesson before rehearsal, but they were gone, along with my sense of pitch.

"Unschooled in love, and ignorant of..." Ignorant of the stupid position I had put myself in.

"The lessons I ought to know." I ought to know better. Why did I think I could do this?

The Old FOTs rustled in their seats and snuck glances at each other. Down in the orchestra pit, Keith tried to magically pull up my pitch with a wave of his baton. I made it through the song, exited stage left, and hid my red face in the darkness of the wings.

My musical faux pas was soon forgotten, though, as Marge came onstage and stood there. And stood there.

In this scene, Marge/Mother Superior explained to Bitsy/Sister Angelica why she was sending Mary to the Vaughn Katt Club. She was also supposed to say the first line.

Silence. I looked at Bitsy, who gazed expectantly at Marge, a sweet, nun-type expression on her too-smooth face. "C'mon, Bitsy," I said in a stage whisper, partly to myself and partly hoping she would hear me. "Help her out."

It's an unwritten rule in theater: You don't let an actor hang himself onstage when there's an audience. Typically, if you "go up" (forget your lines), your fellow actors help you by giving you a hint that the audience won't recognize, maybe a question that leads you to your line, or a different version of your line, or even just one of the words from the line—just something to get your brain back on track. Bitsy, though, just waited, like she'd taken a vow of silence.

Candy/Sister Marvela wasn't supposed to come on until after the song, but she entered stage right. "Thank you for waiting for me," she said, a Candy-created line that explained the lack of action onstage. "I believe we are going to discuss your decision to send Mary to the nightclub as a singing teacher?"

Brilliant. Candy had just encapsulated the entire scene and given Marge her cue for the song, a refrain of "Problem Like a Nightclub." The orchestra began playing. I thought I saw a brief scowl flit across Bitsy's face, maybe because Candy had jumped several of her lines to save Marge. Served Bitsy right.

With a grateful glance at Candy, Marge opened her mouth and sang:

"WHY WOULD I SEND A POSTULANT TO A NIGHTCLUB?"

What Marge lacked in memory, she made up for in volume.

"Why would I have her costumed like a TART?"

Phew. Marge was going to make it through the song.

"I THINK she'll do some good."

Her big voice filled the theater.

"If ANYBODY could."

Marge had star quality. Even when she was miscast, you couldn't take your eyes off her.

"Mary can reach the singing sinners' HEARTS."

But what would we do about the play? It'd kill Marge to be replaced, but we couldn't have her continually forgetting her lines.

"Oh, why would I send a postulant to a NIGHTCLUB?"

She seemed to do just fine with her songs. No memorization problems there.

"Why? 'Cause I trust she'll do THE WORK OF GOD." She finished with a flourish.

I had it! I knew how Marge could stay in the play. I bounced on the soles of my feet, waiting for Marge to come offstage.

When she finally did, I grabbed her by the arm and pulled her into a corner away from everyone. She didn't exactly resist, but it felt like pulling a wet bag of sand. "Marge, I know how you can remember your lines. I can help you."

Marge's eyes flickered with hope. "Really?"

"Really. I know just the trick."

The bag of sand straightened itself up into a semblance of the old Marge. "Me too," she said. "I think I can help you too."

I'd forgotten all about my little singing problem. Some folks might call it denial.

"You wash my back, I'll wash yours," said Marge, and we shook to seal the deal.

CHAPTER 20

"That's it? That's all there is to it?" Marge asked the question loudly, presumably to be heard over the kicking and splashing of her water aerobics class, but mostly because she was naturally loud.

"Yep. It's simple." I had just regaled her with my periodic table *Oklahoma!* story. "You just have to sing your lines." I had to talk loudly too, especially since I stood a nice safe distance from the edge of the pool. Though we both thought we needed all the rehearsal we could get before preview tonight, Marge was adamant about not missing her morning workout, so we decided we could talk during her Water Lilies class at Sunnydale Recreation Center, then follow up with a session at her house.

"But that'll sound weird."

Marge jogged in the shallow end of the enormous indoor pool. Bitsy worked out next to her, the little skirt on her swimsuit floating up and down with each step.

"It'll take a little practice, but I really think it'll work." The water aerobics instructor had turned up the music, so I had to shout. "You start out by singing the words to a tune you know. Then take away the notes, so you just have the rhythm, then soften that rhythm just a bit. The music will help you remember your lines, and the audience will never know."

"I'll give it a try." She tried to smile. "What have I got to lose?" She swung her arms in wide circles, as did the rest of the class. An aerobicizer wearing a glittery pink cowboy hat splashed water my way, and I jumped back.

"I can't believe you don't like the water," said Marge. "I love it. It's the only time my boobs point in the right direction."

I snuck a look at my own boobs, wondering how they'd fair in years to come. They were pretty perky now. So were Bitsy's, which was weird considering she was probably nearing seventy.

"Ever thought about a little lift?" Bitsy said to Marge.

Ah.

"Nah." Marge made a big wave with her arms and accidentally splashed Bitsy. Or maybe not so accidentally. "I make the best of what I got, but I'm not doing anything unnatural. This is what I look like. Those who don't like it can lump it."

"Noodles!" shouted the instructor, a young woman who looked about fourteen next to all the folks in the pool. Marge grabbed a yellow foam noodle from the side of the pool, swung it under her rear, and sat on it, like a kid in a swing. "Now you, chickie," she said to me, kicking her legs as she talked. "When exactly do you lose it?"

Bitsy's head turned slightly in our direction, but I didn't care. Everyone knew there was a problem. I just wanted to fix it. "When I have to sing in front of anything that remotely resembles an audience."

Marge began kicking up a storm. "Do you have stage fright any other time?" she asked, not panting or breaking her stride. She really had some lungs on her. "When you're acting? Or dancing?"

I shook my head. It was one of the mysteries I was trying to solve. I'd been an actor since I was a kid—not in plays necessarily, but I was always pretending to be the Red Queen or Dorothy Gale or Han Solo (I was a big fan of gender-neutral casting). Dancing came naturally too. I didn't even have to think about it. Once a choreographer showed me the steps, it was as if my legs took over. I mean, it was work, but glorious physical work without any mental or emotional baggage.

"Last push!" shouted the aerobics instructor. "Your choice of aerobic activity for two minutes. Go, ladies!"

I wondered if the instructor actually overlooked the one man in the class, or if her instructions were so ingrained she couldn't stop herself. I felt a little sorry for the guy, being the odd man out. Then I noticed the ring of swim cap-clad heads around him, the ladylike laughter that surrounded him. He was a small man, neat and hairless, and in pretty good shape. No pecs or anything, but no flabby man-boobs either. He was a good catch in these parts.

"I got an idea for you," Marge said, powering her way through the last part of the routine, splashing and kicking to beat the band. Beside her, Bitsy trotted daintily like a miniature pony. The pool churned with the efforts of the swimmers, except for the sparkly cowgirl, who just pushed the water around. Maybe she didn't want to lose her hat.

"Nice job, ladies!" shouted the instructor. "See you tomorrow."

The little man got out of the pool first, hoisting himself up a ladder near me. Marge and Bitsy both walked over to the pool steps in the far corner, as did most of the women. I wondered why for just a moment, then realized that I wouldn't want my butt hanging off the ladder for all the world to see, either.

I got in line with the aerobicizers as they filed out of the pool area door, held open by the man from the class. As I passed by, the guy winked at me. Not a friendly "hiya" wink, but a slow lascivious one. He mouthed the word, "Tonight?" I was about to give him a piece of my mind when I heard a soft giggle behind me. Phew. I was not the object of his attention. I wanted to look behind me, but couldn't do so without being obvious. I wished I had Arnie's spy sunglasses.

I followed the ladies into the locker room, now full of chatting, dripping swimmers. The sparkly cowgirl paused in front of a sink where a sign taped to the mirror said, "No hair dye in sink, especially black dye." She took off her cowboy hat to reveal suspiciously dark hair.

Marge stopped in front of an unlocked locker and opened it.

"Wow," I said. "Is Sunnydale so safe you don't need a lock?"

Bitsy, who was spinning a combination lock, stopped and waited to hear what Marge had to say. Marge paused too. That was out of character. Marge was never at a loss for words.

"I don't bring anything worth stealing," Marge finally said, keeping her back to me. She pulled a plastic bag from the locker and sat down on a slatted wooden bench.

"Olive!" said a querulous voice. I looked over to see Fran Bloom, from my neighborhood investigation, dressed in a tracksuit. "Have you found out anything more about Charlie Small?"

At the mention of Charlie's name, a murmur went up among the locker room ladies and several of them looked at Bitsy. I remembered that Charlie had been in her karaoke club. Maybe they sang duets?

"Well..." I began.

"Oh, sorry, dear. Never mind." She waved goodbye as she padded off. "I'm sure that's all supposed to be top secret."

Uh-oh. She might be right. And I hadn't been exactly closed-mouthed about the whole thing.

"So." Marge stripped off her wet suit, plonked it in the plastic bag, and tossed it in the locker. "I have an idea what the problem might be. We can talk through it in the sauna."

"Sauna? I'm not dressed." I nodded down at the t-shirt and jeans I'd thrown on that morning. I'd gotten up earlier than usual to meet Marge and was pretty impressed that I'd managed to dress myself in something clean and right-side out.

Marge barked a laugh. "It's a *sauna*, Ivy. You don't need clothes."

"Oh. Um. I'm not really comfortable being naked in front of others."

"And you're in the theater? How do you make it through the underwear scene onstage?" One of the dance numbers in *The Sound of Cabaret* took place in the dancers' dressing room with all of us nearly naked.

"That's different."

"How?"

"Because it's not me. It's my character."

Marge smiled. "I can definitely help you. C'mon, let's sweat this out in the sauna."

I hesitated.

The very naked Marge walked a few feet and opened a wooden door. “I bet when we come out you’ll be cured.”

That was good enough for me. I stripped quickly and followed Marge into the dark cedary-smelling room. She shut the door, turned up the temperature, and poured a pitcher of water on the rocks. Steam filled the room like a fog. “If we make it really hot we can have the place to ourselves.” Marge laid a towel on a wooden bench and sat down. “So, what do you think about while you’re singing?”

I didn’t have a towel, so I stood instead of parking my bare butt on the bench. “Well, breathing from my diaphragm, and raising my soft palate, and not sliding into the notes and—”

Marge raised a hand. “That’s enough. What do you think about when you’re acting?”

“I’m in character.” I almost added “of course.” What actor worth his salt wouldn’t be in character?

“So you’re thinking your character’s thoughts, right?”

“Right.”

A lady poked her head in. “Heavens!” She waved away the heat and backed out again.

“Works every time.” Marge smiled at me. “Well? Did you figure it out? Your problem, I mean?”

I shook my head, confused. “Roger says—”

“Roger?”

“He’s giving me singing lessons.” Wow, it was hot. I fanned myself with my hand.

“Listen, kiddo. Roger can teach you technique—and it won’t hurt you to learn some—but...Roger’s got a great instrument, but he doesn’t use it like an actor.”

Marge was right about Roger. His rich baritone voice was the type a radio announcer might envy. But his singing was fine instead of great. He hit the right notes, but the music never soared, like it did when Marge sang.

“That’s why he never made it big.” She shook her head.

I'd heard the story. Years ago Roger and Marge were both in an off-off-Broadway musical called *The Improbables*. The show launched Marge's career, but Roger was replaced when it moved to Broadway.

"Only reason he's made it this far is because of his agent. She's crazy about him. In fact, I heard..." Marge stopped. "Sorry. Idle gossip. Now," she said, facing me. "You're more like me." She wiped the sweat off her brow. "It's not necessarily what we got, but how we use it. What Roger's going to teach you won't help with your stage fright. Might even make it worse unless you keep this one thing in mind..." She leaned forward on the sauna bench, boobs swinging dangerously close to her knees. "You gotta be in character when you sing."

"That's it? I got naked for this?" I'm not sure I said it out loud, but I thought it.

"Music comes in when words aren't enough," Marge continued. "It's like you can't contain your love or heartbreak or outrage, so it comes out in a song. If you've done the technical work ahead of time, all you do once you're onstage is be your character, and let that emotion pour out of you."

This was not going to help. Of course I was in character when I was...I sank down on the bench, not caring I had no towel. Marge was right. During my songs, especially in front of an audience, I'd been thinking about singing. I hadn't been in character. How could I not have recognized that simple fact?

"Hello ladies!" Bitsy came in the door. Steam billowed as Marge poured more water on the rocks. Bitsy stayed anyway. "Did I hear that you two are helping each other with your little problems?"

Marge nodded and snaked an arm toward the temperature control, but I blocked her. I couldn't take it any hotter.

"That's so nice of you both." Bitsy hopped up on one of the slatted benches. "You know, I've never had any problem with stage fright, but I have had some experience with 'senior moments.' My husband, you know." She smiled brightly at Marge. "He died of Alzheimer's."

CHAPTER 21

After deploying her little stink bomb, Bitsy left the sauna. Marge got up too. “Let’s go.” She looked like she had the wind knocked out of her.

Things did not get better. When she got to her locker and opened the door, it was empty. No swimsuit, no clothes, no nothing.

“Shit, Marge,” I said. “I’m sorry. I feel horrible. I’m the one who made such a big deal of it being unlocked.”

She shook her head and sank back on the bench without saying a word.

“Tell you what, I’ll drive over to your house and get you something to wear.”

“No!” Even Marge realized she’d shouted. “The house is an embarrassment right now,” she said in a much quieter voice. “Maybe I could borrow something from Bernice?”

I drove to Bernice’s, picked up a t-shirt and a stretchy pair of pants, and met Marge back in the locker room. She got dressed, walked with me into the parking lot, grabbed a hide-a-key from under her car’s back bumper, and unlocked her car. “Good thing I keep my wallet in my car.” Marge slid into the driver’s seat. “Listen, I know we talked about a practice session at my house, but I’m not feeling so well. I’d like to rest before preview tonight.”

“Sure.” I waved goodbye and watched her drive slowly, carefully out of the rec center parking lot.

* * *

"Cuckoo!"

"That is not what I need to hear right now," I admonished the clock on Bernice's wall.

I was worried about Marge and anxious about the show, but there was no way to know if she'd remember her lines or if her sing-in-character advice would help me until we faced an audience. So I decided to tackle another source of anxiety: my lack of progress on Charlie's case.

What had I learned about Charlie Small? He seemed to be a popular guy, and a busy one, on the theater board and in Bitsy's karaoke club. He was a Vietnam veteran, a Republican, and a Christian, a strong enough believer that people didn't think he would take his own life. He was also really depressed after the death of his wife. It wasn't much to go on.

I had the feeling the answer lay not with Charlie's life but his death. I found my black notebook on the counter and flipped through it. I knew the basics: carbon monoxide poisoning in his car, no note. My neighborhood investigation hadn't turned up much of anything except the unusually high number of suicides and the landscaper.

I'd initially thought the idea of a landscaper in this mostly gravel-lawned neighborhood was suspicious, but then I noticed a few around—blowing bougainvillea leaves, trimming orange trees, and pulling the few weeds that managed to survive. Charlie hadn't hired one, but one of his neighbors could have. I made a note to check on that.

Then there was Carl Marks. I hadn't seen him or his car since that night outside the theater, but I felt uneasy just thinking about him. Using my laptop, I logged into a database Duda Detectives used to run criminal background checks and typed in his name. Nothing, not even a parking ticket. Next I tried to find out what type of insurance policy he'd sold Charlie. I called my uncle.

"So how do I do this?" I asked, after giving him the rundown.

"To begin with, go to the Medical Information Bureau website and enter Charlie's information."

I did. I had to pretend I was Charlie, but I got his file. "Done. Now what?"

"Did anyone pull Charlie's medical records recently?"

I looked at my screen. "Yeah. It looks like Carl's company did, about a year ago."

"That means they probably issued him a sizable policy, since insurance companies don't usually bother pulling records for policies under 50K."

"Okay, now how do I find out what type of policy? And who the beneficiary is?"

"Remember how I started this conversation with 'To begin with?'"

"Uh huh..." I was beginning to wish I was in the office so I could see my uncle's face. I had the feeling he was grinning.

"That's all you can find out, at least for now. Then you got some real work to do."

If I had been in the office, I would've considered shooting him with a rubber band.

He continued: "Because the only people who would know more are Charlie's attorney, his beneficiaries, or his insurance agent."

"The guy I'm investigating."

"Right."

Definitely would have shot him with a rubber band.

Uncle Bob chuckled. "Isn't it fun being a PI?"

A few hours later, I was in the greenroom enjoying my first free meal: Chicken Marsala with wild rice pilaf and fresh cut green beans. Though it was only preview, the old FOTs and a few invitees would be there, so dinner was being served.

"How's the chicken?" Roger sat down next to me at the long folding table.

"Wonderful!" In reality, it was a tad dry, but it also wasn't beans.

Roger took a bite of his London broil and chewed. And chewed.

Zeb appeared, as was his way, and set a plate of coconut prawns in front of me. "This is what you really want to eat." I bit into one. It was indeed what I wanted to eat, like a tropical vacation for my mouth. "I've got a lovely pair of coconuts..." sang Zeb, tweaking imaginary boobs.

"A, does everything have to be about sex?" asked Candy, who sat down next to us with a dish of mac and cheese. "And B, you are way too young to know that song."

"Arnie taught it to me. And I'm not all about sex. There's also science—hey! Want to help me test the optimal temperature for maximum enjoyment of mac and cheese?"

"Sure." Candy shrugged.

Zeb grabbed her plate away. "Okay. Be right back." He jogged toward the dishwashing area.

"How's the detecting going?" Candy asked me. I had the sneaking suspicion she was trying to keep my mind off my little singing issue.

After Fran's remark this morning, I realized I probably shouldn't blab everything I knew. I was still figuring out how to reply when Zeb set Candy's new plate of food in front of her. On it were four little piles of macaroni and cheese. "Okay," he said. "Start with the portion at the top of the plate. Taste it and give me a ranking between one and ten, with ten being the highest."

Candy took a bite from the top pile. "Ow!" she yelped. "Hot hot hot!" She grabbed my glass of water, downed it, and glared at Zeb. "I think you just burned off all my taste buds."

"So on a scale of one to ten..." Zeb held a pencil poised above his black notebook.

"OW."

"I'll put that down as a 'one.'"

"Just get me a plate of lukewarm mac and cheese. Now."

"What approximate temperature do you consider lukewarm?"

"Now."

"Hey, kiddo." Marge walked in, looking remarkably better than when I last saw her. "How'd it go today?" she said. "You practice?"

I nodded. It had felt good, concentrating on my character, but since my phobia involved an audience, I had no way of knowing if Marge's advice would help once I was onstage.

"You've been working on the breathing technique I gave you?" asked Roger.

I hesitated. I didn't really want to tell him I'd had additional help. There was always a bit of tension between Marge and him.

"A half hour until places." The disembodied stage manager's voice floated over the PA system and saved me from replying. Instead I wolfed down the last of my chicken, dropped my empty plate at Zeb's dishwashing station, and headed to my dressing room. All the while I kept my fingers crossed. Whatever happened tonight could determine the fate of two careers.

Marge's advice worked. Or I heard that it did. I wasn't really aware of how my voice sounded, or the orchestra, or, thank God, the audience. But after my song, everyone congratulated me—just the way they'd congratulated Marge after her first scene, which went perfectly. I'd stood in the wings and listened. I could just hear the slight rhythm of...what song? I couldn't place it. Later when I had the chance, I grabbed Marge. "Hey, what song did you use to help you remember? I could just barely hear it and it's been driving me crazy trying to figure out what it was."

Marge smiled. "It's that song from *Cats*. The one Barbra Streisand made famous. You know..." She hummed a bit of the familiar tune.

"Of course," I said.

The song was "Memory."

CHAPTER 22

"WHAT GOOD IS STRUTTING YOUR STUFF ON THE STAGE?"

Even in the parking lot I could hear Marge singing the familiar tune of "Cabaret." Everyone could. That woman could belt.

"Come HEAR the organ PLAY." The song blew my hair back as I opened the stage door. I trotted down the hall.

"Eternal life AWAITS you, FRIEND." Marge stood in the greenroom, arms wide, inviting the whole world to..."Come to the CABA—nunnery!"

Oops. But no biggie, really. All of us had a hard time not singing the original words to the songs.

Roger, Bitsy, and the other cast members who were in the room clapped. Everyone was relieved that our headliner was ready just in time for opening night.

"You're in fine form." I gave her a friendly swat on her behind, which tonight had "Star" embroidered on mauve velour.

"Thanks to you, chickie." She crossed the room to the table where she'd left her duffel bag. "You know how I said that music transcends words?"

I nodded.

"I feel so good right now, I just had to sing." She poked me with an elbow. "I noticed your little problem is gone too."

"Knock on wood." I looked around for something wooden to knock on and settled for my head. "By the way," I said. "What was up at your house today? Everything okay?" Around three o'clock a bunch of cars had converged on Marge's house, including a posse car.

"Oh, that." She waved my concern away. "Damn burglar alarm. I punched in the wrong numbers and couldn't find the code. You know how it is." Unfortunately, I did. I set off Bernice's alarm the first night I stayed there and had to run around the house looking for the code, which I found in the nick of time. "I canceled the service," Marge said.

"Was that wise?" said Bitsy, behind us.

"It's Sunnydale," said Roger. "Nothing ever happens there."

"Ivy, join me in a cuppa joe to celebrate our newfound tricks for success?" Marge poured herself a cup of coffee from her thermos.

As she poured more coffee into a Styrofoam cup, I had that knock-on-wood feeling again, like we were tempting fate with our confidence, but said, "Sure."

Marge handed me the cup full of the steaming liquid. "Cheers," she said, knocking her cup into mine. I took a big swig—and spit it out. "Aaaaachhh!" I couldn't help the spitting or the weird noise I made. There was something god-awfully wrong with that coffee.

"What? It's good coffee. I even put cinnamon in." Marge took a sip before I could stop her. Her face turned crimson as she struggled to swallow.

"Omigod, is it poisoned?" asked Candy. The question wasn't as silly as it sounded. Uncle Bob had been poisoned at a theater once.

I sniffed at the coffee. "I don't think so."

"It couldn't be," said Marge. "I made it myself and put it right in the thermos. It's just coffee and cinnamon."

Roger reached for my cup. "May I?"

I handed it over gladly.

He took a small sip. "Ah." He leaned close to Marge and spoke quietly, which didn't really matter because the entire roomful of people was straining to hear. "I think you mixed up cinnamon with cayenne."

Did Bitsy's eyes gleam?

Marge stared at Roger for a moment, then burst into raucous laughter. "I did!" She slapped Roger on the back. "Cinnamon, cayenne, both start with Cs, both sort of brown. Ha!" she said, loudly.

I wondered if anyone else noticed that her smile did not reach her eyes. Marge was acting.

CHAPTER 23

Phew. We'd done it. I sang on pitch, Marge remembered her lines, and from the sound of the applause, opening night was a success.

We had just finished the all-cast bow that marked the end of curtain call when Arnie walked onstage with an armful of red roses. None of us were surprised when he presented Marge with the flowers, but several mouths dropped open as he got down on one knee, Marge's included.

"Think he'll be able to get up again?" Candy whispered to me. I elbowed her, in a nice way.

The audience quieted down. Keith rapped his baton on the top of his music stand, then, his eyes on Arnie, led the orchestra in the tune to "You're the Cream in My Coffee."

"You're the schmear on my bagel," Arnie sang. The audience laughed appreciatively.

"You're the love that is true." His voice wobbled a little with emotion.

"You really are...My shining star." Arnie proffered a small jewelry box to his star, whose mouth was still open.

"I want to marry you."

The audience exploded with applause—and Marge bolted from the stage.

The music halted. The audience stopped clapping. Arnie stayed on one knee for a moment, then slowly slumped back until he sat on the wooden stage. He looked like he'd been hit by an emotional bus.

"Help him up," I whispered to Timothy/Wolf and I ran offstage after Marge.

For a mature lady, she was pretty fast. I ran through backstage to the greenroom, where I saw the stage door to the parking lot close. I pushed it open in time to see Marge jump into her car.

"Wait!" I yelled, but Marge started up the car and roared out of the parking lot like a teenage boy.

When I got back into the greenroom, Zeb and Roger were helping Arnie into a chair.

"I would have never done it," Arnie shook his head, his eyes searching the room, "if I wasn't sure she loved me. I know she loves me. So why do this?" he asked the ceiling. When no answer came, he covered his face in his hands.

"Ivy?" I turned around to see Matt standing next to my brother and Sarah. "I came to pick up Cody and Sarah, but before they left..."

"We wanted to say how good you did." Cody was dressed in a pressed blue dress shirt that matched his eyes. He held hands with Sarah, who wore a pretty flowered dress, her dark hair curling down around her shoulders.

"Why didn't she want to marry him?" she asked me in a hushed voice.

"I don't know," I replied. Arnie was right. Marge did love him. Why not say yes? Or at least something that wouldn't have made her refusal so publicly humiliating.

"Hello, baby!" Candy came up and slid an arm around Matt, seemingly oblivious to the sadness that covered the room like a damp sheet. "Why Cody, you look good enough to eat. And this must be the young lady I've heard so much about." She winked at Sarah. "We all going out for a drink tonight to celebrate young love?"

Matt shook his head. "I'm on duty and—"

"C'mon, just a Coke." Candy wrapped her arms around his neck.

"And Sarah needs to get home. Besides," Matt looked at Arnie, whose shoulders were shaking, "I don't think it's much of a party atmosphere."

"It is a damn shame," Candy said. "He wore his lucky alligator shoes and everything."

"His what?" I said.

"Oh, there's a good story there." Candy caught my eye. "But I'll only tell it over Jack and Coke and chicken wings."

"Don't most people have beer and chicken wings?" asked Cody.

"Now, darlin'," Candy said, "am I most people?"

"Maybe it was because she didn't love him," Hailey said.

"Maybe it was because she didn't think he really loved her," Timothy said.

"Maybe it was because she doesn't think he's really reformed," Candy said.

"Reformed?" everyone said on cue. Actors, you know.

A bunch of us were crowded into a high-backed booth at Chili's, a big basket of chicken wings in the middle of the table. Until Candy's pronouncement, I'd been half-listening to the conversation, too worried about Marge to participate in the banter. But now I paid attention.

"I have it on good authority," Candy sat back in the booth and sucked on a wing, "that our Arnie is a jailbird."

"Really?" I didn't know many (okay, any) jailbirds, but Arnie didn't seem the type.

"What was he in for? Not using moisturizer?" asked Timothy, who, though he played my love interest, was as gay as the day is long. He was also really hairy.

Candy downed the last of her drink and held her glass up to the light.

"Lands, have you ever seen such a poor empty thing?"

"Yeah, yeah." Timothy waved a waitress over. He even had hair on his hands. "Another Jack and Coke over here, please."

I held up my empty glass too. Timothy ignored me. It was worth a try.

"And another amber ale for this lovely lady." That was Roger. I wished I hadn't angled for the drink. I felt beholden enough to him as it was. But what the heck, it was free beer.

"So," said Hailey. "What's the story, Morning Glory?"

"Well, I guess Arnie used to wrestle alligators down in Florida."

"What?" I dipped a wing into some ranch dip. "Arnie's like five foot four or something."

"Those little guys can be mighty strong," Candy said. "Wiry, you know."

Hailey and I rolled our eyes at each other. This story sounded like a "Candy special," a bit of gossip accessorized beyond all recognition.

"Anyway," Candy said, ignoring our eye roll and smiling at the waitress who dropped off our fresh drinks, "one day this alligator was attacking a little boy. Arnie jumped into the swamp and saved the kid, but he ended up killing the gator."

"With his bare hands?" asked Timothy. None of us really believed Candy, but it was fun to egg her on.

"Yep," she said. "Broke its jaw or something."

"How did that put him in jail?" I sipped my drink and decided that free beer actually tasted better.

"I guess it's illegal to kill an alligator," said Candy. "So Arnie went to jail. And I heard he got sued too, by the parents of the boy he saved 'cause the kid still got bit by the gator."

"That was Arnie's fault?" asked Hailey.

"No, no, no," said Timothy. "I've heard of that type of stuff happening. That's why I'll never rescue anyone."

"Good to know," I said. "Remind me never to go hiking with you."

"Like I hike?" Timothy arched an obviously plucked eyebrow.

"The thing is," Candy said. "Arnie got the last laugh after all. He had that dead alligator made into shoes. He wears them every opening night." She sat back in the booth, a satisfied storyteller.

While I was trying to pull up a mental image of Arnie's shoes, I realized that Roger had been quiet during the whole story. "You ever hear any of this?" I asked.

He rubbed a finger around the rim of his whiskey glass. "I don't know exactly what happened," he said slowly. "But, yeah, Arnie was definitely in jail."

CHAPTER 24

The sun shone on my shoulders, music filled the air, and a bunch of brawny men showed off in front of me. No matter what had happened last night, all was right with the world this afternoon.

"Pull!" The shout rose above the theme from "Rocky," which blared out of a portable PA system. I sat on the side of a grassy field, sipped my Diet Coke, and admired the men, especially the one whose biceps were as astonishing as his eyelashes. Jeremy caught my eye briefly and grinned as he and his seven teammates, all wearing dark blue Phoenix Fire Department t shirts, tried to pull their foes over a line drawn in the dirt. I cheered wildly along with the crowd when my team gained ground. Who knew the annual "Guns and Hoses" Police versus Fire tug-of-war was so much fun?

A well-orchestrated tug sent the policemen spilling over the line and tumbling on top of one another like puppies.

"Woo hoo!" I shouted along with dozens of other onlookers as a collective groan arose from the police side of the field. The policemen scrambled to their feet, brushed themselves off, and formed a line to shake the hands of the firefighters, who barely suppressed their glee.

"Third year in a row," said the young woman next to me. Then to her toddler, "Can you show everyone how to make three?" The boy held three chubby fingers in the air as his daddy ran toward him. His mother smiled in my direction, jiggling the baby she held in her arms. "Who are you here with?"

"Jeremy White."

"Jeremy? Wow. We've been wondering when someone would snag him. He is a *catch*."

Her husband reached the little group, swooped his giggling son into his sweaty arms and kissed his wife and baby. All truly was right with the world. Except that my heart hurt, just a little. It always did when I saw happy families.

But suddenly I was in the air, picked up like a toddler by a laughing Jeremy. "Did you see their faces?" he asked. "They were so sure they'd win this year they said they'd double their contribution to the United Way if they lost. And they did. Ha!" He hugged me again to his sweaty chest. I didn't mind.

He stripped off his shirt. Wow. I thought I might faint. The woman with the little boy caught my eye and gave me a "See what I mean?" look. Jeremy grabbed a towel from a duffel bag near me, wiped himself off, and shrugged on a similar but non-sweaty Phoenix Fire Department t-shirt. "I'm starving," he said. "Let's get in line before the police eat it all."

We walked over to the picnic area, where several big barbecues filled the air with the irresistible smell of smoky meat. Jeremy grabbed a couple of paper plates and we got in line. "Hotdog or hamburger?" he asked.

My stomach growled in response.

"I'm having both," he said.

What the hell. "Me too." After all, I had a pretty high metabolism. Plus I'd drop in at one of the aerobic classes at the rec center later.

"So how'd it go last night?" Jeremy asked.

I gave him a quick rundown as we filed through the line, picking up buns and scooping coleslaw and beans onto our plates. I stuck with the good news. Bad news was out of place on a day like this.

"Sorry I couldn't be there," he said, squirting ketchup onto his dog. "When are your folks coming?"

"They probably aren't." My parents and I had what you might call a "cool relationship." Though they lived only a few hours away in the mountain town of Prescott, I usually saw them just once a year, when I drove Cody up there for Christmas.

"Well, it's nice your brother came with his girlfriend."

"She's not his girlfriend." Whoa, where did that come from?

Jeremy looked at me sideways, but wisely ignored my remark. I did too. Whatever was bugging me, now was not the time to think about it. Now was the time to glory in sun and hotdogs and the possibility of romance with a nice guy with amazing pecs.

I had just managed to settle down on a big blanket on the grass with my full plate and Diet Coke (to make up for the other calories) when a familiar voice behind me said, "Olive?"

I turned and felt something slide off my plate and onto my lap. I looked down. Baked beans. Very pretty on my white shorts.

"Oh shoot. Sorry," said the guy who had startled me. Detective Pinkstaff, a friend of my uncle's, probably here to cheer on the police.

I stood up and let the mess slide onto the ground. A couple of nearby firemen burst into laughter. "Hey Jeremy!" one said. "Better hose her down!"

Instead Jeremy stripped off his shirt (again!) and gave it to me. "This should be long enough to cover..." He nodded at my bean-smeared shorts. "I'll wear the other one." He grabbed the sweaty one out of his duffle and put it on. I wondered if there was any way I could get him to take off his shirt again. I bet there was, but maybe not now. Especially since Pink seemed to be joining us.

"Detective Pinkstaff," he said, offering a hand to Jeremy. "But everyone calls me Pink."

"Hey, Detective!" called one of the neighboring firemen. "You here to arrest us for winning?"

"No, just for drinking an open container in a park."

The guys looked at their beer.

"Kidding." Pink turned back to Jeremy, whose beer had stopped halfway to his lips. "We got a permit. Drink away."

Jeremy indicated a spot on the blanket. "Join us?"

I slipped Jeremy's XL t-shirt over my head and wished he

wasn't quite so polite. I liked Pink, a lot actually, but I wanted Jeremy for myself. Plus the detective had asked me out once. He was a good twenty years older than me, thought wrinkles were a fashion statement, and smelled like menthol cigarettes. He was also a really sweet guy, so I was a bit uncomfortable flaunting my fabulous-looking date in front of him.

"Can't stay long," he said, settling himself on the blanket next to me. "Just wanted to see how Olive was getting on with her first case."

"A couple of things seem funky—" I began.

"That's just Jeremy!" said one of the firemen jokers.

"But I can't put my finger on anything."

"It was carbon monoxide poisoning, right?" said Pink.

"Yeah." The firemen had quieted down, probably so they could eavesdrop better. "In his car," I replied.

"What kind of car?" asked Jeremy.

"A brand new Ford Taurus."

"No catalytic converter?" he asked.

"Uh..."

"A car that new shoulda had a catalytic converter," Pink said.

The firemen scooted closer. "See, catalytic converters turn carbon monoxide into carbon dioxide," said one. "That's why they're better for the environment."

"And why it's tough to kill yourself with a car that has a catalytic converter," added the second one.

"But they can be removed," Jeremy said.

"Some people take 'em off to get better gas mileage." The first fireman grinned at Pink. "Cheapos. You know, like policemen."

The detective ignored him. "They're also a pretty hot ticket in the criminal world. Easy to sell for the platinum they contain. Easy to remove too. Car owners don't even realize they're gone half the time."

"Wait," I said. "You're telling me that Charlie could only have committed suicide in this particular car if the catalytic converter had been removed, either by him or by a thief?"

"Yep." This time the firemen and the policeman were in agreement.

I had some investigating to do.

CHAPTER 25

"Na na na na. Na na na na," the firemen sang as I kissed Jeremy. "Hey hey hey, goodbye." I waved goodbye to them all and headed off for Sunnydale. If I made good time, I'd have an hour before I had to be at the theater.

Nope. I don't know where all the people were going in their incredibly slow cars, but by the time I drove past the Sunnydale exclamation points, I only had twenty minutes to spare. I decided to make the most of it, and stopped at the Sunnydale Posse Headquarters.

The building looked like a smallish police station, with flags flying, a gated lot for official vehicles, and a few patrol cars parked outside. I parked next to one of them and headed in through glass doors, only to stop cold at the reception desk.

Bitsy.

The Alzheimer's comment had cemented my dislike of the woman, but there was something else, something sneaky about her that raised my antennae. For one thing, she seemed to be everywhere—the theater, the rec center, the craft fair. And here she was again.

"Ivy! So nice to see you."

Bitsy's sincere-sounding greeting made me feel bad I'd doubted her. But just a little. "You too," I replied.

"Have you seen Marge today? I'm a little worried about her."

I shook my head. I'd called Marge this morning, but no answer. I even went over and rang the doorbell. I heard a dog bark, and then what sounded like Arnie's voice. Good. Maybe they were making up. But whatever was happening, I didn't want to discuss it with Bitsy. "I didn't know you volunteered here," I said instead. A gray-haired woman walking down the hall smiled at me and studiously avoided looking at Bitsy.

"Oh, I do a little community service," said Bitsy.

"More like servicing the community," the gray-haired woman mumbled as she passed me and walked out the glass doors.

Huh.

"What can I do for you—oh dear," Bitsy glanced at the clock on the wall, "in the next ten minutes?"

This was awkward. I really needed some information, but felt like I should keep my investigating to myself.

"Is this about Charlie? How did your neighborhood investigation go?" asked Bitsy.

Guess that particular train had left the station. "I was wondering if anyone had their catalytic converters stolen recently."

"Don't think we'd have that information, but I'll see what I can do."

"I'd also like to find out a little more about the suicides you've had here recently, the manner of death, specifically."

"I'm pretty sure that's not public record, but I'll see what I can do."

"How about the names of the people who committed suicide?"

"Arizona is a closed record state—to protect our privacy, you know, but—"

"You'll see what you can do," I finished.

"Wait here just a sec." Bitsy punched a number into the phone on the desk. "Can you cover the reception desk for me, just for a minute?" she said into the receiver. Then, "Thanks a bunch."

A short-ish man with a comb-over hurried down the hall toward us.

"Thanks, Max." Bitsy got up from her desk and trotted down the hall. She knocked on a closed door and was admitted.

"Having a nice day?" I asked the guy, who now occupied Bitsy's chair. He didn't answer me, just ran a hand over his elaborate hairdo. I decided to give the shy fellow a break and turned my attention to the framed photos on the walls. Most were pictures of posse members in uniform, but there was also a big photo of Maricopa County Sheriff Joe Arpaio. Since the posse was organized under the county, Sheriff Joe was its head honcho. He was also "America's Toughest Sheriff," famous for housing inmates in tent cities, reintroducing chain gangs, and making all inmates wear pink underwear (for better inventory control, he said). I wondered if the sheriff's for-the-public version of the underwear (with "Go Joe!" stamped on them) sold well. I wondered if the Spanish version ("¡Vamos Jose!") was still on offer. I wondered how Jeremy would look in pink boxers. Before I could wonder how Jeremy would look out of pink boxers (I admit I was heading down that path), Bitsy returned.

"It's as I suspected. I can't give you much, but I can put together some information for you. I'm working here again on Tuesday afternoon. Why don't you come by then?"

"Sounds good. See you at the theater." I was about to leave when Bitsy said, "You know, you might talk to one of our posse members, Hank Snow."

My ears perked up at the mention of Creepy Silver Hank. I briefly wondered if they literally did that, stood up a bit more, but directed my curiosity to the matter at hand. "Why him?"

"It's a funny thing." Bitsy shook her head in disbelief. "He's been on every single one of those suicide calls."

CHAPTER 26

"Do you think real nuns get hot?" I asked. I was. Candy and I were walking through the greenroom to our dressing room after curtain call for the Sunday matinee and I was dripping. "Especially here in Arizona. I mean, they wear all this black fabric." Yards and yards of it, if my costume was any indication.

"Darlin', have you been under a rock? Most nuns just wear normal clothes today." Candy opened the dressing room door for the both of us. "Probably because they got too hot."

Made sense to me.

"But we could ask my cousin," she said.

"She's a nun? One who wears a habit?"

"No, but she was." Candy sat down and took off her too-tight shoes. The costumer didn't have nun-looking shoes in a size twelve, so Candy squeezed her enormous feet into size elevens every night. "In a past life. She was beheaded. S'got the birthmark on her neck to prove it."

I began taking off my habit. The veil and wimple came off pretty easily, but the habit itself had way too many folds. I pulled it over my head, engulfing myself in a sea of sweaty black rayon. "Wouldn't it be really hard to climb the Alps in habits?"

"I don't know." Candy sighed happily. I bet she was rubbing her feet, but I couldn't see because I was still stuck inside my nun costume. "The girls in the movie wore dresses. Maybe the Alps aren't so hard to climb. Or maybe there's a back way."

Since I still had black fabric covering my face, Candy couldn't see my look of doubt.

"I think you're just complaining 'cause you want to wear your curtain costume for bows," she said.

Busted. In our play, Mary makes the Vaughn Katt dancers some new, less-skimpy costumes out of drapes. Mine was adorable, a short flirty skirt and lace-up Bavarian-style bodice. I looked like that girl on the German beer label.

"That costume is sexy, in an innocent sort of way," Candy went on.

I could see the light at the end of my habit and struggled toward it.

"Sort of like Cody's girlfriend," Candy said as I finally emerged. I managed not to make the "she's not his girlfriend" statement again, but just barely. "She's cuter than a sackful of puppies." Candy continued. "What's her name?"

"Sarah."

"Sarah." Candy was down to her undies and putting on her street clothes. "Do you think they've done it yet?" She stepped into her jeans.

"Candy! What is with you lately?" Candy was always sassy, but lately she'd been a bit over the top, inappropriate even.

"I know." She zipped up and sat in her chair with a sigh. "I'm getting as bad as Zeb. I think I'm just feeling restless."

"Why? I thought things were good." Candy had Matt, a job that worked with her schedule, and she was never without acting work of some kind.

"I just wonder what I'm doing here." She peered at herself in the mirror. "I think I'm getting crow's feet."

I put those two thoughts together. "You're worried that you're wasting your youth in a dinner theater in Arizona."

Candy looked at me in the mirror. "You're getting to be a pretty good detective." She shrugged. "If I'm really going to be an actress, I'd better hop to it."

She had a point. But I didn't want to talk about it, because then I'd have think about it too.

"But something's up with you too," Candy said. "Every time I say Cody's name lately you frown," she said. "And I don't think you said 'boo' to his girlfriend when she came on opening night."

Didn't I? Maybe not. "I was probably hot and grouchy because of this ridiculous nun's outfit, which did I mention is a stupid costume for curtain call?"

"Yeah, you just did."

"None of the audience can even tell who's who," I finished.

"'Cept for Marge," said Candy, pulling a hot pink t-shirt over her head. "'Cause she looks like an apple doll nun."

Marge had tried lighter foundation during dress rehearsal but she looked like a kabuki nun. "Apple doll nun" was a step up.

"She said anything to you?" Candy corralled her unruly curls into a ponytail.

I shook my head. Ever since Friday night, Marge had slipped into the theater at the last possible moment as to avoid all of us offstage. She remembered all her lines and did a decent job of the show. I'm sure none of the audience could see the pain behind her eyes, but we could. And judging from Arnie's long face and unusually demure demeanor (even his cigar looked limp), the two hadn't made up.

As worried as I was about Marge, I had other things on my mind, like the catalytic converter conundrum, and Hank. I was sure the two were connected. But how? Maybe if I could tail Hank, I'd find out the link. But not only was my car the only yellow, fire-prone VW around, I was one of the few under-fifty folk in Sunnydale. He'd peg me in an instant.

Candy smoothed her nun's habit as she hung it on the rack in the dressing room. "I kinda like my habit," she said, smoothing the fabric. "Because—"

"La la la," I sang. "I don't want to hear about playing 'Naughty Nun.'"

"*Because*," Candy continued, "it's so different from clothes anyone wears, yet you sort of disappear into it." I wondered if she was referring to my tendency to get stuck in the costume, which I seemed to do with regularity. "It's like you're hiding in plain sight."

Oh.
Oh.
Perfect.

CHAPTER 27

It was Monday morning and way too early, but Bitsy had told me Hank was due at the posse at six a.m., so I dutifully got up at the crack of dawn, got dressed in my habit from *The Sound of Cabaret*, and drove Bernice's golf cart to my first stakeout location. The cart wasn't exactly what I thought of as a nun-mobile, but it did fit Sunnydale better than my VW, and I thought there must be nun golfers somewhere.

I parked around the corner from Hank's street where I could see his one-story Spanish-style house. My plan was to follow him to see if he cased any potential victims' houses or did anything else generally suspicious. I had reread the chapters on tailing people in all my PI handbooks and brought the recommended gear: notebook, mini tape recorder, and camera. I also skipped my morning cup of coffee. "Don't want to lose someone because you have to make a pit stop," one of the books warned.

After twenty minutes of waiting (during which I heartily regretted my no-coffee decision), I finally saw Hank back out of his drive. I slunk down in my seat so he wouldn't see me. This was when I realized that golf carts are not the best vehicles to hide in. No doors, you know.

Luckily Hank didn't seem to notice. He drove to the posse station, parked out front and walked in the entrance.

I pulled around to where I could see the official posse parking lot, where all the cop cars were kept behind locked gates. Though the posse was made up of volunteers, their cars were exact copies of

Maricopa County patrol vehicles, down to the radio antennas and flashing lights.

After a few minutes, Hank strolled into the lot, started up a car, and pulled out of the lot. I turned on my mini tape recorder. "Hank pulled out of the lot at 6:10 a.m., driving a posse car, license plate HDB 8913." I waited for him to pass by, and pulled out behind him, staying as far behind him as I could without losing him.

Over the next hour, I tailed Hank, making note of his route and of every house he slowed down in front of or stopped at. Twice he stopped for a smoke, once in a church parking lot, once near a golf course, both times looking around to make sure no one saw him.

"Note to self," I said to my tape recorder. "See if it's against the rules for posse members to smoke." I was pretty awake now, but when Hank pulled into a 7-Eleven I was really happy. Coffee!

I didn't know how long he'd be in there, so I needed to move quickly if I wanted a cup. I grabbed the spare pair of glasses I'd found at Bernice's house, put them on as an added disguise, and dashed into the 7-Eleven.

Or at least as far as the curb.

Peering through Bernice's glasses, the curb looked lower than it really was. Not only did I trip over it, I caught my foot in my habit too.

"Oh dear, are you all right?" said the first woman who rushed to help me.

"Have you broken anything?" said another man.

"Are you European?" said another.

"What are you talking about?" a woman (probably his wife) said to him.

"You know any nuns around here who wear habits?" he asked.

"Are you here for the golf?" said another woman, pointing to Bernice's cart.

"Ja," I said, trying to disentangle myself from my habit. "Sprechen sie Deutsch?" I really hoped no one did speak German since I only knew the few words I'd learned from the play.

"Olive?" said the next voice. Oh no. I peered up through Bernice's incredibly thick glasses to see mirrored sunglasses. Hank shifted a full paper bag to one arm and pulled me to my feet with the other. Pretty strong for a sixty-something guy.

"Almost didn't recognize you in that getup," he said. "Until I heard your voice." Even speaking German? This guy was good. Or he'd been onto me for a while. "You should be more careful."

Was there an undertone of menace in his carefully modulated voice? I couldn't tell, and I couldn't see his eyes through those damn sunglasses. I shivered a little despite my hot polyester costume.

A packet of Twinkies started to slip off the top of Hank's grocery bag, which was full of chips and cookies. Hank let go of me, caught the Twinkies, and stuffed the bag in his car. "Why are you dressed like that?" His walkie-talkie crackled and a voice said, "Stand by for a nine-oh-one."

"Ten-four," said Hank, sliding into his driver's seat.

"It's a promotion for the show." I'd come up with this nun disguise excuse earlier, but now it sounded pretty lame. "Everyone," I said in a loud cheerful voice, "come see *The Sound of Cabaret* at Desert Magic Dinner Theater. Dancing nuns!"

"Didn't she just say she was German?" someone grumbled.

"With Marge Weiss, Arizona's Ethel Merman!" I said, trying to distract from my gaffe.

A few "oohs" from the crowd, then Hank's flat emotionless voice from inside his patrol car: "Not anymore. There's been an accident."

CHAPTER 28

I raced over to Marge's house as fast as Bernice's golf cart could go. By the time I rounded the corner to the cul-de-sac, all of the official vehicles were gone. Hank couldn't have been more than a few minutes ahead of me, but he, too, was pulling away. A few onlookers lingered. Wait, was that Carl Marks?

I squealed to a stop in Bernice's drive, but by the time I jumped out of the cart, the mustachioed man I thought I saw had disappeared.

I approached a woman I vaguely recognized as a neighbor. "What happened?"

She stared at me. "I didn't know Marge was Catholic."

What? Oh, I was still a nun. "She's not. I don't think. It's just—what happened?"

"It depends on who you talk to," said a silver-haired man. He pulled a pipe filled with tobacco out of his shirt pocket, extracted some matches from another pocket, and lit one. "There are two sides to this particular story, plus a few pertinent details." He drew on his pipe a little to get it lit. "I found her."

"Is she okay?"

"That depends on your definition of okay."

Arghh. I knew I could probably get a ton of information out of this storyteller, but I was not feeling patient. I took a deep breath and held it. Sort of like meditating, but not.

"I was having my morning constitutional when I heard Marge's dog barking up a storm. Not only that, but I heard another sound over and over—a man's voice. It said, 'Let's go, Gorgeous! Let's go, Gorgeous!' Again and again."

I released my pent-up breath as quietly as I could and took another.

"I rang the doorbell and knocked and knocked," he continued. "No answer, just that dog and 'Let's go, Gorgeous!' So I called 911. The firemen got in using her lockbox and found Marge on the floor in the garage, bleeding from the head. Must have had a tumble."

"But she's okay?" The words came out in a whoosh with my breath.

He puffed on his pipe thoughtfully. "I guess it's understandable she'd be confused after a fall like that. But it's more than that. The paramedics figure she got up for a glass of water or something, got confused and made a wrong turn, and fell down the step into the garage, where she hit her head. But that's not what Marge says."

"What does she say?" I tried hard not to throttle the slow-talker.

"She says somebody tried to kill her."

I had just parked Bernice's cart in her garage when my cell rang. I didn't recognize the number but I picked up anyway.

"Ivy?" It sounded like Arnie. And it sounded like he was crying. "I'm at Sunnydale Hospital." He took a big shuddering breath. "Marge is here."

"I heard."

"And she won't see me." He barely got out the "me."

"I'm so sorry, Arnie."

A few sniffles. "But here's the thing." An enormous honk of a nose blow. "She says she'll only see you."

It only took me ten minutes to get to the hospital parking lot, even via golf cart. I parked, jogged to the hospital entrance, stopped at the information desk to find out where Marge was, and made my way to the ER, where she lay in bed behind a curtain. Along the route, people were inordinately polite to me. Probably because I still wore the nun habit. It would have taken me twenty minutes to get there if I'd tried to get out of the dang thing.

Marge's eyes were closed. Aside from the gauze bandage wrapped around her head, she didn't look too bad, partly because of her perma-tan. I mean, it would be hard for her to look pale.

"Marge?" I said softly.

Her eyes flew open. "I'm Jewish," she said.

"Uh-huh."

"And I'm not confusing. Convening. Converting."

Ah, the nun's habit. "Marge, it's Ivy." I got closer so she could see me better.

"Is it nighttime?"

A window was visible from Marge's bed. The sun shone brightly in a cloudless sky.

"It's morning."

"Then why are you wearing that?" She nodded at my outfit, which I wore as a costume for the show. At night.

"Oh. I was...undercover. How are you feeling?"

"Like someone used my head for a...you know, that game you play with alleys and gutters and pins?"

"Bowling?"

"Yeah, a bowling ball." Marge gently touched the back of her head and winced. "Listen, chickie." I was relieved to hear the old nickname. Maybe everything would be okay. "I need you to do a couple of things for me. First of all, they're not going to let me go home for a few days. Lassie needs someone to take care of him." Lassie was a him? "But he doesn't do so well in other people's houses. You'll need to move into my place for a while."

I nodded. I'd call Bernice, but I was pretty sure she wouldn't mind if I kept an eye on her house from next door, especially under the circumstances.

"The second thing—God, my head hurts."

"You want me to get a nurse?"

Marge looked at me blankly. "What for?"

"To give you something for your head?"

"Nah, I'm fine."

I wasn't so sure about that. "You said there was a second thing you want me to do."

"Yeah." Her hands plucked at the cotton blanket covering her.

"Marge," I said gently, "the second thing?"

She scrunched her forehead in concentration, then looked at me, her eyes focused again. "You're a detective." I was about to object, but this didn't seem the time. "I want you to find whoever did this to me."

"Did what, Marge? Can you remember?"

She screwed up her face again. "Not really. I just know there was someone in my garage."

"How do you know?"

"Lassie. He started going apeshit, barking like a crazy dog. I got up to see what was going on and heard something in the garage. I opened the door and stepped out and someone came at me."

"Did you see who?"

She shook her head. "That's all really foggy. I just remember a shape where it shouldn't be, then I heard Lassie hitting that damn doggie doorbell Arnie gave me."

"Doggie doorbell?"

"It's a big plastic button. You train the dog to push it when he wants to go out. Arnie recorded his own voice on it so it says, 'Let's go, Gorgeous!' Lassie hit it again and again, over and over. I bet that's what scared the intruder away."

And what the neighbor heard. I smiled when I made the connection.

"That's right." Marge had a glimmer of the old sass in her eyes. "Not only did Lassie rescue me, I was saved by the bell."

CHAPTER 29

After throwing my sweaty disgusting nun's habit into the washer at Bernice's house, I walked next door to Marge's. Her house was similar to Bernice's: stucco exterior and red tile roof, but the front yard boasted a patch of grass shaded by a Palo Verde tree, all surrounded by a short decorative iron fence. Maybe for the dog?

I felt a thrill of nosy excitement as I unlocked the door with the key Marge had given me. I loved snooping and I'd never been invited inside Marge's house. I stepped into the cool interior. The click of toenails on the tile announced the dog, who rounded the corner in the entryway and skidded to a stop. I couldn't tell right away if Lassie was a he or she, but I could tell the dog wasn't a collie. It was a black pug. Lassie looked at me, then walked around me and peered out the open door.

"Sorry, it's just me." I shut the door. "Want to go for a walk?" Lassie's whole butt wagged. "Let's go find your leash." He or she snorted in agreement.

A niche in the entryway held an abstract statue made of red and purple glass. On closer inspection, I could see it was an artist's rendition of the comedy and tragedy masks. Pretty cool.

Didn't see anywhere Marge might put a leash in the entryway, so I padded down the white-tiled hall. Lassie pushed ahead of me. I rounded the corner and walked into a big open room that looked like it served as living room and dining room, with an open kitchen attached. Lassie stepped on the red plastic button by the patio door. "Let's go, Gorgeous!" I recognized the sound, and not just from Marge or the neighbor. I'd heard it the day I had come over to check on Marge, the morning I hoped she and Arnie were making up.

"Let's go, Gorgeous!" The pug's buggy little eyes pleaded with me. I slid open the door. "There you go." Lassie ran out the door to another small patch of grass and lifted his leg. Definitely a he.

Lassie trotted back inside, relieved. Me, I was the opposite of relieved as I stared past the dog at a turquoise nightmare. Marge had forgotten to tell me she had a swimming pool.

I'd figure out what to do about that later. I shut the door. Lassie stood near what must be the door to the garage, looking at me meaningfully from beside an empty water bowl. I picked it up, then opened the door. This must be where Marge...

The bowl dropped from my hands. There were bloodstains on the step, on the concrete floor of the garage, on the doorframe. Correction: there was blood. Still wet. The sweet metallic scent of it filled my nose.

I held my breath, thinking I might be sick. Instead, after a few seconds, a switch flipped on in my brain and I began looking at the scene clinically. It looked like Marge had hit her head on a small brass hook fastened into the doorframe—for keys, maybe? Most of the blood was on the top of the step, but some had dripped down onto the garage floor. There were smears and dog prints, plus several sets of partial footprints. The paramedics? Or an intruder? I followed some of the prints to a door that led to a small side yard landscaped with gravel and a few morning glory bushes. I stared at the gravel, which looked slightly disturbed. Were those footprints or coyote tracks? I made a mental note to keep Marge's little tasty pug close by and went back into the garage. More prints led out the garage door. I pushed the button for the opener, waited for the door to rise, and walked outside, where I could see more faint footprints already fading in the Arizona sun. Seemed unlikely an intruder would exit this very visible way. I suspected Marge's rescuers made the prints while getting her into the ambulance.

I walked back into the garage, closed the door, and stared at the scene. I'd never thought about who cleaned up the blood.

Paramedics would need to get victims to the hospital, so I suspected it wasn't their responsibility. I was afraid it was mine now.

A cold nose nudged my shin. When Lassie realized that I noticed him, he ran back to his water bowl, which was still where I had dropped it on the garage floor.

"Sorry, buddy." I picked up the bowl, stepped around the blood, and went through the door into the kitchen to get some water for the poor thing.

That's when I noticed the first list, written on a large fluorescent yellow Post-it and stuck to the counter between the sink and the coffeepot. It said:

1. Throw out old filter full of coffee.
2. Fill coffeepot with water to top line.
3. Pour water into back compartment of coffeemaker.

The very detailed list went on, ending with, "Put CINNAMON in coffee. Smell or taste before adding!!!"

Looking around, I noticed another Post-it stuck above a desk. On closer inspection, it was a list of instructions on how to pay bills, down to affixing the stamp. Another one in the hall prompted Marge to make sure she had her keys, driver's license, and insurance card in her purse. And one mounted near the front door reminded her to take keys and a poo bag when walking the dog. The last line read, "The dog's name is Lassie."

Oh, Marge.

CHAPTER 30

"Do you know how to clean up blood?" I admit it wasn't the most romantic opening, but I did kiss Jeremy "hello" right afterward. And being the nice fireman-type he was, he took my question in stride.

"I do," he said, stepping into Marge's foyer. "Is everything okay?"

"Yeah. It's leftover blood."

"Good." He stooped to pet Lassie. "Then let's eat first. I'm starving." He gave one last scratch to the dog, whose butt wriggled with glee at his touch. I understood the feeling.

Since it was Monday, one of my nights off, I'd asked Jeremy to dinner. I originally planned to have him over to Bernice's house, but when I'd called her with the news, she insisted I stay at Marge's and take care of Lassie. I promised to check on her house and plants once a day.

Jeremy followed me into the living room. "This blood have to do with your investigation?"

"No." I wasn't getting anywhere with Charlie's case, and it was eating at me. Not only was I beginning to feel like a dud as a detective, I was afraid I was letting down Uncle Bob. And Amy Small. Not to mention poor Charlie.

Jeremy stopped in front of the sliding glass door. "Nice," he said, admiring the view.

It was nice. It was a nice view on a nice night with a nice guy, and I needed to stop thinking about blood and investigations and live in the moment instead.

"Right on the golf course." Jeremy's eyes followed a golfer's swing.

"You play golf?" I asked. Jeremy and I were still in that getting-to-know-you stage. It was partly a function of our crazy schedules, partly a gentlemanly approach on his side, and maybe a bit of self-protection on mine. I had fallen hard for a fellow actor last fall and gotten burned. Ha. Bet I was safe from that with a fireman.

"I chase a little white ball around. Don't know if you could call it 'playing.'" Jeremy turned to see me smiling at my private fireman joke. "What's funny?"

"It's just good to be with you." I smiled again as I walked into the open kitchen to stir a bubbling pot of chili-scented black beans. I had sprung for some ground beef for tonight's feast, but just couldn't seem to get away from the beans.

"You too." He hugged me from behind. Ohhhh. I relaxed into his arms and chest. I'd never had a boyfriend who spooned with me, but this must be what it felt like. Safe, but sorta sexy.

Jeremy kissed my neck. Definitely sexy. "Can I help you with dinner?" A man who offered to cook? Even sexier.

"We're having hamburgers. Help me with the grill?"

"Sure thing." Jeremy went out through the sliding glass door to the awning-covered patio, Lassie trotting behind him. Through the window, I watched Jeremy stop and look at the pool. His face was turned away from me, but his shoulders rose and fell with a deep breath. Then he walked over and turned on the grill. The flames illuminated his face and his eyes shone—wait, were those tears? Jeremy caught me watching and grinned, his dimples deepening into shadow. Any trace of sadness disappeared.

"Alright." He came back into the kitchen, Lassie following behind. "Hamburger?" he asked, opening the refrigerator.

"Already made into patties and everything. They're next to the coleslaw."

I was sort of proud of myself. I mostly cooked one-dish dinners: spaghetti, beans and rice, omelets, that sort of thing.

Tonight we had three whole courses. Four, if you counted the chocolate ice cream in the freezer. Which I did.

Jeremy stood in front of the open refrigerator. "I hope it's not you who needs to remember what goes in the freezer and what goes in the fridge."

I must have missed a Post-it in the refrigerator. "It's a long story," I said. And since he was starving and the story involved blood, I added, "I'll tell you after dinner."

Later, over bowls of ice cream on the patio (a good safe distance from that damn pool), I filled him in.

"You really like this Marge, don't you?"

"Yeah." Lassie sat curled at my feet, his little body warm against my ankle.

"And you believe her?"

I wasn't sure why I believed Marge, but I did. I nodded slowly.

"Do you think maybe you believe her because you like her?"

"Maybe," I conceded.

"You're a detective." He called me a detective! I really was going to have to get that PI license soon. "Let's look at this like two investigators," Jeremy said.

"Like *two* investigators?"

"Caught that, did you?"

"I *am* a detective," I said in my best noir-ish voice.

"And I'm applying to be an arson investigator." Jeremy grinned broadly. "Who knows, maybe we'll even work together someday."

I didn't know how many PIs worked with arson investigators, but I hoped I'd be one.

"First of all, is there any evidence of confusion on her part?" Jeremy sat forward in his chair.

I thought about the conversation at the hospital, the cayenne in her coffee, the note reminding her of her dog's name. "Yeah."

"Then why don't you think she's confused about what happened?"

"I did a little research and learned that dementia at this stage doesn't usually involve hallucinations. Marge was sure she heard Lassie barking and hitting the doggie doorbell—"

"Could that just have been Lassie wanting to go out?"

"She also saw a person in the garage." And before he could ask, "She wasn't sure if it was a man or a woman. Just saw a shape."

"And then she hit her head?"

"Yeah." I grimaced. "That's what I need your help cleaning up. She seemed to bleed an awful lot."

"Head wounds can do that. And a concussion can make people confused about what really happened." Jeremy's golden eyes were serious.

"Okay," I said. "I'll keep an open mind about the intruder bit. Now I have something to ask you. Why did you look so sad earlier? When you came outside?"

"Oh." Jeremy sat back up and his face closed like a door shutting. "I worked an accident yesterday. Little kid in the family pool." He shook his head. "He didn't make it."

I could tell he didn't want to talk about it, so I got up and kissed him instead. He kissed me back, then pulled me into his lap and kissed me some more. His lips were soft but insistent. He pulled me close to him with one hand, while the other caressed my hair. Then he stopped.

"I can't stay tonight," he said, a little out of breath.

"That's okay."

"I want to."

"Good."

"But I don't too."

"What?" I sat up straight.

"No, no, no," he said, petting my hair again. "It's a good reason. See, I really like you, and I want to take it slow. I think we might have something here, and I don't want to rush it."

I nodded. Wow.

"But soon," he said. I nodded again.

"And now that I've spoiled the mood," he said, hoisting me off his lap. "Let's go take a look at this blood."

I was a bit disconcerted by the way the conversation changed direction, but I did want his help. "We see this type of situation a lot," he said as we walked through the house to the garage, Lassie at our heels. "You know, LOLFDGBs."

"What's that?" I took the bait as I opened the door.

Jeremy smiled broadly. "Little Old Ladies Fall Down Go Boom." Then he looked at the accident scene. His dimples disappeared.

"What is it?" I asked.

"She must have fallen backward and hit her head here." He indicated the key hook I'd noticed earlier.

"Yeah?"

"Usually, when someone's going down a step," he said, "they fall forward."

CHAPTER 31

"Is Hank working today?" The next morning I sat at Marge's kitchen table, talking on my cell and holding a nearly empty yogurt container for Lassie to lick. I was pretty sure it was good for him. Probiotics, you know.

"Not until Thursday," said Bitsy. Perfect. I didn't want him around when I picked up the information about the suicides. "Do you want to leave him a message?"

"No, I'll just catch him later. See you in a few."

I jumped in my Bug and headed to the posse station. Bitsy met me at the reception desk. "Here you go, dear." She handed me a manila file stuffed with papers. "These are all the incident reports from the Maricopa County Sheriff's Department for this area over the last several months."

"Why not the posse's reports?"

"Since we operate under the sheriff's department, all of our logs go to the county."

"So they respond too?"

"Sometimes. We do a lot of health and welfare checks, that sort of thing. The sheriff's department only responds if a call is serious. Fire comes too, for medical emergencies, and in case they need to use the lockbox to get in."

I remembered the lockbox in front of Charlie's house. And Marge's. "Do posse members have access to the lockboxes?"

"Oh, no." Bitsy shook her head. "We don't have that kind of authority. Posse members aren't even allowed to go into the house unless they're invited."

I opened the file and skimmed the first page. Then the second.

And the third. "This is it?" I asked. "This is all the information?"

Bitsy came out from behind her desk and stood next to me, close enough that I could smell her makeup. She ran a pink fingertip down the report and stopped at one line. "See here? It says 'dead body.'"

It didn't say much else. The report listed the date, time, location, and description of calls the county officers had responded to. Nothing that would let me know if a dead body was a suicide or if a burglary involved the theft of a catalytic converter. Even worse, there were no actual addresses listed, just locations like "400 block S. Arnold Palmer Court." Could this really be all the information available?

Bitsy seemed to read my mind. "If you could find the names of the people who died, you could get their autopsy reports." I inwardly groaned. The last time I'd applied for one, it took a month to get it. "And if you wanted to know about catalytic converter thefts, specific reports might have information about what was stolen. Of course, you'd need to have the exact addresses of the burglaries to request the reports." She smiled brightly like what she told me was good news instead of a gigantic pain in the butt. How in the world was I supposed to find exact addresses and names when all I had was "400 block S. Arnold Palmer Court?"

That led me to another question that'd been bugging me: "When a posse patrol car receives a call, they must get an address to respond to, but do they get a name as well?"

"Of course not. That would be a privacy issue."

Then how did Hank know it was Marge who'd had the accident?

"And is it against the rules for a posse member to smoke on duty?"

Bitsy pursed her lips together in disapproval. "Of course." Her eyes focused on something behind me. "Why, Hank! What are you doing here? I just told Ivy you wouldn't be in until Thursday."

I turned around. There was Creepy Silver Hank, wearing a pearl-buttoned Western-style shirt, cowboy boots, and his mirrored sunglasses. He stood stock-still but tightly wound, like those guys in the haunted house who jump you when you walk past.

"Decided to stop in and check my schedule," he said. Then to me, "Thought your name was Olive."

"Ivy's my stage name."

"That right?" Hank spoke so slowly and deliberately that I wondered if he was drunk. I stepped a little closer to him to see if I could smell alcohol. Nothing.

"Ivy's in *The Sound of Cabaret* with me." Bitsy patted her perfectly coiffed white hair.

"What's that you got there?" Hank jerked his chin at the manila folder I held.

Bitsy said, "Ivy's interested in—"

"It's just something for Uncle Bob," I interjected.

"But Ivy, I thought you wanted to talk to Hank about—"

Dammit, Bitsy. "Thursday would work better. I've got to run right now."

"Alright then." Hank started to leave, then turned back to me. "I got my eye on you." He left.

Bitsy seemed oblivious to the threat hanging in the air. "Didn't even check his schedule."

That's because Hank wasn't there for his schedule. I was pretty sure he was there for me. I watched through the glass doors to make sure he got in his car. Didn't want him waiting for me in the parking lot.

"I've got to get going too." Bitsy took her purse from a desk drawer. "I need to be at the theater early. An added rehearsal, you know." She looked down at the floor, a look of contemplative sorrow on her face, like a sad nun. "It's too bad about Marge," she said. "Didn't even get a chance to perform in front of that big producer." She waved goodbye as she walked out the posse doors.

How did Bitsy know about the producer? As I followed her out the door, I tried to remember if Roger had said the visit was secret when a bigger fish grabbed my mind's pole: The extra rehearsal. Bitsy now had Marge's role.

CHAPTER 32

If I hadn't known better, I would have thought I was driving up to a resort. The one-story Spanish tile and stucco building occupied a prime piece of real estate with views of the desert and the bare rocky hills to the west. A wide circular driveway served as a place to drop off guests, who were greeted by the cool sounds of water splashing from a massive fountain near the front door. It was only when you stepped inside Mountain View Care Center that you knew its true function.

A few people dozed in wheelchairs in the front room. A woman with beautifully coiffed salt-and-pepper hair said "Good afternoon" to me as I entered, while a man sitting on a pastel flowered couch mumbled to himself. Thankfully the place didn't smell of urine and Lysol like I'd feared, but it still had that smell peculiar to hospitals and nursing homes—not a horrible smell, and yes, probably some mix of bodily and cleaning fluids, but weirdly unidentifiable.

A smiling young woman behind a desk greeted me concierge style: "May I help you?"

"I'm here to see Marge Weiss." I hoisted the paper grocery bag I carried. "I've brought her some things from home."

She asked me to sign into the visitors' log, then gave me directions to Marge's room. Off I went, passing a short round woman determinedly pushing a squeaking walker toward the front doors. A young aide in pink scrubs came up behind her and touched her gently on the shoulder. "Effie, it's Tuesday. Your family will be here *tomorrow*."

I found Marge's room and knocked on her closed door. I heard a soft, "Come in."

The room's walls were cream with just a hint of blush. The sturdy whitewashed southwestern-style furniture was stylish and practical, and a large picture window opened onto a courtyard where twittering birds bathed in a smaller version of the fountain out front. The whole effect was calmingly cheerful.

Marge was not calm or cheerful.

"Why are you still in bed?" I watched her kick off her blankets and put them back on again.

"No reason to get up," she muttered, not looking at me.

This was not the Marge I knew, but I proceeded as though it were.

"So." I sat down in a chair next to her bed, put the grocery bag next to my feet and pulled a wheeled bed tray in front of me. "I brought your hairbrush, mascara, powder, some blush," I placed each item on the little table as I named it, "a couple of lipsticks—I thought you'd want more than one color—a sweater," this I placed on the bed next to Marge, "and most importantly, lots of chocolate." I handed her a smaller paper bag I'd filled with M&Ms. "Oh, and...ta da!" I set a thermos on the bed tray. "Some of your own coffee, with cinnamon in it."

Marge held the paper bag full of M&Ms. She hadn't opened it.

"It's okay for you to have the chocolate. I checked with the nurse."

"Of course it's okay," Marge snapped. "I'm demented, not diabetic." Her face softened immediately. "I'm sorry, Ivy. I just can't believe this is happening." She put down the bag of M&Ms.

I couldn't either. Just a few days ago she was wowing the audience at Desert Magic Dinner Theater. "I bet this will be temporary. They'll get a treatment plan figured out for you and you can get back onstage where you belong." I had no idea if any of what I said was realistic, but it felt like the right thing to say. "Everything's fine at the house. Roger is going to take care of your pool as well as Bernice's." When he came over for dinner and pool duty last night, he immediately offered to help. "And Lassie is just a little lovebug."

"Ha!" Marge's laugh startled me. She picked up a red tube of lipstick I'd put on the tray. "This isn't lipstick." She took off the cap to reveal a little spray nozzle. "It's pepper spray. One of the gadgets Arnie bought me."

I took the pepper spray from her under the guise of examining it. It really did look like a lipstick—maybe slightly longer than a regular tube, but obviously good enough to fool me. I slid it into my purse when Marge wasn't looking. Didn't think it was quite the thing to give to a confused person.

Marge opened her powder compact and examined herself in the small mirror. "How is Arnie?"

"Brokenhearted," I said truthfully. I scooted closer. "Won't you just let him—"

"No." She shut the compact lid like she was closing a case. "Don't you see? This is why I couldn't marry him. I was afraid I might do something like this, and now—"

"Wait a minute. I thought you said an intruder caused all of this."

"That's right."

"Then stop blaming yourself. Can I at least tell Arnie—"

"No." Marge snapped her mouth shut like a turtle's.

"Okay." I felt awful for both of them. "Let's figure out what really happened. If you still want me to investigate, that is."

Marge still had that no-lips turtle look, but she nodded stiffly.

I helped myself to a few of the M&Ms I'd brought. "To begin with, is there any chance there was something slick on the garage step where you fell?" Jeremy said this could be the other reason Marge fell backward, that she slipped and her feet went out from under her. "Maybe you had a glass of water with you?"

Marge shrugged. "I don't think so."

"Who has keys to your house?"

"I can't remember."

"Yes, you can."

"I can't remember anything. That's why they're going to keep me here."

"Marge, stop feeling sorry for yourself. They *will* keep you here"—I hated being harsh—"unless you help me prove it's not necessary. Now think. Who has keys to your house?"

It worked. Marge straightened up in bed and squeezed her eyes shut, trying to concentrate. "Arnie, of course, and Bernice. I think that's it...oh. There's that lockbox outside too."

"Good. Great. Thank you." It actually wasn't that helpful, but it was a start. "Do you ever leave your keys where someone might be able to pick them up?" It was a long shot, but maybe someone had made a copy before Marge realized they were gone.

"I don't know."

"Marge," I said sternly.

"I guess someone could have picked them up when I'm swimming."

Omigod. The unlocked locker. I about choked on an M&M.

"Your keys were stolen that day I was with you, weren't they? Did you ever get your locks changed?"

"I forgot."

I didn't say anything. I didn't want to kick that horse.

"And someone could have picked them up at the theater. I just leave them in my purse in the dressing room."

I was about to give Marge an Uncle Bob-style lecture about preventing burglary, but an M&M got in the way and I bit my tongue. Literally. "Ow!"

"You okay?" Marge looked directly at me for the first time. She looked depressed—sagging mouth, drooping eyes, frown lines on her forehead—but her eyes were clear and focused.

"I juth bit my tongue." A corner of her mouth twitched. "Tho," I said, playing up my temporary disability, "how elth could thomoen have gotten into your houth?" A definite tug on her lips. "Did you let anyone in rethently?"

"Sure." Marge wasn't exactly smiling, but her face was animated and she hadn't answered with "I don't know." Success.

Then her face drooped again. "Well, not *recently*. I couldn't. The Post-it lists...I couldn't let anyone see them."

"Of course." I nodded understandingly. "How about before you put them up?"

"Well, Arnie, of course, and Bernice..." Bernice's name kept coming up. I really wished I could use her as a suspect, but it'd be awfully hard to pull off a caper from New Zealand.

"The guy who fixed my dishwasher..." Marge waved away the question I was about to ask. "I don't remember the name of the company, but there's paperwork in one of the kitchen drawers. I think that's it." She sat back against her pillows, looking better than when I'd arrived. The power of getting something done, I guess.

"Oh, yeah," she said. "Colonel Carl Marks too."

"Carl Marks?" His clipped mustache and too-expensive shoes flashed into my head.

"What a name, huh? Wonder if his parents had a clue," Marge said, almost smiling. "He gave me a viatical settlement."

"What's that?"

"It's the reason I can afford this place." Marge waved at her room, which I now realized was a private one. "And a fancy way of saying that Carl bought my life insurance policy from me."

CHAPTER 33

"Hi, Olive-y."

"Hey, handsome." I trapped my cellphone between my neck and shoulder so I could use both hands on the fire extinguisher.

"Will you go on a picnic with me at Encanto?"

I sprayed the still smoking engine of my Bug, emptying the extinguisher. "Sure." Encanto was the greenest park in town and our favorite picnic spot.

"With me and Sarah?"

"Okay." I got back in my car to wait for the engine to cool down. Better than standing in the sun on the side of the road. It was only ten o'clock in the morning, but it was already hot, especially if you stood next to a car that was recently on fire.

"On Sunday?"

"Oh, Cody, I've got a matinee."

"After?"

"You bet."

"What's that noise?" he said as a semi driver honked, probably because I hadn't made it completely onto the shoulder.

"Just traffic. Gotta go," I said. "See you Sunday."

Before I got back on the road, I wrote myself a reminder to get a new fire extinguisher. Seemed like my car was catching on fire more often these days.

Given my flaming car and all, I was pretty proud that I made it into the office in time to get a bunch of work done before Uncle Bob showed up. He came in at noon, carrying a white bag that smelled of Thai curry.

"Hi," I said. "I'm just getting ready to eat my lunch. Which is just a poor little peanut butter sandwich. On stale bread." A minute later, a nice plate of red curry with beef sat in front of me.

"All of those background checks done?" Uncle Bob asked as he settled down with the rest of the Thai food.

"Yep. I also typed up two reports, and researched viatical settlements."

"Viaticals?"

Though I'd done the research for Marge's case, I had a feeling it might apply to Charlie's too. "I have a call in to Amy," I said. "You know, they sounded like scams to me, but I guess they're legal." Basically, viatical settlements, also called life settlement contracts, enable people to sell their life insurance to a buyer before the insured person dies. The person selling the policy gets an infusion of cash and the person buying it benefits whenever the policyholder dies.

"Viaticals really helped out a lot of AIDS patients during the bad times," said Uncle Bob, an unusually serious look in his eyes. "By the time they were really sick, they couldn't work. They needed help and healthcare. And a lot of their families...weren't around." He sat back in his chair, his lunch untouched.

"You knew someone?" My uncle rarely divulged anything about his personal life.

"My next-door neighbor." He smiled. "You would have liked him. He gave great big parties where he'd play the piano and have everyone sing corny old songs." Uncle Bob straightened up and took up his fork. "Now, I guess, the settlements are mostly between older folks and buyers. Pretty much for the same reasons."

My cell rang. Amy. After we'd exchanged pleasantries, I told her I was close to having some news and just had a few questions for her. "Did your dad happen to have a viatical settlement?"

A pause. "As a matter of fact, he did." Another pause. "It was a bit strange, because he didn't really need the money. The one he sold was a fairly new policy, and not a big one. I was still the beneficiary on his other policies."

"Do you know who bought his policy?"

"I can't remember right now, but it was a weird name, the name of someone famous, like Robert Kennedy or—"

"Carl Marks?"

"Yeah. I think that was it. Do you know him?"

"Sort of." I frowned at the image of the mustachioed man that crept into my mind. What he did might not be illegal, but I still didn't like it. "Oh, and Amy, did your dad ever talk about a burglary?"

"A burglary? No, and I'm sure he would have told me."

"Did he have any complaints about his car, maybe about the gas mileage?"

"No." She sounded puzzled.

I didn't want to ask the next question, but I needed to know. "So he never told you about removing his catalytic converter?"

"What? No. Why?...Oh." A gulp. "I never thought about the mechanics of how Dad..." Another noise, like she was holding back a sob.

"I'm sorry, Amy. Just one more question." I scrolled down my computer screen. "I can see that your dad's car was sold after his death, but not who to. Do you know who bought it?"

"Yeah, it was one of his neighbors. Larry Blossom."

"Really? One of your dad's neighbors bought the car—" I almost said "that he killed himself in" but stopped myself just in time.

"I know," Amy said. "But Larry said he'd always liked it, and of course he got a really great deal. I mean, Dad only had the car about a month. It was brand new."

I thanked Amy and hung up. Huh. Would someone planning to kill himself buy a brand new car? I let my mind wrestle with the idea for a moment, then asked my uncle.

"It's possible," he said. "You never know what people are thinking. Maybe Charlie wanted to go out in style."

I nodded. I didn't agree, but I nodded.

CHAPTER 34

Larry Blossom lived on the same street as Charlie, Bernice, and Marge. I strolled over the next morning, past a Realtor pounding a "For Sale" sign into Charlie's gravel front yard. Guess things moved quickly around here.

I walked up to the house and rang the bell. A man opened the door.

Oh no.

"You look an awful lot like a nun who was around here the other day," said the slow-talker from Monday.

"That was me." I handed him my uncle's business card. "I'm Olive Ziegwart with Duda Detectives. I'm looking into the death of Charlie Small." Larry had been out of town on the days surrounding Charlie's death, so I didn't meet him during the neighborhood investigation.

The gray-haired gent looked me up and down. "And the nun outfit?" The pause plus the four-word sentence took about a minute. At least it felt like it did.

"I was undercover."

He laughed. "I'll say you were. Come on in." He stepped back into the dark cool interior.

I stepped just over the threshold, hoping that staying near the door would signal the fact that I was in a hurry. The foyer smelled not unpleasantly like pipe tobacco. "I only have a minute, but I wanted to ask you a quick question." Please let it be a quick answer. Please. "You bought Charlie's car, correct?"

"I sure did. Some people might think it's strange, buying a dead man's car, but—"

"Do you know if—"

"*But,*" Larry gave me a look that said interrupting was rude, "I liked Charlie. I liked his car. I didn't see an issue."

I decided to get right to the point. "Do you know if the car has a catalytic converter?"

"Well..." Larry took a pipe out of his front shirt pocket, searched around in another pocket, pulled out some tobacco, and began filling his pipe. Being direct didn't seem to have saved me any time. "You're supposed to have one, you know. Greenhouse gasses or something."

He pulled out a book of matches from a pants pocket, discovered it was empty, and patted his pockets until he found another matchbook. I thought I might scream.

"But here's the thing." Larry lit his pipe. "You do get better gas mileage without one. And not buying so much gas is good for the environment too." He waved out the match and put it in an ashtray on a nearby credenza. I was afraid I might grow moss. "Still, I don't think I would have taken it off. May even get a new one. Car makes a lot of noise without it. Like a bad muffler."

"Did Charlie take off the catalytic converter himself?"

"Think he had someone help him." He puffed thoughtfully. "Maybe whoever told him he'd save on gas."

"Any idea who that was?" A long shot, sure, but what the heck.

Larry thought. And thought. I waited. Uncle Bob would have been proud.

"You know," he said, "I think he said it was someone from the theater. He was on the board, you know."

I nodded. "Thank you." I turned to go.

"I heard you saw Marge," Larry said. "She doin' okay?"

"Okay," I said. "Not great, but okay." I had my hand on the doorknob when I thought of something. "I know you found Marge that morning, but did you see or hear anything before her accident? Maybe earlier?"

"Nope," Larry said. "Just a landscaper."

CHAPTER 35

I called Marge as soon as I left Larry's. "Do you have a landscaper?"

"A what?"

"A landscaper?"

"Who is this?"

"Oh, sorry. It's Ivy."

"Who?"

"Ivy Meadows. I'm taking care of your—"

"Is this some sort of joke?" Marge slammed the phone down.

I hung up, hoping this was not a sign of things to come, and still wondering about the landscaper. I'd ask Arnie. Maybe he would know.

But when I got to the theater that night, I was distracted by a near-barf. I had just sat down at the greenroom table with a plate of mac and cheese, when...

"Oh! My!" Bitsy gagged, slammed down her iced tea glass, and ran from the room.

"She better not have the flu," Timothy said, pulling some hand sanitizer from a pocket. He slathered it on his hairy hands, then offered it to me. "Want some?"

Instead I picked up the glass, sniffed at the cloudy tea and nearly gagged too. I got up and strode back to the kitchen with the glass. The head cook, a silent woman whose hairnet was so tight she always had little triangles on her forehead after dinner, looked up at me, then quickly down at the pot of soup she was stirring. Zeb saw me and stepped behind the industrial-sized dishwasher.

"Come out, Zeb," I said. "We have to talk. Now."

He shambled out from his hiding spot. The kitchen staff stopped chattering.

"This glass of Bitsy's..." I held it aloft and waited.

"It was an accident." Zeb looked at the floor.

"I didn't see anything," said the cook, unbidden.

"I must have used the glass I did my science experiment in," Zeb said. "I was testing the enzyme activity of blended liver."

"A liver smoothie!" said one of the prep cooks.

I didn't say anything, just held the glass up high.

"Really." Zeb produced his black notebook from his kitchen apron pocket and showed it to me. "See, right here it says—"

"Zeb." I put down the stinking glass. "I believe you used this glass for a science experiment. I do not believe that using it for Bitsy's iced tea was an accident."

The rest of the kitchen staff floated away but stayed within earshot.

"I don't like 'Bitchy.'" Zeb thrust out his chin. The few hairs there stood straight out in defiance.

I waited. I didn't like Bitsy either, but apart from the Alzheimer's remark, which could have been innocent, I couldn't put my finger on why.

"She's a nympho."

That wasn't the reason. "If that ain't the pot calling the kettle black." I had picked up a few of Candy's southernisms. Sometimes they just fit the bill.

"No, really. She hit on me." Zeb shuddered. I did too, but not because I believed Zeb. According to him, everyone from the cashier at Trader Joe's to his math teacher was hot for him. No, it was the image—fictional or not—of almost-seventy-year-old Bitsy with sixteen-year-old Zeb that made me squirm. "She's after Arnie too, if you hadn't noticed. Can't decide if she wants a young buck or an old goat."

"You make that up yourself?" I asked.

"I am not your average dishwasher," he said with pride.

If that ain't the truth.

* * *

I watched Bitsy that night. Zeb was right. Anytime Arnie came into the greenroom, Bitsy ended up next to him, laughing at his corny jokes, touching his arm, listening to him with an annoyingly coy tilt of her head.

On my way out of the theater after that night's show, I saw her waiting by the stage door, dolled up in a figure-hugging red suit, high heels, and a tiny black patent leather clutch. I heard Arnie in the hall behind me, humming a little around his ever-present cigar. I let him pass, then dropped back around the corner so I could spy on them.

Arnie turned the corner. "Yowza." He whistled in admiration. "I love a woman in red."

"Thank you," said Bitsy, with that stupid head tilt. "I have a date."

I watched Arnie to see if he looked jealous. I suspected Bitsy was looking for the same thing. I didn't see it. What I did see was the stage door open to reveal Bitsy's date.

Colonel Carl Marks.

"Carl!" Arnie smiled and thrust out a hand at the colonel, who wore well-cut slacks and an open-necked shirt under a sports coat. Arizona formal wear.

"So you two know each other," Bitsy said.

"Everyone knows the colonel here," Arnie said. I was beginning to think that was true.

"Colonel," I said, stepping around the corner. "Just the man I wanted to talk to." Carl's and Bitsy's smiles dimmed perceptibly. "Seems to me I've seen your car around an awful lot."

"Checking out my 'hot rod,' are you?" Carl said to me. He gave Bitsy a lascivious smile.

I shook my head in mock confusion.

"And I could have sworn you were married."

"I am." Carl stared past me. Out of the corner of my eye, I saw Bitsy's face redden, but I kept my gaze on the colonel. He popped a piece of gum in his mouth, then shifted his eyes to my face. "This is a business meeting." Ah. A lie.

"But you're retired."

The colonel smiled directly at me, lying again. "I still do some work for my friends." His gum chewing amped up.

"Like Charlie and Marge? I heard you recently gave them viatical settlements."

"A viatical settlement? Marge?" Arnie about dropped his cigar.

"She didn't tell you? Oh, buddy, I am so sorry." Carl patted the much shorter Arnie on the shoulder in a gesture so patronizing I wanted to slug him.

"Does this mean…?" Arnie's words and his cigar hung mid-air.

"Yeah," said Carl. "You're no longer the beneficiary of Marge's life insurance policy." He opened the door and held it for Bitsy. "I am."

CHAPTER 36

Arnie had just left the theater after Carl and Bitsy when Zeb came skidding around the corner. "Ivy!" His eyes were wide. "I need your help."

"Okay." I wondered what could make the normally unflappable kid hyperventilate.

"My notebook—the one where I write down all the data from my experiments—it's gone."

"Okay." Still wondering. A missing notebook didn't seem like such a big deal.

"And if I don't get it back—" Zeb gulped back a sob. For the first time, I noticed his pimply young face had old eyes.

I put my arm on his shoulder. "Zeb? I know this is important, but—"

"You don't understand. I haven't input any of that data yet and I have to do it in order to get the extra credit and I need the extra credit to be eligible for this special summer science program and I need the science program—"

"Whoa." I was afraid he would pass out if he didn't take a breath.

"I need the science program," Zeb kept going, "so I can get a scholarship so I can go to college and I need to go to college so I can get out of the house and away from—" He finally stopped and looked at me with those old eyes. *Oh.* I remembered that one of those eyes had recently been blackened by "someone in gym class."

"That's why you're at the theater all the time?"

"I don't want to talk about it," Zeb said. "I want to find my notebook. I think Bitsy took it."

"Okay." I wanted to do more than that, to keep this kid safe, but maybe finding his notebook was a start. "How do you know it's been stolen?"

"I keep it in my apron pocket. I always hang up my apron on a hook in the kitchen when I use the bathroom so the apron strings don't fall in the—"

"I get it," I said. "Go on."

"My notebook isn't there. And one of the guys saw Bitsy hanging around the kitchen by where we hang the aprons. He figures she took it for payback."

After a short discussion, we decided to search Bitsy's dressing room. I didn't think she could have taken the notebook with her. The patent leather clutch she carried was too small.

"But just me," I whispered to Zeb as we walked down the hall. "I'm going in alone." He opened his mouth to protest. "It's easier to explain one person in the dressing room than two."

"I can keep watch."

"Okay, but don't be too obvious. Stay away from the door."

"Right. And I'll cough if I see someone coming."

"Great." We stood in front of Bitsy's dressing room door. "Now shoo."

I slipped into the dressing room. Hairspray still hung in the air—Bitsy must have re-lacquered herself before her date. The room, which used to be Marge's, was slightly smaller than the one Candy and I occupied, but meant for one person—a star's dressing room. I flipped on the lights that ringed the mirror. A pink makeup kit, about the size of a tackle box, sat on the edge of the counter that ran underneath the mirror. Not much else on the counter, no makeup or brushes scattered about, no cards or scripts or stolen black science notebooks.

I popped open the lid. Zeb's small spiral-bound notebook was right on top. As I grabbed it, the movement caused the kit to shift slightly toward the edge of the counter. I steadied it with a hand underneath so it didn't fall.

Huh. There was something taped to the bottom of Bitsy's

makeup kit. I lifted it up so I could see. A 6x9 manila envelope was duct-taped to the underside. I set the kit on the counter, closed it, tipped it up, and carefully peeled the tape away. It'd be easy to put it back on without Bitsy noticing. The envelope wasn't sealed shut, just closed with the little metal hook thingie. I slid its contents—several pieces of folded copy paper—onto the counter. I unfolded one sheet. Oh. Just a copy of one of our reviews. I started to fold it again when something caught my eye. About halfway down into the review, the critic had written, "As the Mother Superior, Marge Weiss delivers a powerful performance." In this copy, though, "Marge Weiss" was scratched out and "Elizabeth Bright" written in. Bitsy's real name. I put that review aside and unfolded another sheet. This one said, "The sold-out crowd was almost certainly there to see Marge Weiss..." Again, Marge's name was inked out and replaced with Bitsy's. I quickly unfolded the other pieces of paper. All the same, with Bitsy substituted for Marge in each review.

I didn't like the tension that crept up my neck. I shook it off. Maybe this was just Bitsy's way of staying inspired, by imagining she was the star. Nothing really wrong in that. Then I unfolded the last sheet of paper. It was a copy of a photo that ran in the Sunday *Arizona Republic* the week before opening. In the picture, Marge/Mother Superior smiled down at Hailey/Mary, looking kind and wise—even with the word "bitch" scrawled in a heavy hand across her face.

A coughing fit in the hall—Zeb's cue that we weren't alone. I shoved all the papers back into the envelope and re-taped it to the bottom of the kit. More coughing, then footsteps and a man's voice. "I'm on it. But this is the last one, right? Right?" I put the kit back on the counter. I must have made a noise because the footsteps stopped outside the dressing room door. "Wait, I think someone may be..."

The dressing room door opened. Roger held his phone to his ear. His eyes flitted over me, his face hard in the bright lights of the dressing room. "Yeah, I did hear something," he said into his phone. "Gotta go, Debra. Catch you later." He hung up. "My agent." He shook his head. "Not happy that I'm retiring. And speaking of which, you need to be retiring for the night too. They're getting ready to lock up." Roger now stood near me, too close, as always.

"Of course." I thought fast, conscious of the question in Roger's eyes. "Bitsy said I could borrow some..." I scratched my nose, which was one of my "tells," but which also gave me an idea. "Calamine lotion." I itched my arm for good measure as I opened Bitsy's makeup kit.

"It's the water hazards," said Roger. "The golf course tries to keep the mosquitos down, but they're pretty persistent."

I pulled out a likely looking tube and showed it to him, keeping the label away from him. "Found it." I'd have to find a way to get the pink tube of lotion back into Bitsy's kit later. Now I had to figure out how to pick up Zeb's notebook, which sat on the counter next to the makeup kit.

"Aaah! Mouse!" I pointed behind Roger. When he turned to see, I slipped Zeb's notebook into my shorts pocket.

"Missed it," he said, turning back to me.

"Slippery little buggers. Speedy too." Who knew I'd ever be happy that the theater had mice?

As we walked into the hall from Bitsy's dressing room, I caught a glimpse of Zeb, half hidden behind a corner. I nodded slightly toward the parking lot, where I could hand off the notebook. He nodded back, then disappeared.

"By the way, you sounded great tonight." Roger smiled at me as he held the stage door open. "I wouldn't be surprised if you found yourself in New York one day pretty soon."

"Yeah." I smiled back—a bright fake smile. Just like Bitsy's.

CHAPTER 37

Dammit! I reached for the fire extinguisher in the backseat. It wasn't there.

I jumped out of my car as flames shot skyward and ran across the pebbly shoulder, putting a good safe distance between the car and me. Black smoke billowed from the engine and orange flames engulfed the back of the Bug. Shit. The fire was way worse this time, and I'd forgotten to put my new fire extinguisher in the car.

Or had I? I could have sworn I put it in the car after buying it. Sirens interrupted my thoughts as a fire truck careened around the corner.

Once the fire was out, I declined the ride the tow truck driver offered. Marge's house was just a mile away. The walk would give me time to clear my head and maybe air out my burnt-rubber smelling clothes.

As I walked, I called Uncle Bob to tell him I wasn't going to be in the office that day. I decided to play down the event so he didn't worry. "My car had a little fire. I think it needs more than duct tape this time. Maybe a hose or two." Or an engine.

"Olive! Are you *trying* to burn yourself up?"

Good thing I'd played it down.

"You need to stop driving that P.O.S. It's dangerous."

I let him go on so I wouldn't have to say anything that wasn't technically true.

"What does your fireman boyfriend say? Is he happy you're driving that fire hazard? Doesn't he think it's dangerous?"

"Um..."

"Let me guess. You haven't told him about that fire-magnet you drive because you're afraid he would tell you to stop driving it. Right?"

Of course Uncle Bob was right, but I decided that silence was a good enough affirmation.

He blew out a breath. "You promise you'll have a mechanic look at your car right away?"

"I promise. Right away." Especially since it was being towed to a repair shop.

"Good. So," he said in a calmer voice. "You said duct tape wouldn't work?"

"Yeah."

"Duct tape?" he repeated.

"Yeah." I wondered where he was going with this.

"Did you know its real name is duck tape? Like the bird?"

Aww. He was trying to make me feel better by offering me one of his trivia tidbits. "I did not know that."

"Yeah. They came up with the tape during World War II to keep the guys' ammo cans dry. It did the trick—like 'water off a duck's back.' So, 'duck tape.' Nice, huh?"

I love my uncle.

I was just beginning to feel better, thanks to my talk with Uncle Bob, a nice walk in the sun, and the sight of a family of quail running in a little line ahead of me. Then I stepped through Marge's front door. Something was wrong.

Lassie didn't greet me. I started to call out to him, then stopped. I wasn't sure what to do if someone was in the house, but I opted for quiet. I also took my cell out of my bag as I crept silently down the hall. I saw no sign that anything was amiss. But I also didn't see Lassie.

Was that a noise from the backyard? I stopped and listened, concentrating hard. Yes. I punched 911 into my cell so I could hit "talk" in a second if need be. I kept going, staying near the wall. No one in the great room, but the noise in the backyard was clearer—splashing? And barking, definitely barking. Oh God, Lassie must have fallen in the pool!

I threw open the sliding glass door and rushed out. I spotted Lassie running around the perimeter of the pool, yapping. Then I realized there was someone in the pool. Then I realized it was Arnie, swimming laps with his glasses on and his cigar still firmly between his teeth. Then I realized he was naked.

"Oops!" I heard him say before I turned my back. "Sorry, kid. I like a little swim au natural and got no pool at my house. Didn't think you'd be home."

Lassie ran up to me, panting, then back behind me toward the pool. From all the splashing I gathered Arnie was getting out. "Okay, safe to turn around."

I did. Arnie had fastened a big blue towel where his waist would have been. Out of his clothes, you could see Arnie wasn't fat, just sort of square—his shoulders, waist, and hips were all about the same circumference. "Didn't mean to scare you," he said, padding over to me, Lassie jingling at his heels. "Weren't you going into the office this morning?"

I nodded, remembering that I had said so at the theater last night.

Arnie glanced up at a corner of the covered patio, then sat down in a chair, peering at me through water-spattered glasses. "Everything okay?"

I sat across from him. "My car caught on fire." Arnie's eyes grew enormous behind his thick glasses. I waved away his worry. "It's nothing new. Just a little more serious this time. Are *you* okay?"

"You're thinking about last night? About Marge selling her insurance policy?" Arnie picked up Lassie and sat him in his lap. "You know, I thought my heart was already broken, but..." He petted Lassie with great tenderness. "It's not about the money. I mean, sure the theater could use it, but...I love that woman." Arnie's eyes filled with tears that spilled over. "Damn. Never cried when I was young." He took off his glasses to wipe his eyes. "It's an age thing. Now I cry at the drop of a hat. Happens to a lot of us. Like Charlie Small. Cried like a baby after his wife died. Couldn't even say her name. Poor devil."

Maybe Charlie did kill himself. Everyone had said he was miserable. But I didn't have time to think about it because Arnie's remark about the theater jogged a memory: Marge on her way to that charity gig right after Charlie's death. Hadn't she said something about the theater being in trouble?

Lassie, settled comfortably on Arnie's lap, began to snore. Loudly. You wouldn't believe how loud that dog could snore, like a bear on top of a freight train.

Arnie chuckled. "Marge used to use earplugs at night."

"I'm going to buy some today," I said. "By the way, what's that thing on Lassie's collar?"

He fingered the small plastic object dangling from Lassie's neck. "It's a Pet Cam. You know, a camera for the dog. I bought it for Marge." Did his eyes flick toward that corner again? "Thought she'd get a kick out of seeing things from Lassie's point of view."

Arnie's eyes started to glimmer, so I decided to distract him and satisfy my curiosity at the same time. "I heard a story about you the other night," I said. Arnie waited. I swear his ears stood up a little straighter, like Lassie did when he was waiting for a command. "It was about your shoes."

He relaxed. "A tragic tale. Just heartbreaking." Arnie's ears waggled as he spoke. "But a great story all the same." He settled back in his chair and patted Lassie on the head, which woke the dog up and stopped him snoring, thank God. "I'm an impresario, you know."

I didn't know. I didn't even know what the word meant exactly, but it sounded impressive.

"I love arts and culture, but I got no talent. I do have a good imagination and a head for business."

I'd give him the good imagination bit. Maybe that's why he thought he was good at business.

"So I produce and present, help shows get up on their feet. That's how I met Marge. Produced her one-woman revue called *Margelous!*"

Lassie lifted his head and stared at Arnie. "I know, horrible name," Arnie said to the dog. There *was* something of the critic about the pug. "Anyway, I was struck dumb with love the moment she opened her mouth and said, 'You call this a dressing room?'" He stopped, a faraway smile on his face.

"And your shoes?"

"Yeah. So," Arnie sat up a little straighter, "years ago, before I met Marge even, I had this great idea to produce an alligator wrestling show in Florida. Got the idea after running into a guy named Leroy when I stopped to fill up at a service station. He was pumping gas, but said he used to be an alligator wrestler. Still did it for county fairs and church fundraisers."

Church fundraisers?

"Later I was at a friend's house when I heard on the TV they'd captured this old alligator who'd been terrorizing a neighborhood. 'Sherman,' they called him." He leaned toward me. "Seemed like fate, you know? Those two things happening back to back? So I adopted the alligator and set up a show. Started out with just a little tourist trap with a wrestling area, gift shop, and picnic tables, but I had plans for a full-blown amusement park with a roller coaster in the swamp and everything."

A swamp roller coaster. I'd ride that.

"Still think it would have been a great idea. If only Leroy hadn't been drunk that day. And if someone had remembered to feed the alligator." Arnie shook his head. "Poor Leroy. Not much left to bury."

"Your shoes?" I squeaked, trying not to think about poor Leroy.

"Yep," Arnie said. "Sherman shoes."

CHAPTER 38

After seeing Arnie out, I stood in the front foyer, thinking. During our conversation, Arnie's eyes kept sliding to a particular place on the patio. Was he lying about something? I didn't think so. The first time he did it was after he asked if I was going into the office. It was a question. No need to lie. The second time was after he talked about buying the Pet Cam.

"Lassie!" I called. The pug trotted over and gave me a dog smile, pink tongue lolling out the side of his mouth. I checked the thing that hung from his collar, which did indeed say, "Pet Cam." What else had Arnie said? "I bought it for Marge." That seemed like the truth too—the gadget was much more likely to be an Arnie purchase. I walked through the house and out the sliding glass door to the patio, Lassie at my heels. I sat in the chair Arnie had recently vacated and looked at the corner of the covered patio, as he had.

Now I knew why the Pet Cam comment had made Arnie glance up. In the upper corner of the patio, close to the roof and nearly hidden by a light fixture, was a camera.

At the Costco website, I learned that the home security kit Arnie bought included a camera, motion sensor, dimmer for lights, and a door open/close sensor. I combed through Marge's house, found each component of the kit, and took them all down. Gave me the heebie-jeebies to think anyone was watching me. Even though that was sorta what I did when I investigated someone. Huh.

I put that thought away in the garage cupboard where I stored the security kit, just in case Marge had asked Arnie to install it. Then I grabbed Marge's car keys. I had a moment of hesitation about using her car without permission, but after our conversation yesterday, I was afraid she'd say no because she couldn't remember who I was.

I drove to the theater in her big, loud beast of a Buick and got there before the rest of the cast, just as I'd hoped.

Uncle Bob always told me that invisible people make great witnesses. Hotel maids, busboys, janitors—people tend to talk in front of them without registering them as people with ears. With this in mind, I went straight to the kitchen.

Zeb was putting his white apron on over black pants and a white Oxford shirt when I came in. He smiled shyly, which was unusual for him, and motioned me closer. "I just wanted to say thanks for getting my notebook last night. And to ask," he scuffed the toe of his sneaker against the floor, "that you don't say anything about...you know."

Now that I knew Zeb's secret, I wondered how I ever missed the signs, like the fading bruise near one wrist. "No worries. I don't even know what you're talking about." He smiled. "Unless you want to talk about it." He shook his head furiously. "Okay," I said. "But the offer stands if you ever change your mind. And now, there's something you can do for me."

"Why, Ivy," Zeb affected a Cary Grant-type voice, "have you come to your senses, and my arms?" The old Zeb—or Zeb's old way of making it through life—was back.

"Nice. But not what I'm looking for. What I really want..." I crooked a finger at him, and he came closer, "is information. You ever hear anything about the theater being in trouble?"

Zeb glanced around us. The cook was at the far end of the kitchen, along with a few guys chopping vegetables and speaking to each other in Spanish.

"Yeah," he said in a quiet voice. "In fact, about a month ago, Arnie and one of the board members came through here, yelling like crazy. The one guy kept saying that this show—*The Sound of Cabaret*—was going to bankrupt them, and the board wasn't going to let—"

"Ivy!" sang Candy as she came through the door, followed by a bunch of hungry actors. "Heard your car caught on fire again."

"Again?" said Roger, who was right behind her.

Uncle Bob must have told Cody who told Matt. I shrugged. "Yeah, this time even duck tape wouldn't do it. Hey," I said to the group as Zeb disappeared into the kitchen, "did you know the real name is '*duck* tape?'"

All through dinner I regaled the cast with trivia, Uncle Bob style. Afterwards I followed the older nuns back to their dressing room.

"You here to join our game?" one of them asked. The nuns weren't onstage much, so they whiled away the time playing poker.

I shook my head and shut the dressing room door. My purpose was twofold. First, I slipped Bitsy's pink tube of lotion out of my pocket and onto the counter. That way, someone would find it but not trace it back to me. As for my second reason for being there: "I just need a little advice."

They gathered around me, all talking at the same time.

"You want to know about men or money?" asked the tall nun.

"Or maybe how to get men with money?" added the short one.

"If you get that figured out, let me know," the chubby one said.

"I guess it's sort of about money," I said. "I work in downtown Phoenix, and with gas prices, this commute is killing me." They clucked understandingly. "I heard that removing my catalytic converter could help me save on gas. Any of you ever heard that?"

"Sure."

"Yeah."

"Of course."

"Did you hear about it here at the theater?" A little direct, but I couldn't think of a better way to angle the question.

Another chorus of "yesses."

"Any chance you remember who was mentioning it? Maybe whoever knows about it could help me remove mine."

The little group shook their heads. "You see, everyone's been talking about it. Here, at the rec center—"

"Even at church."

"It's a hot topic here in Sunnydale," said the tall nun. "On account of all the catalytic converters that have been stolen."

CHAPTER 39

Saturday mornings are meant to be spent in bed, especially when one has been out drinking with one's cast on Friday night. I would have adhered to this very practical rule if only my stupid car hadn't caught fire and made me miss work yesterday. Instead, I sat at my "desk" in Uncle Bob's office, sipping from an enormous cup of to-go coffee and hoping it would jumpstart my sluggish brain.

"Hey, you." I heard the jingle of my uncle's keys as he opened the door. "How'd you get here?" Uncle Bob didn't usually come in on Saturdays, either. Maybe he wanted to keep me company. Or make sure I showed up.

"I borrowed Marge's car." I was really going to have to stop doing that. I could get in big trouble if I ever got pulled over. But right now I didn't know what I was going to do about a car. My mechanic had told me that my Bug was toast. "Burnt toast," he cracked. Good thing he had a day job.

Uncle Bob eased his bulk down into his chair with a groan. "Remodeling is a job for much younger men." He looked at me. "You gonna get those invoices out today?"

"Yep. Then I'm going to work on my case." I drained my cardboard cup.

"Good. You need to have something to report. Even if it's nothing. You know what I mean?"

I did. I needed to show that I'd been methodical in my research, not just farting around or relying on hearsay. "I'm going to see what I can find out about catalytic converter thefts in Sunnydale."

"You might call the posse," Uncle Bob said. "They might be able to tell you a bit more."

"I already tried tha—" I stopped. Shit, I'd forgotten I told Hank I'd see him on Thursday. I'd been too busy talking to slow-talking Larry Blossom and just plain forgot.

"Try Googling it."

I did that while I waited for Uncle Bob to leave the office. Several new sources reported that catalytic converter thefts were on the rise in the Phoenix area. The thieves mostly did their dirty work in public areas like mall parking lots. Some victims never realized their cars were missing converters until they took them in for service. I didn't really learn much more than what Detective Pinkstaff had told me at the picnic.

Finally, Uncle Bob went to the bathroom. I dialed the posse. "Hi, this is Olive Ziegwart with Duda Detectives. I need to leave a message for Hank Snow."

"Why, hello, Ivy," Bitsy said in her sweetly insincere voice. "He's working dispatch today. I'll connect you."

"No, that's—" A click and some Muzac. Before I could decide whether it would be smarter to just hang up, Hank picked up. "Dispatch."

"Hey, Hank, this is Olive Ziegwart, Bob's niece? I just wanted to say I'm really sorry about Thursday."

Silence. Then, "Thursday?"

"Yeah. I know I said I'd be in to see you, but—"

"This Thursday?"

"No, I...never mind. I found out what I needed."

"You did, did you?"

What was with this guy? "Yeah."

"Good." That must be how he said goodbye because he hung up right afterward. I didn't have much time to ponder Hank's strange behavior because Uncle Bob returned. I busied myself finishing up the invoices.

Once I was done, I put my mind toward a new problem. Arnie had never really finished his story about the alligator. I especially noticed how he skipped any mention of jail. "Do you think it's against the law to kill an alligator?" I asked Uncle Bob.

"I wouldn't think so, unless it was an endangered type. Or maybe rare. Did I ever tell you I saw an albino crocodile once? Really creepy. It looked like a statue made out of marble or something. Then it moved." He shivered. "Moving statues. Creepy." His fingers flew across the keyboard. "Oh. I'm wrong."

"What?"

"I'm wrong." My uncle was still distracted by whatever he was reading on screen.

"Sorry, I didn't quite hear you." I'd heard him perfectly.

"I'm wro—oh sheesh." He threw a paper clip at me. "Stop disrespecting your boss and listen up." He cleared his throat for emphasis. "You can only kill an alligator in Florida if you have a specific license. If not, it's a felony, punishable by up to five years in prison."

"So someone could have gone to prison for killing an alligator?"

"Looks like it. But doesn't smell like it." Uncle Bob tapped the side of his nose. "Better dig a little deeper." He looked again at his screen. "Hey, did you know that alligators don't have any vocal cords?"

"Nope."

"They suck air into their lungs and blow it out to make noise."

"Sounds like someone I know."

"Are you trying to get fired?"

I wasn't trying to get fired, and I did respect my boss (and his advice), so I dug deeper, using the databases Uncle Bob subscribed to. Candy's and Arnie's stories were both true. Arnie had run a swamp-themed tourist attraction, there was an accident involving an alligator, and Arnie did go to prison for an offense related to the Swamps are Scary! Theme Park. But not for killing an alligator, or even for making him into shoes. For fraud.

* * *

Turns out Arnie may have been the impresario behind Swamps are Scary!, but he was not the principal investor. The money that built the park was from a man who thought he was putting his money toward a dry-cleaning franchise. When the park went alligator-belly-up, the investments were gone and Arnie went to prison.

When I told this to my uncle, he frowned. "How's Arnie connected to your case?"

"He's Marge's boyfriend, and the producer of the theater."

"And?"

"And I think Marge's attack and Charlie's death are related."

"Why?"

"They live in the same block and know a lot of the same people, like Arnie. Marge was attacked in her garage. Charlie was killed in his garage. They both had viatical settlements from Carl Marks." Out loud it sounded lame, even to me. "And there have been a suspiciously large number of suicides in Sunnydale recently."

My uncle shook his head. "You're beginning to sound like—never mind. Just go look up the incidence of suicide in the elderly."

I did. I found that older adults made up 12 percent of the U. S. population, but accounted for 18 percent of all suicide deaths. I found that the number seemed to be increasing as baby boomers headed into their "golden years." I found that elder suicide could be underreported by as much as 40 percent, the deaths disguised as accidents, overdoses, and dehydration and self-starvation. And I found that the mean-spirited Pastor Scranton may have also been well-intentioned: "suicide contagion" was a real issue that could seriously increase the number of suicides in a community.

As if that weren't depressing enough, right before I was leaving for the day, Uncle Bob said, "You hear from your mom lately?"

"Mom? No."

"She called me. Went on a rant about Cody."

"That's new." It wasn't, and it was the reason she and I didn't talk much. Not only did my parents still blame me for Cody's accident, they were not exactly happy when I encouraged him to move out of their house and into a group home so he could have a life of his own.

"She doesn't like the thought of him having a girlfriend. She actually used the word 'dangerous.' Like Cody might blow up or something." Uncle Bob looked at me. "Cody told me you met her. Sarah, I mean."

I nodded. "I'm going on a picnic with them tomorrow. At Encanto." I didn't say anything else.

"Good," said Uncle Bob. "I knew you'd be on his side."

CHAPTER 40

"Roger says he has a surprise for you."

Candy's words stopped me as I was about to leave our dressing room after the Sunday matinee. "Do you know what it is?" I asked. Candy was very good at wheedling secrets out of people.

"No, dang it all. He wouldn't spill the beans." Her voice was muffled as she slipped a short flowered dress over her head. "But he says we'll all find out in the parking lot."

"Firecrackers, you think?" I tried to imagine things that one might do in the parking lot. "Or maybe a keg?"

"Maybe it's a party." Candy zipped up her dress. "Maybe because he's going to propose to you or something."

"Omigod. You don't think that's a possibility, do you?" My heart beat faster. I knew Candy was kidding, but I also had the feeling I was playing with fire.

"Nah. Not if he learned anything from Arnie's mistake." Candy stepped into her shoes. "Let's go see what it is."

We went out into the parking lot, squinting in the bright sunlight after hours in a dark theater. Across the lot, actors gathered in a little ring, close to where I'd parked Marge's car (which I was still driving without permission). As we neared, they parted to reveal Roger sitting on the hood of a car. A car with a big red bow on the grill.

Seeing me, Roger patted the hood. "Guaranteed to not catch on fire!"

A laugh from the actors and a nervous titter from me. A car?

Roger bought me a car? He couldn't have. I opened my mouth but nothing came out. A car?

"It's all yours." Roger slid off the hood and walked toward me, car keys in hand.

I finally got my tongue in first gear. "But..." Unfortunately, my brain was still stuck in park, so that's all that came out.

"No, buts," said Roger. "I'll explain over a beer." Then to the crowd, "Who wants a ride to the bowling alley in Ivy's new car?"

The car (not *my* car—there was no way in hell I was keeping it) was a blue four-door Taurus, used but in good condition. It held four people comfortably, but seven could cram into it, as I found out on the way to the bowling alley. "I can't keep this!" I shouted to Candy over the noise in the car.

"Hell's bells." Candy turned on the radio, as if the din wasn't loud enough. "Of course you can."

"But—"

"Just hear him out first, okay?" Candy decided to see how loud the radio would play (loud), and I stepped on the gas. As uncomfortable as I was with the whole scenario, I have to admit it was nice not looking over my shoulder for smoke.

About fifteen minutes later, I grabbed a tray of beers and wound my way through a gaggle of senior bowlers to the two lanes where my actor friends sat tying their bowling shoes. "Get this—bowling and beer for just over five bucks," I said, handing out plastic cups of beer.

"And free pool." Candy sighed happily, looking around at the rows of pool tables, indoor shuffleboard courts, and well-lit bowling lanes. "I could live here."

"Really?" Roger asked Candy as she passed him a beer. "Wouldn't it be weird being surrounded by old people?"

"What, like you? Aren't you old enough to live here?" She poked him good-naturedly, missing the steel that glimmered briefly in his eyes.

I passed out all the drinks and sat down next to Roger. "So." I took a deep breath. "This was incredibly sweet of you, but I can't—"

Roger shook his head and scooted over next to me, too close, as usual. "Let me explain."

All of the actors leaned in. This was going to be good.

Roger looked into my eyes. "I see potential in you. The kind of potential I had when I was your age." A few cast members grumbled into their beers. "A lot of you have potential," he added, "but Ivy is the only one with an exploding car." The grumblers acquiesced. "I don't want you to end up like me," Roger said to me. "Fifty and doing dinner theater in Arizona."

"And retiring to a custom-built house in Mexico," I said.

"To be thus is nothing; But to be safely thus." Before I could figure out why Roger was quoting *Macbeth*, he went on. "I know it seems a bit much. I just want to give you the chance I never had."

"If she won't take it, I will," Candy said. "The chance and the car."

"Candy, can I tell you something without you being offended?" Roger said.

Candy nodded.

"I don't think your future lies onstage."

Ouch. We all felt that one.

"Wait, I'm not finished. I think you could make it in film."

"Really? Do you know anyone—"

"Hold on, Candy." I set my beer down. "I'm not ready to move on." I dug the car keys out of my bag and handed them to Roger. "I just can't—"

"I hadn't finished either." Roger addressed the group. "Could you all give us a minute alone?"

"Yeah," I said. "Go pick out bowling balls or something."

After everyone had "oohed" and nudged each other and finally left, it was time to talk straight to Roger. "I have a boyfriend. I'm not available."

"Ivy." Roger sat back, giving me personal space for a change. "I'm not after your body." He shook his head at me like I was a silly schoolgirl.

I felt my face flush, but I persevered.

"People, *men*, don't just give cars to other people."

"Men don't?" The corners of Roger's mouth tugged up.

"You know what I mean. I can't pay you for this car. In cash or in...any way."

"I don't want you to pay me back. As your mentor, I consider this an investment in your career—"

"But—"

"And a cheap investment at that."

"Cheap? That car must be worth—"

Roger raised a hand to stop me. "Here's what I want you to consider. The guy from Mooney Productions will be here next Saturday. I think your chances with him are really good. If things go well, you'll be in New York soon. You won't need a car there, so you can sell it and give me the money. I bet I won't even take a hundred dollar loss. And the only way you'll have to thank me is in the playbill of your first Broadway show." He held the car keys out to me.

If things didn't work out with the producer, I could pay Roger back eventually. And if I did go to New York, it would be like having a free car for a month or two. I studied Roger's face. He looked sincere, almost fatherly. And I really needed a car. The doubt in the back of my mind faded to a niggle. Enough to ignore.

"Okay." I took the car keys back from Roger. "Thank you."

"All clear!" Roger said to the hovering actors. They ran back to the table like their beers were going to take flight.

"I'm keeping it," I said to Candy. "At least for now."

My cell buzzed in my shorts pocket. I looked at the display.

"Jeremy!" I said as I walked away from the thunder of balls hitting pins (and from interested ears).

"Hey, I just found out I'm going to have tomorrow night off. What do you say to a movie?"

"Aaah. I can't. I have a voice lesson."

"How about after?"

"My lesson is with Roger. He's also going to help me with the pool. With *both* pools." Yes, I left out the fact that I was cooking him dinner and that he had just bought me a car. Didn't seem like the right time for that discussion.

"All right." It did not sound like it was all right.

"I'll make it up to you on Tuesday night. I'll fix you dinner. And dessert. And if you want to come down here and play pool afterward, I'll let you beat me."

"Sounds good." Jeremy did sound better. "See you then."

One beer later, I'd just finished throwing a gutter ball (my specialty), when my cell buzzed again.

"Hey, Matt," I said as I picked up.

Candy handed me another beer. "Why's he calling you?"

I put my finger to my lips. It was hard enough to hear in the bowling alley without Candy adding to the noise.

"Ivy?" said Matt. "Are you on your way?"

Boom! "Woo hoo!" Hailey squealed. "Steee-rike!"

"Guess not." Matt sounded pissed.

"On my way to?" Oh shit. "Are you guys at Encanto?" It was Sunday. Cody's picnic date.

"Yeah. Guess we'll eat without you. Too bad, Cody baked cupcakes and everything."

"No. I, um, I'll be there in...crap, with traffic it'd be—"

"An hour. Don't bother. Sarah has to get home."

"Tell Cody I'm—" I didn't get to finish before Matt hung up.

CHAPTER 41

The next morning I made a big pot of coffee, extra strong. I needed it. I only slept about four hours between worrying about the car-Roger deal and feeling guilty about Cody.

But I had work to do, hence the coffee and the early-for-me rise time of eight a.m. I needed to go into the office in the afternoon, but now I wanted to work on my dead body map. I sat down at Marge's kitchen table, spread out the large map of Sunnydale I'd bought, then went through the sheaf of reports Bitsy had given me. I found twelve dead body calls. I wrote down the addresses (such as they were), then pinpointed each location on my map, marking the blocks in red. After an hour and another pot of coffee, I had plotted a driving route past all the locations.

"C'mon, boy!" I said to Lassie. He followed me out the garage door and into my new car. It was parked next to Marge's car, which Arnie had driven back here last night.

I rolled down the passenger window for Lassie, who stuck his head out the window and snorted with happiness. I felt the same way. How nice to have a car that just ran. That started right away when I turned the key. That stopped without me having to pump the brakes. That didn't require a fire extinguisher, which was good since I never did find the one I'd bought. I didn't realize how much my old car had stressed me out until I had one that didn't. I'd figure out how to handle Roger. The car was worth it.

First stop, Jack in the Box. All that coffee was doing a number on my empty stomach. "I'll have a Sausage Croissant, an order of hash browns, and a Junior Bacon Cheeseburger." The burger was for Lassie. He didn't seem like a breakfast eater.

Once we'd both wolfed down our meals, we began the trek past all the dead body locations. I planned to scope out the areas, then conduct a neighborhood investigation in each block so I could find out which house the dead body had been found in, and maybe even the manner of death.

After the fourth location, I noticed an interesting pattern. Each block had a house for sale. Well, not for sale any longer—all the signs had big "SOLD" stickers plastered across them. The fifth location did not have a house. It had a lot where a house had been razed. So did the eighth location. Locations six, seven, and eleven had "FOR SALE" signs with sold stickers. In locations nine and twelve, new houses occupied the lots. You could tell they were new because, like Carl Marks' house, they were obnoxiously big, three times larger than the neighboring houses. They stood on the lots like bullies shouldering their way into the prime spots without regard for their neighbors, whose views would now consist of tall stucco walls instead of cactus and oleander.

"Lassie," I said to the pug, who was licking the Jack in the Box wrappers for the third time. "I have an idea." Most of the houses were for sale by the same Realtor, Jean Wilson, who was also the agent listed on the sign in Charlie Small's front yard. I dialed Jean's number and asked if I could talk to her about Charlie's house.

"Sorry, we just closed that sale," she said. "In fact, I'm at the house right now."

"I'm a minute or two away. Could you hang on 'til I get there?"

"Well...alright. I have a few things to finish up anyway."

I zoomed back to the Charlie/Bernice/Marge cul-de-sac. I'd just parked the car in Marge's driveway and had opened the car door when Lassie decided to help with the investigation. He jumped out ahead of me and ran over to Charlie's house, where Jean Wilson was smoothing a "sold" sticker onto the sign.

"Lassie!" I jogged over to get him, but not before he lifted his leg on the woman's sign. "No!" I grabbed him by the collar and pulled him toward me, clipping a leash on his collar. "Sorry."

"I'm sure most of my signs have been peed on." Jean, a

heavyset woman dressed in loose linen in shades of tan, straightened up as if she'd just been hit with an idea. "I wonder if I should hose them all down."

"Probably a good idea," I agreed as Lassie proceeded to water a yellow hibiscus.

Jean began walking toward a gold Cadillac parked on the street, so I trotted next to her, Lassie behind me on his leash. "I'm the one who called you about Charlie's house. So it's sold? That seems pretty quick."

"We got our asking price," she said. "And with this type of house, I don't mess around."

"What do you mean, this type of house?" I had an idea, but wanted to hear it from her.

Jean dropped her voice. "A house where somebody died. By Arizona law, I don't have to tell interested parties about the history of the house, but around here, neighbors talk. It makes it tougher to get a good price."

"I bet they talk even more about a suicide. Like Charlie's."

"Couldn't stop the gossip if I tried." Jean unlocked her car door with a beep of her little remote.

"So you sell those houses cheaper? Maybe there's a particular buyer?" All of the monstrous new houses had similar designs.

Jean dropped ungracefully into her driver's seat and looked at me with narrowed eyes. "Just who are you?" Sensing her change in tone, Lassie gave a low growl.

I pulled out a business card. "Olive Ziegwart with Duda Detectives."

"Well," she said, with a snort that sounded a bit like my four-legged associate. "You're a detective. You figure it out."

CHAPTER 42

So I did. Jean must have known it wouldn't be difficult. Property ownership is public record. Once Lassie and I were back in the house, I booted up my laptop at Marge's kitchen table and started investigating. First I went to an online homes-for-sale site and typed in the addresses of the for sale/sold/razed houses I'd circled on my map. After finding their selling prices, I looked up the comparables in the neighborhood. Sunnydale houses typically sold for $200,000-$300,000. Jean's "dead body houses" had all gone for around $40,000 less. Using the Maricopa County Assessor's site, I dug a little deeper and found that nine of the twelve "dead body" houses had been bought by Underwood Holdings, whose offices were in Bogota, Columbia.

The new owner of Charlie's house wasn't listed on the site. The sale was probably too recent. I called up the assessor's office.

"Just a moment," said the woman who answered the phone. "I may have it...yes, just came in. The new owner for that property is..."

I mouthed the words silently on my end of the line as she spoke them: "Underwood Holdings." I didn't know what all of this meant, but I was sure it meant something.

I patted myself on the back for a job well done, then patted Lassie on the head for good measure and told him to be a good boy while I was gone. I headed to the office, whizzing down the 101 in my new car, which would actually go the speed limit without smoking and shuddering and threatening to drop car parts all over the freeway. I felt great.

Then I walked into my uncle's office.

"Cody called me last night. After you stood him up." Uncle Bob leaned back in his chair and crossed his arms, daring me to say something that would exonerate me. "Nice, ruining your brother's big date."

I cringed. He was probably not exaggerating. When Cody got upset, he got loud and agitated, and had trouble sitting or standing still. Not the best atmosphere for a date. I dropped my purse on my desk. "I can explain."

"You'd better."

I told him the whole story, leaving out the part about my potential move to New York. My gut contracted as I explained, like someone was tightening a lug nut in my stomach. "That's my new car right there." I gave Uncle Bob an actor's smile and pointed out the window at a nearby parking lot, where the afternoon sun bounced off the Taurus' windshield.

Uncle Bob looked out the window, then back at me. "What does this Roger guy want?"

"I told you, he wants to give me the chance he never—"

"I don't buy that. Not for a minute."

My squeezed gut wasn't sure about it either, but my head reminded me about the producer's visit.

"You'd better figure out what this guy wants from you, and if you want to give it to him." My uncle shook his head. "Or give back the car right away."

I wished I could tell him that I'd probably sell the car in a month or two when I moved to New York. That fact made all the difference. Instead I nodded.

The office landline rang. "You answer it," said Uncle Bob. "I gotta go. Client meeting." As he walked out, he didn't jingle his car keys the way he usually did.

I picked up the phone. "Duda Detectives. This is Olive. How may I help you?"

"Olive? Olive Ziegwart?"

"Yes?"

I rarely received calls at this number and didn't recognize the tearful female voice.

"Thank God I found your card." A still-unrecognizable snuffle. "I need to hire you."

"Um, could I have your name?" I didn't think Candy would play an un-funny joke on me, but I also couldn't figure out who was—

"Oh, sorry. It's Cheri."

Still no clue.

"Cheri Marks. Carl's wife." Ah, the belly-ringed exhibitionist. My uncharitable thoughts slapped me in the face as the woman on the phone began crying in earnest. "He's missing."

CHAPTER 43

I was about to knock on the door of Cheri and Carl's house when it opened and I was nearly bowled over by someone striding out.

"Whoa!" The someone caught me before I tumbled backward. I looked up into mirrored sunglasses.

"Olive." Hank tipped his hat, then continued on his way without another word, like a black-hatted cowboy out of an old movie.

"What?" I said to Cheri, waving in Hank's general direction as she ushered me in. It was all I could say, as if Hank's "man of few words" thing was catching.

"He's from the posse." Cheri wore booty shorts and a sports bra, all black.

"But..." Again, nothing more. I really wished my mouth and my brain would reconnect ASAP.

Cheri didn't seem to notice. "See, I called 911, but they said it wasn't an emergency. So then I called the police and they filed a missing persons report, but they didn't seem very helpful, so I called the posse. Then that nice man..."

"Hank," I managed to say.

"Came over to see if there was anything he could do."

"And?" I was beginning to enjoy this one-word conversation style, especially since Cheri was supplying me with good information.

"Once he found out that Carl wasn't senile and that you were on your way, he said he couldn't help me." Her bottom lip started to tremble.

"Hey, it's going to be okay." Uncle Bob had warned me never to say that to a client, but it just slipped out. Cheri bit her lip and nodded.

I put an arm around her slender shoulders.

"Let's go sit down and you can talk me through what you know." I led her to a black sofa in the black room, where an eerily silent shark circled on the enormous flat screen. "Maybe you should change that to something less..." What's another word for morbidly creepy? "Shark-y?" Cheri picked up a remote. The shark disappeared and the screen filled up with jellyfish: moon jellies glowing and floating and pulsing. Very relaxing, actually.

Cheri relaxed too. She told me how she wasn't really worried when Carl didn't come home Thursday night, since he "sometimes stayed over at one of his poker buddies' houses if he had too much to drink." On Friday she went shopping and to the gym afterward, but started to worry when she got back in the early evening and Carl still wasn't home. "I heard somewhere you couldn't file a missing persons report until three days or something"—that's not actually true, but I didn't want to interrupt her—"so I called today."

I jotted down all the information in my black notebook. "You said you filed a report with the police? Was that the county sheriff's office?"

"I don't know." Cheri sat up and her leg began jiggling. "I just called the number the 911 operator gave me."

"You said they didn't seem very helpful?"

"They took a report and stuff, but," she bit her lip again, "they said they couldn't do much since he's an adult and..." Cheri squeezed her eyes shut, like she was trying to block something out. "It appears he left voluntarily."

"What? Why do they think that?"

"His car is gone, his wallet is gone, his phone is gone...it even looks like he took some clothes with him."

"But you don't think he would leave—"

"Not the Carl I know."

I looked around me, at the big new house, at the enormous flat screen, at Cheri's expensive workout clothes, and asked the question I'd wondered about ever since I met the colonel: "How do you afford all this?"

"Oh, Carl's a really good insurance agent. *Was* a really good agent," she said. "Plus we're in debt. Big time."

Ah. "Could Carl be trying to run away from his debts?"

"Carl would never run away from anything. He's a retired Marine, you know."

"Any chance he would have disappeared because someone was investigating him?"

"Who?"

"Me." Cheri laughed out loud. I was startled by her change in mood, and also slightly offended. "I was investigating him in connection with Charlie Small's death."

"So he sold Charlie a policy. It's not illegal." She laughed again. Quite the mood swings. "You're the perfect person for me to hire."

"Why?" I had thought she might cancel the deal once she knew about my investigation.

"You've already done a lot of the work."

I continued my investigation by asking Cheri more questions about Carl's personal life, his background, and the debts he'd incurred. Then I asked her to find a recent photo of Carl and to make a copy of the police report while I checked out the house.

I didn't find anything interesting until I got to the bedroom. "Cheri?" I shouted from the walk-in closet. "Could you come here a sec?" I heard the slap of her bare feet on the slate tile, then muffled footsteps as she entered the bedroom, which was carpeted in thick shag pile. Black, of course.

"Yeah." Cheri pouted at Carl's side of the closet, which was only half-filled with clothes. "He took a lot of his stuff with him."

"It's not that," I said. "It's *that*." I pointed to the corner of the closet, which held video equipment: a camera, reflectors, lights, even a boom mike. "Carl was into filmmaking?"

"You could say that." Cheri laughed.

I made a note to research "inappropriate laughter."

"He made sex tapes."

"What?"

"You know, amateur porn."

I didn't know what to say.

"He's good," Cheri said, leading me out of the room and down the hall. "He even won an award at the HUMP! Festival in Seattle last year." She opened the door to another room, probably meant as a guest bedroom. "He's his own editor too." A couple of desks lined one wall and held a computer, editing equipment, and two large monitors. Another camera leaned against one wall.

As a normal person, I didn't want to even think about the question that formed in my mind. As a detective, I needed to know the answer. "Did you and Carl participate in the films? As...talent?" I couldn't make myself refer to them as actors.

"Sure." Cheri shrugged. "Us and others."

"Did Carl ever...perform...without you?"

She nodded.

"That didn't bother you?"

"We have an open marriage."

I noticed that she didn't answer my question. Instead she led me back into the big black room, where the blue light that infused the underwater film scene lit the room, but just barely. "That's one reason we have this room set up like this. It's a screening room." Cheri headed back toward the kitchen. "Let me get that photo and report for you."

I waited in the black room, where the jellies pulsed rhythmically. I no longer found it relaxing.

"Here you go." Cheri handed me a photo of Carl with an award (I really hoped it wasn't from the HUMP! Festival) and a copy of the police report. I still had one question. "That nice posse member...did he wear his sunglasses indoors?"

Cheri nodded.

"Even in this room?" I waved at the black hole of a space.

"Yeah. But what does that have to do with—"

"Great, thanks." I shook her hand. "I'll keep in touch, and let you know when I find something."

I didn't tell her that I had already found something. That I had seen Carl hours after Cheri had last seen him on Thursday. At the theater. With Bitsy.

CHAPTER 44

Someone rapped on the door. Not the front door, where normal, trustworthy people knocked. The back patio sliding glass door. I grabbed a butcher knife from a wooden block on the counter and approached the door hesitantly, trying to stay out of sight. Another knock and a voice. "Ivy?"

Roger. Phew. I opened the patio door. "What are you doing—oh."

It was Monday night, time for our singing lesson and dinner date. Roger stepped in, carrying a bottle of wine. He raised an eyebrow at the sight of the butcher knife.

"I've been worried about intruders," I explained. Not just Marge's intruder, but Creepy Silver Hank and the maybe-missing colonel.

"They don't usually knock." He carried the bottle of wine to the kitchen. "I already took care of both pools. I wanted to get it done before dark."

That's why he came round to the back. I followed him into the kitchen and put the knife back in its wooden block. Roger opened a drawer and pulled out a wine opener. "Want a glass before our lesson?" He turned and took a step toward me, so that he was a good twelve inches too close to me, as usual.

I shook my head. "Actually, this isn't a great time." In ten minutes, Cody would be home from his job at Safeway and I wanted to call to apologize. "Can we postpone tonight's activities?"

"Uh, uh, uh," Roger scolded me as he pulled the cork from the bottle. "A promise is a promise."

* * *

"But you promised to be there!" Cody said when I finally talked to him on Tuesday evening.

Marge's doorbell rang. "I know." I continued the conversation on my cell as I walked down the hall. "I'm really sorry." I opened the front door, waved Jeremy in, and kissed him quietly on the cheek. Lassie ran to greet him, butt wriggling in anticipation of a scratch.

"You promised," Cody repeated.

"I forgot," I said, motioning Jeremy into the great room. "It was an accident. A mistake. Everyone makes—"

He hung up.

"What's going on?" Jeremy set a six-pack of Kilt Lifter down on Marge's table, twisted open a beer, and handed it to me. He got one for himself and we sat at the table, where I gave him the short version of the picnic-bowling alley story, leaving out the new car part.

"You stood up your brother?" Jeremy looked at me over his beer.

"I know."

"Don't you like his girlfriend?"

I considered Sarah, her soft voice and shy smile. "No, she seems nice."

Jeremy waited. He would make a good investigator.

"I guess I'm uncomfortable with Cody having a girlfriend. I'm not sure he can handle it."

"Why not?"

"Because—" I started to say "because he has a brain injury," but stopped. Why did I think Cody's disability precluded a romantic relationship? "I guess I need to think about that." I stood up as a way of changing the subject. "What do you say we go All-American tonight—have pizza delivered and hit the bowling alley afterward?" I grabbed the rest of the six-pack and headed to the kitchen. Lassie followed me. Jeremy too.

"Sounds good," he said. "What's this?" He stopped at my dead body map, which I'd spread out on the counter between the kitchen and the dining room. "Planning to buy some golf course property?"

I put the beer in the fridge and joined Jeremy. He was right. All of the addresses bordered golf courses. Sunnydale did have more golf courses than the typical town, but still.

I explained to Jeremy that the map represented "dead body houses," and that all of them were for sale or recently sold to Underwood...I stopped. "And they would be worth even more than the comparables I looked up because they're all golf course properties," I said, shaking my head. "I should have caught that. Thanks."

"Glad to be of service, ma'am." He tipped an imaginary cowboy hat.

"Hey, maybe you can help me with another investigation question."

He stepped closer to me, so our hips touched.

"Are you trying to distract me?" I asked.

"Maybe." Jeremy smiled, but he didn't move.

I plowed ahead. "Do you think someone could place an unconscious person in a car?"

"You're thinking about Charlie?"

I nodded. If Charlie's death wasn't suicide, somebody put him in the driver's seat. Maybe someone dressed as a landscaper.

"It's tough, but not impossible. It would depend on a lot of factors: the weight of the body, the strength of the person carrying him, even how easy it is to get into the car. Here, let me show you." Jeremy scooped me up in his arms. It felt wonderful.

"So I guess you're strong enough and I'm light enough." I wasn't really that light, around one-twenty if I weighed first thing in the morning.

"Yep."

Lassie barked in consternation. "It's okay, boy." I kissed Jeremy to show the pug that everything was all right. And because I wanted to.

Jeremy kissed me back as he carried me toward the garage door. I wondered if he'd carry me toward the bedroom later.

"In the scenario in my head," I reached down to turn the doorknob, "this would all take place in the garage."

We went through the door and down the step. "The perpetrator would break into the garage..."

"'Perpetrator,'" said Jeremy. "I like it when you talk detective to me."

"And lure the victim," I said "victim" especially for Jeremy, "into the garage, where he—"

"Or she."

"Could a woman do it?"

"Maybe a strong woman and a smaller victim. Not real likely, but you should keep your mind open." Jeremy shifted my weight in his arms.

"Okay. Where he or she had already prepped the car to fill with exhaust quickly, and had the car door ajar, waiting." I leaned down and helped Jeremy open Marge's car door. "The attacker knocked the victim unconscious, with chloroform or something like it, and put them in the car." I went limp for best effect.

Jeremy bent down and slid me into the car seat. "It's kinda hard to not bump the body against the door frame," Jeremy said. "But you can do it."

"So my theory could work?"

"It *could*."

Ha. My theory held water. I was very pleased with myself until Jeremy straightened up and looked across the top of Marge's car at the blue Taurus next to it. "Whose car is that?"

CHAPTER 45

Jeremy didn't carry me to the bedroom. "No one just buys someone a car!" He wasn't shouting, but close. "There have to be strings attached."

I nearly told him that I wouldn't have it for long, but that would mean telling him I might leave. I kept my mouth shut. And he left.

So I was especially thrilled when I came into the dressing room on Wednesday evening to find a gorgeous bouquet of white lilies and red roses with a little card that said, "From your biggest fan." I texted Jeremy, "Thanks for the flowers! So sweet. XXOO." Wanting to share the Jeremy story and its happy ending, I went to the greenroom in search of Candy. Instead I found a very angry nun.

"What did you do?" Bitsy spat at me.

"Funny, I was going to ask you the same question."

She pulled me into a corner and hissed in my ear. "I don't know what you think you're up to, but you—" Bitsy's face had turned the same shade as her lipstick.

"I what?" Open-ended question. Another one of Uncle Bob's PI tricks.

"You said or did something to Carl, and now he's gone."

"Why do you think I did something to him?"

"He kept asking about you during our date, whether you were an actress or a detective, and how good you were. In fact, he was so distracted that he had a hard time getting it—"

"Stop." I cut her off. "I do not want to hear the gory details.

How do you know he's gone?"

"He was supposed to see me last night and didn't show. Not only that, but his wife called this morning to ask if I'd seen him. Found my name in his calendar."

"Did you know he was married?"

She whipped around away from me, her black veil nearly thwacking me in the face. "You are not investigating me, young lady."

Now I was.

After the show, I went back to Marge's place and turned on my laptop. I began with the basic criminal checks. Lassie snored under the table (wow, that dog could snore) as I sorted through Bitsy's dirty laundry.

Or lack of laundry. Elizabeth "Bitsy" Bright's offenses stemmed from wearing too few clothes. She had several misdemeanors and warnings regarding "lewd acts" and "indecent exposure." In other words, sex in public places. Eww.

Although I found Bitsy's predilection pretty icky and a good reason to never use the rec center hot tub again, public sex didn't seem like something she'd want to cover up (pun intended). I was sure Bitsy was hiding something, but what? Wait, the women in the rec center locker room had looked at Bitsy when I mentioned Charlie. Could he have been one of her naked partners in crime?

I plugged his name into my database. Nothing. If he'd dallied with Bitsy, he hadn't done it publicly. Or hadn't been caught.

I tried a different database, one that listed civil court records as well as criminal offenses. Bingo. Bitsy was hiding a husband. She had been married to Clement H. Thornberry, a resident of Prairie Home Care Center in Grand Island, Nebraska, for forty-six years. No divorce. Not only that, but Brian Thornberry, also of Grand Island, had filed a domestic abuse protection order on behalf of his father, Clement. Against Bitsy. Elizabeth "Bitsy" Bright was forbidden to threaten, assault, or have any contact with her husband. Bitsy's son had made sure his mother couldn't get anywhere near his dad.

I thought again about the reviews I'd found in Bitsy's dressing room. The restraining order indicated she was capable of violence. Bitsy was too, well, bitsy to have overcome Charlie or Marge, but did she orchestrate the attacks? And where was Carl? Why had he disappeared, and was it just coincidence that Bitsy was the last to see him?

CHAPTER 46

"Lord, I am so tired." I'd called Jeremy on the way from Uncle Bob's office to the theater. I didn't usually make calls while on the freeway (I know that distractibility and speed are not a great combo), but decided that five miles an hour down the 101 did not count as driving. "Crawling," "creeping," or "journeying across the desert at a camel's pace," maybe. Driving, no.

Besides, I needed to talk. First of all, it would help keep me awake. Between Lassie's snoring and my mind cataloguing the new info about Bitsy, I was operating on about four hours of sleep.

Secondly, when Jeremy never responded to my text last night, I realized I had been hasty. Though the flowers were a gift from "my biggest fan," the card didn't say who exactly that was. I had the sinking feeling I might have made a big mistake.

But I'd been raised to tap dance around any potential conflict-raising topics, so instead I babbled on about not much at all. "Hey, I took my foot off the brake," I said into the phone. "I think I moved about a foot. That's progress, right?"

Silence.

"I wonder why they call it 'rush hour?' No one could rush if they wanted to."

Nada.

"I'm really looking forward to you coming to the show tomorrow night."

"Me too."

Success!

"That way I can see this Roger guy who bought you a car and

maybe meet whoever buys you flowers," Jeremy said. "You know, check out the competition."

I tried to reassure Jeremy that he had no rivals for my affection, but I could no more get myself out of that emotional traffic jam than I could sprout wings and fly above the physical one. So I was tired and grouchy when I finally got to the theater.

I scarfed down a plate of cold tater tots and chicken wings that someone (probably Zeb) had kindly left me in the dressing room, slapped on some makeup, threw on my costume, and made it to the greenroom five minutes before places.

"Ivy, hon, you look like something the cat drug in," Candy tutted at me.

"Jeez." Arnie stopped in front of me, chewing on his unlit cigar. "You could pack for a weekend away with those bags."

I thought I'd covered up my puffy eyes and the dark circles under them. "Thank you all for your concern," I said with as much grace as I could muster. "I'm just having a hard time sleeping." I tried not to yawn. It wasn't just the previous night. I hadn't slept well since I'd moved into Marge's house, probably because I was either trying to listen for an intruder or trying not to listen to Lassie snoring.

"Hell, I'm not concerned about you," said Arnie. "I'm thinking about the show. You're supposed to look sixteen, you know."

Bitsy gave a little cough, then smiled innocently at me. I thought about the ace I had up my sleeve and smiled back. I wasn't sure yet what to do with my newfound information, but I wasn't going to keep it to myself forever.

"I'll try some more cover-up." I started toward the dressing room. This was bad. The producer was coming the day after tomorrow. I finally had my singing issue fixed, but now I was going to look "like something the cat drug in?"

Arnie caught up with me in the hall. "Okay, so I am a little worried about you."

"It happens sometimes," I said. "I just can't sleep, then it goes on for days until I somehow break the cycle."

"That used to happen to Marge too." When he said her name, his whole face drooped, ears included. "Hey." His ears perked up. "She's got some Ambien at home. You should give that a try, just to 'break the cycle,' like you say."

"I don't think I should take—"

"It's perfectly safe, she's not using it, and you'll sleep like a baby. What have you got to lose?"

I dragged myself through the show that night, feeling all the time like I was some underwater ballet performer instead of a perky cabaret dancer who could climb the Alps.

After the show, I stopped at Bernice's to water her plants, went back to Marge's, walked Lassie around the block, and then read my copy of *The Complete Idiot's Guide to Private Investigating* for an hour and a half, trying to tire myself out. I crawled into bed, shut my eyes and..."ZZZ...hngggGGng...ZZzzz...Snrkllllll." How could a little dog make so much noise? And what was that noise in the backyard? I threw back the covers, jumped out of bed, and peeked through the blinds to see—absolutely nothing unusual. Of course. I looked at the clock: almost three a.m. I gave up and flipped on the light.

"Snork!" Lassie woke with a start. Hey, maybe he'd stay awake if I kept the light on. After all, he could sleep during the day when I wasn't trying to.

"ZZZzzz, ZZZZhngggg."

Nope. I padded into Marge's bathroom. Whoa. Was that me in the mirror? Not only did I not look sixteen, I looked a good ten years older than I really was. That decided it. One little Ambien surely couldn't hurt.

Marge's medicine cabinet held bottles of Aleve, Motrin, several kinds of cold and allergy medicines, and a few prescription pill bottles: Ambien, Vicodin, and Gabapentin. I shook an Ambien into my hand, started to take it, and stopped.

I was taking allergy pills (spring in Phoenix, you know) and mixing drugs made me nervous ever since the time I downed my allergy meds with a big pot of coffee and was up for forty-eight hours straight. The least I could do was hop online and see if there were any drug interactions.

After a quick search, I learned it was okay to take my allergy meds with Ambien. I was about to shut down the computer and go to bed when something caught my eye. Gabapentin was listed in the "Do not combine with" category. I read further. And further. And knew I was not going to sleep that night at all.

CHAPTER 47

I am easily distracted. It's not that I'm fluttery or nervous. It's just that so many interesting things tend to happen at one time. It's one of the reasons theater is good for me. I can't be distracted during a play—I have to stay in character and focused on the people onstage with me. My distractibility is both a good thing and a bad thing when it comes to PI work. Good, because I observe and collect a lot of information. Bad, because once I learn something new, the old piece of information goes into a mental file cabinet where it languishes among dusty folders until something reminds me to pull it out again. Something like my conversation with Marge.

As I walked through the entrance of Mountain View Care Center, veering around folks parked in wheelchairs in the corridor, I planned my talk with her. The drug issue was obviously the most important, but I had other questions, and I thought I'd better ask them first.

I found Marge in the dayroom, a bright sunlit room where the scent of citrus air freshener overpowered the nursing home smell. She was watching *Good Morning Arizona* on a TV mounted on the wall, along with a half dozen other residents. I sat down next to her and gave her a sideways hug.

"You look good," I said. She did look better. Her hair was combed nicely and she wore a red polka-dotted shirt. Rather than clashing with the flowered chair she sat in, it made her look a bit like the Red Queen presiding over Wonderland. "Can we go back to your room to talk?"

"That room gets so stuffy. Let's stay here."

"But..." I looked around the other people, several of whom were openly eavesdropping. One even waved.

"Don't worry, chickie. Some of them won't know what we're talking about, some won't have anyone to tell, and most, like me, won't remember this conversation five minutes later."

I shrugged and jumped right in, raising my voice over the background TV chatter: "Do you have any enemies? Anyone who might want to hurt you?"

"Nah."

"Even at the theater?" This was what I really wanted to know.

"Ah. You mean Bitsy, right?"

I nodded. "What does she have against you?"

"You know. I had a bigger role, a nice house on the golf course, and a great boyfriend. I don't take it personally." She chuckled a little, a good sign. "Bitsy's got second-itis, big time."

"Second-itis?"

"Second place is never good enough. She wants to be first at everything. Everyone has to love her best. You heard about the Sunnydale Poms incident?"

"I did." A tiny wizened lady sat up straighter on the couch.

"Me too," said the man next to her.

I shook my head. The Sunnydale Poms were a group of over-sixty cheerleaders. They were pretty awesome and pretty famous, performing at conventions and marching in big parades.

"Bitsy was in the Sunnydale Peps, kind of the second string, like a pep squad. But now she's in the Poms. They had an opening after one of them fell and broke her ankle during a parade. A couple of people swear they saw Bitsy trip her."

The couch couple shook their heads.

"People," said the man.

So Bitsy's sweet exterior disguised a bitter inner life. I wondered if Arnie knew, which led me to my next question: "You said she might be envious of your boyfriend..."

"Oh, god, is she after Arnie now? Figures." Marge shook her head, disgusted. "You heard of ambulance chasers? Bitsy's a hearse chaser. First one to go after any recent widower. She even tried to get her hooks in poor Charlie Small, when all the world could see how much he missed Helen."

"Tried to?"

"He was having none of it, but she wouldn't let up. Charlie finally dressed her down but good at an opening night party a few months ago."

"In front of everyone?"

"Yeah. It was great. When she left the room in a huff, all the women cheered."

The tiny lady on the couch tittered. I thought about telling Marge about Bitsy's marriage, but a yawn caught me instead.

"Lassie keeping you up at night?"

I nodded.

"That's why I got sleeping pills. Between old age, my restless leg, and that dog, I wasn't getting a wink."

"I actually wanted to talk to you about—"

"I ever tell you about the time Arnie got his sleeping pills mixed up with Viagra?" Marge did a little Groucho Marx eyebrow wiggle. "He was up all night."

The couch couple laughed, then looked at each other, got up quickly, and padded down the hall, his hand on her waist.

"Seems like you're doing really well," I said. "Have they figured out some medication for you?" Maybe Marge's doctors had already figured out what I thought I knew.

The smile slipped from her face. "No. I'm just having a good morning. Yesterday I thought my yogurt was face cream." She tried to crack a smile but couldn't hold it.

"I may have some good news. Are you still taking Gabapentin?"

"Yeah. For my restless leg."

"I did a little research last night and found that Gabapentin can have really serious side effects, including unsteadiness and dementia. Not only that, but combining Ambien with Gabapentin makes them worse. And," I added, having noticed Marge's well-stocked liquor cabinet, "they say you shouldn't drink while on it, either."

Marge stared at her hands. She slowly lifted her chin, then looked at me, a plea in her eyes. "Are you saying what I think you're saying? That I might not have dementia?"

"I think you and your doctor should look into it." I handed her a sheet of paper. "Here's a list of all the medications I found in your medicine cabinet, along with the phone numbers of the pharmacies where they were filled." I couldn't get info about Marge's prescription history, but I hoped her doctor could get access. I pointed at the bottom of the page. "I also wrote down every vitamin and supplement I found in your house, just in case there's an interaction."

Marge reached over and clasped my hands in hers. "Thank you."

"Don't thank me yet," I said. "I still haven't figured out what happened the morning you were attacked."

"So you believe me?"

"I do." I thought about what Jeremy had said about most people falling forward down the steps. Marge had fallen backward, like she'd been startled or even pushed by an attacker. "You were found in the garage. Do you think the intruder came in through the garage door? I've heard it's pretty easy to do." Uncle Bob had shown me a YouTube video called, "How to break into a garage in six seconds."

Marge shook her head. "That's the one way he couldn't have gotten in. I had the whole shebang fixed and secured after that break-in I had last month."

"Wait, someone broke into your house?"

"Nah, just the garage. You know the only thing they stole?" Marge shook her head in puzzlement. "My catalytic converter."

CHAPTER 48

"I can't believe I didn't ask Marge about her catalytic converter." I paced my uncle's office, really annoyed with myself. I'd driven there straight after my visit to the care center.

"You got a file, right?" Uncle Bob leaned back in his office chair. "Isn't your research in there?"

"Of course." I threw myself into my chair. "But that was Charlie Small's file, and..." I didn't want to tell Uncle Bob I hadn't flipped through it lately...oh, what the hell. "And files don't work for me, because if I put something in a file, I can't see it. I am the poster child for 'out of sight, out of mind.'"

Uncle Bob pursed his lips in thought, then pushed himself away from his desk and went out the office door.

A minute or so later, someone knocked. I opened the door to see my uncle. Or rather a large whiteboard with my uncle's legs sticking out from under it.

"Hold the door for me, will ya?" He wrangled the whiteboard into the office, smacking it into a bookcase. "Try this," he said. "You can put your research headings, suspicions, and suspects on it. The whole gambit."

"Like in a squad room on TV."

"Like in a squad room on TV." Uncle Bob grinned. We both loved cop shows.

"But where'd it come from?"

"We got a shared conference room down the hall. No one in the building ever uses it."

"You just took the whiteboard out of the conference room?"

"I left a Post-it."

I spent the rest of the afternoon in geek heaven—using squeaky markers to write all the pertinent information onto my big beautiful whiteboard. Now everything connected to the case was in one place: the number of suicides, house sales, golf course lots, catalytic converters, and viatical settlements. I listed everyone I knew who was connected with Charlie, which included Carl Marks, neighbors, everyone at the theater, and all the people at Charlie's church and various clubs. Since Hank was Uncle Bob's friend, I didn't write him down. But I didn't forget him.

I also made a pit stop at a garage after work on the way to the theater. "This may be a weird question," I said, pointing to my new Taurus. "But can you tell if this car has a catalytic converter?"

After ascertaining that my car did have a catalytic converter, I drove to the theater, made sure Jeremy's ticket was at will-call, and headed down to dinner. Afraid my love of coconut fried shrimp was beginning to show on my thighs, I ordered a chicken breast, wild rice, and asparagus.

A few minutes later I sat down next to Candy, who was wolfing down a double order of my favorite dish. I looked at my grilled chicken breast so sadly that she plopped a shrimp on my plate. "Just one won't do you any harm."

"Jeremy's coming to the show tonight," I said.

"Your biggest fan."

I nearly grimaced but caught myself in time to fake a smile. I hadn't told anyone that the flowers weren't from Jeremy. I didn't know who had sent them. I had told Jeremy that they were from Uncle Bob, but it wasn't true. White lies in the name of romance were okay, right?

Candy grinned at me. "Ever noticed that all your boyfriends' names start with J?"

"Huh?"

"Jason, Jeremy..."

"Jeb," said Zeb, popping up out of nowhere.

"Your name is Zeb," I said.

"I could change it." Then in a louder voice, for the benefit of the whole table, he said, "Guess what? I got my extra credit and my science teacher says I'm a shoo-in for the summer program. I am officially a science geek."

We all congratulated Zeb and I shook his hand, which was a mistake because he grabbed it and began kissing up my arm, Pepé Le Pew style. I swatted him back into the kitchen, ate my dinner, and prepared to go onstage.

But nothing could have prepared me for that night.

After the Wolf and Teasel dance, Timothy/Wolf kissed me, as he did every night. But this time, he didn't do so in the tender, seductive manner he usually employed, but instead grabbed my ass and French kissed me, with lots of disgusting slobbery tongue. I had to kiss him back or break character. What us actors have to do in the name of art. As soon as we came offstage, I turned on him. "What the hell was that?" I wiped my lips for extra emphasis.

"You don't have to do that." Timothy actually looked hurt. "I was just trying to—"

"To what? It's not choreographed, it's not necessary, and unless you've been fooling all the people all the time, it's not something you want to do with girls, so why?"

"I was told I needed to sex up the character, that I was coming off too gay."

"Well, you could have warned me, is all I have to say."

Blechh. Imagine being unexpectedly French kissed by your hairy brother. Blechh.

The rest of the show was okay. Bitsy didn't have Marge's voice, but she made a decent Mother Superior; I sang well, and we all escaped the Nazis.

But when Jeremy met me in the greenroom after the show, his smile was tight. "You were great." He kissed me and gave me a single wrapped rose. "*This* flower is from me."

We walked in strained silence toward Jeremy's pickup. I'd

decided to leave my new car at the theater. No use rubbing salt in the wound. Roger said he'd give me a ride to the show tomorrow.

Jeremy drove the short distance to Marge's house, pulled into the drive, killed the engine, and turned to me. "Ivy," he said. "I don't know if I can take this. I mean, I knew you were an actress when we met. I was willing to put up with your screwy schedule since mine isn't exactly normal." He looked away from me. "I might even be able to get past your skimpy costumes..."

I thought about the even more provocative costumes I'd worn in the past and kept silent.

"But man," Jeremy said. "It felt horrible, watching those old guys in the audience ogle my girlfriend. And what if we had a family?"

I had a fleeting glimpse of Jeremy tossing a laughing little boy into the air. My heart nearly stopped.

"How would I explain why Mama was half-naked onstage?"

"But—"

"But what was even worse tonight," Jeremy clenched his fists in his lap, "was watching that guy kiss you."

"Jeremy, he's gay. Timothy, the actor playing Wolf, is—"

"He French kissed you! I could see that all the way from the audience."

"He's never done that before toni—"

"And he groped your butt. What's worse, you looked like you enjoyed it."

"My character is supposed to look like she enjoys—" A quick glance at Jeremy's face told me this was not the way to go. "Listen, please just come inside for a drink and I can explain. Please?"

Jeremy didn't say anything, but he did get out of the car, slamming the door as he did. I let us into Marge's house, tossed my keys on the table into the hall, and headed toward the back of the house, Lassie at our heels. I'd get us a couple of beers, and we could sit on the patio and talk this through. We could.

But as we walked through the house I felt a breeze, saw the door to the back patio open, and heard a splash from the pool.

"What the hell?" Jeremy said, before I could say it.

We crept to the back door and peeked out into the night. A man was swimming in Marge's pool, a black silhouette against the turquoise light of the pool. When he got to the shallow end of the pool, he noticed us, stopped, and climbed out of the pool. Roger—wearing the briefest, tightest Speedo I had ever seen.

"I'm sorry." He nodded at Jeremy, but spoke to me. "I thought it was my night with you."

Jeremy turned on his heel. "Wait!" I yelled, running after him. "I don't know what's going on, but—"

Jeremy stopped so abruptly I nearly ran into him. "I don't either and I don't want to. I think you're part of a screwed-up world and I don't want any part of it." He shook his head, like he was getting me out of his system. "I'm sorry. I really liked you." He left, not even bothering to shut the door behind him.

I ran back toward the pool. Roger reclined in a lounger, looking unperturbed.

"Why in the hell did you do that?" I shouted at him. "And what are you wearing?" I picked up his wet towel and tossed it over his Speedo bits. "We are not a couple, Roger! You and I, I mean. Jeremy and I, on the other hand, were, until—" I burst into tears. "What the hell?!" I wailed.

"I know we're not a couple," said Roger. "And—"

"Let's go, Gorgeous!"

Roger sat up. "Is that Arnie?"

I ignored him. "Shit. I need to walk the dog." I stomped off toward the house, but not quickly enough for Lassie. "Let's go, Gorgeous!" Arnie's recorded voice said again. I turned back to Roger. "You'd better be gone by the time I get back."

CHAPTER 49

It was Saturday, the day the big producer would watch the show. I'd been looking forward to this day for weeks and now it just sucked.

I sat at Marge's kitchen table with a cup of really strong coffee and Lassie curled up at my feet, snoring like a grizzly with a head cold. I punched my uncle's number into my cell. "Do you mind if I work from home today?" I had planned to go into the office since Jeremy and I were supposed to go hiking on Monday.

"You sick?" he asked.

I thought about saying yes. After all, I was heartsick. But instead I said, "Jeremy dumped me last night."

"I'm sorry, sweetheart." Uncle Bob's voice was gentle. "Listen, why don't you take the day off, come in Monday instead?"

"I want to work. Get my mind off..." My throat tightened. "Things."

"Why'd he dump you?"

"Because I'm an actor. Because I have a weird schedule and wear skimpy costumes and kiss people onstage."

"And because you let someone buy you a car?"

Sometimes having an observant PI uncle was really annoying. "Yeah," I admitted, "that too." And because I really didn't want to talk about how I'd screwed up, I changed the subject. "I can work on that new Colonel Marks case, do some research from here."

"You sure? There's a handsome man in a Hawaiian shirt and a good-looking whiteboard here. One of 'em might even buy you lunch."

"Thanks, but I think Lassie will be enough company for the day."

"Marge's dog is named Lassie?"

"Yeah. But he's a boy." I wondered just how long Marge had been confused.

"Ha! The dogs who played Lassie, they were all male."

"Yeah, but were they pugs?"

I said goodbye to my wonderful, lovely uncle, and went into the kitchen for another cup of coffee. As I stood at the counter, I remembered the safe, sexy feel of Jeremy's arms around me as I cooked, the way his dimples deepened when he smiled at me, the tender heart he showed me when talking about the drowned little boy. I put the coffeepot down. I didn't want coffee. I wanted Jeremy.

An involuntary half-sob escaped my lips. Tears blurred my vision, and I leaned on the counter, my head in my hands. The thing was, Jeremy was right. And I didn't know what to do about it.

Theater had saved my life after Cody's accident. It gave me a place where I was encouraged to express my emotions, where I felt appreciated, where I was part of a "family." But theater was not necessarily conducive to long-term relationships. Not only did it come with all the baggage Jeremy had talked about, there was a bigger problem. If I wanted to make it big in theater, I'd have to leave Arizona.

Which I had never told Jeremy. Which meant I'd been leading him on. Which meant I deserved to get dumped.

Choking down another sob, I felt a moist nose nudge my calf. Lassie had woken up and was standing near my feet. He bumped me again, looking at me with concern. I gathered him up and went to the sofa, where I held his warm little body against mine and cried for the way I'd treated Jeremy and the breakup that I deserved.

CHAPTER 50

I never had a pet—too messy, my mom said. The depth of feeling people had for their dogs and cats had always baffled me. Sure, animals were cute and fuzzy, but c'mon, weren't they just substitutes for real relationships?

After half an hour of unconditional love from an animal who barely knew me, I now understood how real that connection could be. Lassie had sat with me and cuddled me and looked at me worriedly while I cried. The pug had wormed his curly little butt right into my heart.

Now that I was cried out, I wanted to get to work, but I also wanted to be good to my new best friend, who was still curled on my lap. "How 'bout if I work outside this morning?" I said, gently scooting him off of me. "And you can water the plants and look for rabbits?" He seemed amenable, so I padded to the kitchen, grabbed a cup of coffee, put my laptop under my arm, and slid open the door to the back patio. "C'mon, boy."

I set myself up at the patio table. A memory flashed into my mind: a smiling Jeremy sitting across the table. "*Carl*," I said to myself sternly. Lassie, who'd been sniffing the concrete floor around the table, raised his head to look at me. "I am thinking about *Carl*." Lassie went back to looking for old leftovers on the ground, and I went to work.

I first wanted to get a more complete picture of Carl Marks, figuring that knowing who he was might lead me to where he was. I searched my databases. No criminal history that I could find. Yes, he really was an insurance agent. He'd been investigated by the

Arizona Department of Insurance Fraud Unit (for what I couldn't tell), but not disciplined. Owned six houses so far. No word on whether they all had black rooms. He'd been married four times, no kids. Born and raised in Nebraska, then moved to Arizona.

Huh. At the craft sale, didn't he tell Bitsy he was from the South?

The craft sale.

I went inside, grabbed my bag off Marge's counter, and dug around in its depths until I felt the tissue-wrapped bundle the earring vendor had given me. Yes. Her business card was still taped on top. I called the number on the card. "Hi, you probably won't remember me, but I bought some peacock earrings from you at the craft sale."

"You're right. I probably won't remember you." The earring vendor laughed at herself.

"Anyway, you said that Colonel Carl Marks had ordered some custom work from you."

"Yes." A change in her voice. Tight.

"Did he ever meet with you?"

"Yes." Tighter.

I waited a few seconds. Nada. "Did he, ah, try to sell you anything?"

"Yes." A pause, then the words spilled out. "He not only tried to convince me I needed a 'life settlement contract,' but he hit on me. Awful, all hands. Wouldn't take no for an answer. Haven't had to deal with that type for twenty years. Slimeball."

"I'm really sorry. Thanks for the information."

"By the way, I remember you now. I bet those earrings look wonderful against your blonde hair."

After she hung up, I went back outside. The sun had warmed the concrete beneath my bare feet, but not my now-cool cup of coffee. I sipped it anyway, flipping through my mental snapshots and trying to remember what the earring vendor looked like. That's right: late fifties or so, curly graying hair worn long, a bit more Bohemian-looking than most of the ladies I'd seen around here.

Had Carl really been attracted to her? Was he just trying to sell her insurance? Or maybe he wanted her for one of his films?

I wondered if Bitsy was in a Marks production and nearly choked on my coffee. Eww. Couldn't imagine anyone would want to see that. Wait. Maybe that was the point. Maybe Carl was not just into porn, but blackmail.

He was also still in the insurance business. Had he lied to Cheri about that? After all, she'd said he didn't work as an insurance agent anymore.

No, she didn't. I heard her words in my head: "Carl's a really good insurance agent. *Was* a really good agent." That could mean "retired." Or it could mean "dead." Was Cheri lying to me? Or had Carl been lying to her?

My coffee cup was empty, so I went back inside to the kitchen to make another pot. Lassie jingled and snorted behind me, probably hoping for some food. I didn't disappoint him.

"Why did Carl leave?" I asked Lassie as he chomped noisily on a jerky treat. "If Bitsy was telling the truth and he was asking about me, he must be afraid I'm going to find something. Blackmail, maybe? Maybe Bitsy or some other woman had enough?" The dog stared at me as I poured water into the coffeemaker. "There's also the Nebraska connection. Maybe Carl knew Bitsy's family there. Maybe he found out about Bitsy and her husband, and she offed him. Or maybe Cheri wasn't as okay with her open marriage as she said, and *she* took him out." Lassie looked doubtful, in a puggish sort of way. "You're right," I said. "The fact that he came back to the house and got some clothes makes it unlikely he was the victim of foul play." The coffeemaker burbled. "So what is it about Colonel Carl Marks?" Lassie tilted his head. "Do you think I should run his license plate?"

I hadn't run the plate after Uncle Bob warned me it was a pain in the butt to get the records and it was unlikely I'd get much more than his name and address. But what the heck. I thought I might be able to get past the first problem.

"Hey, Pink," I said into my cell. "Any chance you could run a plate for me? It's one of Uncle Bob's cases. There might be a beer in it for you."

"Are you trying to bribe a police officer?"

"No! No. Shit."

Pink chuckled. "Kidding. Give me the number."

"D...OD...one five six eight."

"Are you singing?"

I *was* singing, and I was right about the lack of info I'd get from the license plate. Pink told me the car was registered to Carl Marks at his Sunnydale address. No warrants. No outstanding traffic tickets. Everything about Carl Marks seemed aboveboard.

Wait. Everything about Carl Marks seemed aboveboard. But not about *Colonel* Carl Marks. None of the information I'd found included the military title he was so proud of. I went back to my computer and started searching through Carl's military records. Or rather, I searched *for* his military records. He didn't have any. No stint in Vietnam, no stateside service, nothing.

In Arizona, impersonating a public servant was a class one misdemeanor "if such person pretends to be a public servant and engages in any conduct with the intent to induce another to submit to his pretended official authority or to rely on his pretended official acts." The federal Stolen Valor Act of 2013 also made it illegal to pretend to be a war hero to obtain tangible benefits. I wasn't sure if posing as a decorated colonel in order to curry favor with potential insurance clients counted as breaking the law. I was sure that it was a low-down despicable thing to do, especially to all the real veterans Carl dealt with. Like Charlie Small.

CHAPTER 51

"Asshole," Pinkstaff said when I called and told him about Carl. "I'll check with the district attorney on Monday about the bastard's legal standing and see what can be done."

"Asshole" was apparently Carl's new name, as it was the first thing Uncle Bob said when I called him too. Then he said, "Hope you find him. I'd like to take him down a peg, for all the guys who really served."

"Like Hank?"

"What?"

Lassie snorted from under the kitchen table. Okay, it wasn't the smoothest transition, but I had to know more about Hank. I'd run over to Trader Joe's at lunchtime, and there he was. Hank wasn't following me this time. He was loading up his cart with junk food while singing along (loudly) to "Good Vibrations" as it played over the store's PA system. I don't think he even saw me, but I couldn't be sure since he wore his mirrored sunglasses.

"Hank's a vet, right?" I remembered the Vietnam Vet cap he had in the fishing boat. Hank had checked in with Cheri "just to be nice." Maybe he had found out about Carl the asshole too. Maybe he did something about it.

"Yeah." My uncle's voice sounded puzzled. "He was one of the last to serve in Vietnam. Got called up a few months before the war ended."

"He have any problems when he came back? Pain from old injuries? PTSD?"

"I don't think so. What are you—"

"Why does he always wear those mirrored sunglasses?"

"I think it's something to do with his eyes. Maybe they're prescription or something."

Or something. I asked the question I'd been leading up to: "Do you think Hank could have a drug problem?"

"No." My uncle was firm. "What's all this about, Olive?"

"Okay, here's my theory." I looked at the photo of the whiteboard I so cleverly snapped before I left the office yesterday. "I think it's suspicious that we have an abnormally high number of suicides—"

"These are old folks, right?"

"Wait, there's more." I looked at the photo again. I loved that whiteboard. "All of the people who supposedly killed themselves lived in houses on golf courses. Each of their houses sold quickly, way under value, most of them to the same offshore holdings company. Several of them were razed to make way for really expensive houses."

"You're thinking real estate is the motive?"

"Yeah." Lassie snorted again. Everyone's a critic. "I think Marge was an intended victim of the same scheme. She lived on a golf course, had her catalytic converter stolen, and was attacked in the garage near her car. She also sold her life insurance policy to Carl, as did Charlie."

"Okay..." I could tell Uncle Bob was considering the case I made.

"And," I took a deep breath, "Hank was on the scene in every single case."

"That's right," said my uncle. "If you had been at that meeting the morning you burned down your apartment, you woulda known that Hank made sure to be at the scenes, because he was uncomfortable with all those suicides too."

"What? Why didn't you tell me?"

"Hank's always been a conspiracy theorist type. And to tell you the truth, he seems a little paranoid these days. Plus you were doing a good job investigating all by yourself," I mentally patted myself on the back, "and I didn't think you'd be silly enough to suspect Hank." I stopped the mental patting. "Do you have any other suspects besides Hank and this Carl guy?"

"Maybe."

My uncle sighed exaggeratedly over the phone. "I've said it before, you've got good instincts, but you can't follow them alone. You gotta find actual evidence."

"You're right. And uh, sorry about suspecting Hank."

"No worries. He has been acting a little hinky these days, so it's understandable. But," he said, cutting off my next question, "Hank would never hurt anyone."

I hung up, stood up, and began pacing the floor, hoping the movement would jog something loose in my mind. Lassie got up and followed close behind me, snuffling and snorting.

Evidence. I needed evidence. I opened the door to Marge's garage and examined the area where she had fallen. Jeremy and I had done a good job cleaning up the mess. Too good. Even if we hadn't, I didn't remember any fingerprints, and the footprints I saw probably belonged to the paramedics.

I shut the door, went back into the house, and paced some more, Lassie still at my heels. I suspected that the mysterious landscaper spotted before Charlie's death and Marge's attack was a fake. I figured that was the killer's ruse: Look like he (or she) was on official-type business, break into the garage when no one was looking, somehow overcome the victim, and then put the unconscious person in the idling car. Oh, and I guess he would have had to steal the catalytic converter earlier.

Lassie snorted. It did seem awfully convoluted. I paced faster. Lassie did too, jingling and snorting, distracting the hell out of me. Enough. I couldn't stop the snorting, but I could sure as hell do something about the damn jingling. I took Lassie's collar off. He shook his head, maybe happy to be free of the collar or maybe trying to jingle all by himself. I went to put the jangly thing on the kitchen table, when I stopped. On the collar, amongst Lassie's rabies and ID tags, hung the Pet Cam. Of course. I couldn't believe I hadn't thought of it earlier. Okay, okay, at the time I had been distracted by the discovery of Arnie's surveillance system, but still.

I found a USB cable among a tangle of cords by Marge's computer, connected the Pet Cam to my laptop, downloaded a bunch of photos Lassie had "taken," and there it was.

Evidence.

CHAPTER 52

"You were right. Someone was in your house." I called Marge as soon as I saw the Pet Cam pictures. "I have evidence."

"Thank God!"

I examined the incriminating photos. Marge must have turned the Pet Cam on when she heard the intruder, setting the camera to take photos every minute.

"You have pink fuzzy slippers, right?" The first photo showed the back of Marge's slipper-clad feet.

"Yeah."

The second photo was the real evidence. It looked like it was taken just after Marge opened the garage door. "I've got a photo from Lassie's Pet Cam that shows your feet and someone else's." In it, Marge's slippered feet faced another pair of feet wearing white leather athletic shoes. "Do you know anyone who wears white tennis shoes?"

"Just everyone."

"Yeah. I was afraid of that." The photo showed only the front of the white sneaker. I could just see the tip of a gray identifying mark that could have been part of a letter announcing a brand name, or a Nike swoosh, or even a curved stripe.

"How do you know these pictures were taken the night I fell? I could've been talking to Bernice or something a few days earlier."

"Well, these first two photos showed just feet, first yours, and then yours and the attacker's. The next photo was of the doggie doorbell."

"Still."

"The next to last photo was of you, lying down in a pool of

blood. And the last picture..." The fuzzy red image looked like a close-up of Marge's face, taken by a camera smeared with blood. I swallowed the sentimental lump in my throat and patted the very good dog at my feet. "Was Lassic, trying to save you."

I hung up with Marge, but not before she told me her doctor was checking into the possibility of medication-induced dementia. "So I may not be crazy. And someone did attack me. Ivy, I'd kiss you if I could."

I still had work to do. I could prove someone was in the house, but who? I thought about the tennis shoes and my list of suspects. Carl definitely had white tennis shoes, the really expensive ones that had set off my radar. Hank (who was still a suspect in my book) wore black shoes with his posse uniform. I tried to think if I'd seen his shoes when he was out of uniform at Trader Joe's or in the boat at Lake Pleasant. Couldn't remember. Arnie usually wore dress shoes, but probably had a pair of sneakers in his closet. Bitsy often wore white tennis shoes, but I couldn't imagine her (or Arnie for that matter) having the strength to put an unconscious person in the car, the way Jeremy had shown me.

Jeremy. My heart actually hurt at the thought of him. Why so much? After all, we weren't even all that serious yet.

The happy family at the firemen's tug-of-war flashed into my mind. Was it our potential future I mourned? Maybe. That and the fact that Jeremy might be right. The "screwed-up" world of theater might keep me from having any sort of normal relationship.

I shook my head. No time to mourn lost near-love. I had a murder to solve, and the producer was coming to the show tonight.

A knock and Roger walked in the unlocked front door.

"What the—" I looked at the clock. "Shit." It was time to go to the theater, I wasn't ready, and I'd forgotten to call and find a ride who wasn't Roger. My car was still in the theater parking lot. I waved Roger out of the room. "Just go. I'll take Marge's car."

"Then you'll have two cars at the theater." I was about to tell him I'd deal with it when he said, "And I think we should talk."

He was going to get a talking-to, all right. "I need a minute." I scooped up Lassie and put him outside the back door. "Pee now," I said, "walk later." I ran to the bedroom, threw some clean undies and tights in a duffle bag, grabbed my purse off the dresser, came back, let Lassie in, hoped he'd peed, and said, "I'm ready."

Roger was looking through the photos on the table. "What are—"

"Pet Cam photos." I pointed to the clock. "Let's go." I didn't want to spend any more time in Roger's company than was absolutely necessary.

I followed him out to his borrowed car. "About last night," he said, "I did that on purpose." He unlocked the doors remotely.

"No shit, Sherlock. I didn't think you'd just happened to show up at Marge's half-naked and unannounced for the first time ever."

Roger got into the car. "I also sent you the flowers. And told Timothy to French kiss you."

"Nice. Thanks. The ass-grab too?" I slid into the passenger seat.

"He improvised that." He started up the car. "Don't you want to know why I did what I did?"

I stayed silent. I had a pretty good idea.

"It's not what you think."

I continued to hold my tongue.

"You know how I've been mentoring you? The lessons, the car, this introduction to the producer?"

I stiffened. Here it came, the tit for tat bit.

"If you had ended up in love with that guy, you probably would have thrown away your chance at the big time. Stayed here in Phoenix and had kids or something." He shook his head as he pulled into the theater parking lot. "I've seen it too many times."

I was about to protest, then stopped. If the relationship with Jeremy had progressed to love, I might have stayed.

"You've got to realize something about the theater, Ivy." Roger turned to look at me. "If you really want to make it, you have to give it everything you've got. Don't let anything—or anyone—stand in your way."

CHAPTER 53

I carefully parted the velvet curtains so I could check out the audience pre-show. A man with black glasses and a neatly trimmed salt-and-pepper beard sat at a table in the front row, perusing the program. Had to be the producer. He was the only one sitting by himself, except for—

Really? Yeah, it was him, mirrored sunglasses and all. I hadn't figured Hank for a musical theater guy. Was he following me again?

I let the curtains fall and went back to the greenroom, where I shook off the producer-and-Hank nerves by taking deep breaths, doing head rolls, and practicing tongue twisters. As I said, "The sixth sick sheik's sixth sheep's sick" for the third time, Candy walked in. Normally the very definition of "high energy," tonight she dragged her feet, a rubber ball that'd lost its bounce. She plopped down onto the old sofa and sat there, still in her scrubs from the care center. "I broke up with Matt."

I sat down too, and put an arm around her.

She leaned forward, hanging her head. "I really liked him." Candy, who was notoriously fickle, had broken a relationship record with Matt. This wasn't just a bit of fun.

"Then why?" I rubbed her back gently.

Raising her head, Candy caught sight of the clock on the wall. "Lordy, is that the time?" We both stood. The sadness slipped off her. "I figured it was time to fish or cut bait. I'm fixin' to leave town." Her face brightened like a Christmas bulb. "I'm moving to L.A. I've got a friend I can live with, and she's going to introduce me to her agent. I'm going for it!" She did a little happy dance. Maybe she was the definition of "high energy" *and* "resilient."

A bunch of eavesdroppers congratulated her. "And when were you going to tell your very good friend Ivy?" I couldn't believe Candy had made such a big decision in secret.

"I wanted to tell Matt first, and didn't want you to have to hide anything when you saw him." Candy shook her head. "Did he tell you we were finally goin' on a double date? A picnic or somethin' with Cody and his girlfriend. Would have been fun." Her face grew serious again. "I *really* liked him. Maybe even..." She trailed off. I thought I knew what she was feeling, that pull between the love of acting and, well, love. Maybe it was good that Jeremy broke up with me.

"Don't worry, dear," Bitsy said. "He's a nice, handsome boy with a good future. Some lucky girl will snap him up." She patted Candy on the shoulder and walked away.

Candy deflated like a balloon. "How does she do that? Say something sweet as honey that makes you feel like crap?" She slunk back to our dressing room.

I'd had just about enough of Bitsy and her passive-aggressive maliciousness. "So, *Mrs.* Bitsy Bright," I said loudly enough that a few actors turned around. "I think we need to talk after the show."

Bitsy coiled into herself, like a rattlesnake about to strike. But I had my big boots on, metaphorically speaking, so I smiled at her and followed Candy into our dressing room

I told her about my breakup with Jeremy. After a good cry and a couple of MoonPies (she kept a stash for emergencies), we were ready for the show. I tried not to think too much about the producer. Who had seats at a front row table. Who was about to decide the trajectory of my life.

Thanks to Marge's advice, once I was onstage as Teasel all thoughts of the producer vanished. Maybe I was really becoming an actor. I sang "Sixteen Going on Twenty-One" beautifully, executed the grand jeté in our dance number perfectly, and even managed to kiss Wolf with something that resembled virginal passion. I could almost see the lights of New York.

Then came "Dough, Ray, Me." All of us dancers sang together

with Mary, “Dough, the rent, the bucks I owe...” Except for me. I opened my mouth and out came, “D...OD...one five six eight.” Carl’s license plate number. The Sunnydale street scene flashed into my mind: Carl’s red Ferrari, Roger in running gear, the lady with the schnauzer.

What the hell? My singing memorization trick had never backfired on me before. Teasel the dancer disappeared and Ivy took over as one part of my brain scrabbled around trying to figure out what was going on, while another part recognized that I was onstage in front of an audience (and a producer) and tried to shut the detecting part down. In self-preservation, I stopped singing and just mouthed the words.

Luckily, no one seemed to notice. In fact, during intermission, there was a knock on our dressing room door. Roger stuck his head in. “The producer loves you.” He blew me a little kiss and closed the door. Candy, who had just heard how Roger torpedoed my love life, gave me a “what the hell are you doing?” look. I ignored it, like I ignored the license number jingling away in the back of my mind and the Sunnydale street scene that continued to loop through my consciousness. I had a show to do.

CHAPTER 54

I tried to slow my breathing as I waited in the wings for Act Two to begin. I/Teasel sang the opening line. I *had* to be in character. I took a deep breath, shucked off Ivy, and became Teasel. I put myself in her shoes, in pre-World War II Austria when the Nazis were closing in and Jews were in definite danger.

The music began, the stage lights went to black, and we Vaughn Katt dancers took our places onstage. The lights came up, dimly.

I looked around us at the ruined stage, the up ended chairs, the curtains the Nazis had spray painted with swastikas. I sang, "The nightclub tonight...lacks the sound of music..." My voice quavered a bit with the fear Teasel felt but was perfectly on pitch. The other dancers joined me in the song, which ended with rousing applause from the audience.

The rest of the scene went great too: Mary, who had run away to the nunnery, returned to the cabaret to proclaim her love for Captain Vaughn Katt, and together they hatched a plan to disguise us dancers in nuns' habits so we could escape across the Alps unmolested. I snuck a peek at the producer, who smiled as he scribbled in a notebook. My heart soared as I exited into the wings.

While the Captain and Mary sang a love ballad onstage, we dancers had to make a quick costume change for our last two numbers, which we performed already disguised in our habits. The idea was that the Captain and Mary and all of us pretend nuns sang at a festival that offered a slightly easier escape route, while some of the real nuns posed as cabaret dancers to keep the Nazis occupied.

I kicked off my sparkly heels (I shared them with a nun actor who was changing into a cabaret dancer costume) and ran to the place where Lori, my dresser, always waited with my costume in hand, ready to pop the habit over my head, fasten my wimple and veil, and help me slip into sensible nun shoes.

Lori wasn't there. I looked around frantically. Everyone else was almost ready—it was amazing how quickly you could get changed with help. I not only had no help, I had no costume. The music began for our next number. "Hold!" I stage whispered to anyone who might hear. "Hold!"

No one heard. The rest of the dancers rushed onstage just as Lori ran back to the wings, habit in hand. "I don't know what happened." She threw the habit over my head. "I set out your costume just like always, but when I got here it was gone." The music for the next song began. Dammit, couldn't they tell they were a nun short?

Lori quickly fastened my veil and wimple. "I never did find your shoes." The captain began to sing, "Edelweiss belongs to me..." Finally dressed, I flew onstage. Which, I realized as I ran, was really stupid.

This particular song was a strange combination of "Edelweiss" from *The Sound of Music* and "Tomorrow Belongs to Me," which is sung by Hitler Youth in *Cabaret*. It was supposed to show that we were subtly thumbing our noses at the Nazis, and to bring the audience to tears. Instead there were titters as I ran onstage two lines late, veil flapping and bare feet slapping the stage.

We had just finished the song to modest applause when Bitsy, whose Mother Superior did not do double duty as a cabaret dancer, said, "Teasel, wherever are your shoes? How are you going to climb the Alps in bare feet?" These lines, of course, were not in the play. They were meant to draw attention to my bare feet, which I was sure were Bitsy's doing.

"Someone stole my shoes." Not the best bit of improv, but the only words I could think of. They were also a trigger: The Sunnydale street scene took center stage in my mind again. This time, I saw shoes.

Roger's running shoes.

His white running shoes with a gray swoosh.

"Shoes," I mumbled again as I stared at Roger.

"To be thus is nothing; But to be safely thus." The *Macbeth* line he had quoted at the bowling alley—Macbeth speaks it as he plots a second murder in order to make sure his first one brings his promised future.

Omigod. The good-looking captain with the great baritone voice who saved his Jewish dancers was a serial killer.

The music began for our next number, "So long, Gute Nacht." My mouth was already open, so I sang, "There's a loud kind of banging from the cymbals on the stage..." Or rather, I tried to sing. Now that I'd slipped out of character, I couldn't carry a tune. At all. I also couldn't tear my eyes away from Roger-the-murderer (who studiously ignored me), but out of the corner of my eye I saw Keith wince and pull his baton up. So I was flat. I thought briefly of the producer in the audience. It didn't matter. All that mattered was figuring out what to do next.

"So long," I sang (really, horribly flat) as I exited offstage right. Candy waited there for me. "What happened?" she whispered. Everyone must have heard my out-of-tune singing over the PA system.

"Gute Nacht..." sang Bitsy as she walked offstage left.

"I think our Captain is a killer," I whispered back, keeping my eye on Roger.

"Farewell!" sang the Captain and Mary. They exited stage left, and the lights went to black for a quick scene change.

"Come again?" Candy asked.

"Gotta go." I hurried onstage for the final number, "Climb Out of the Gutter." The lights came up to reveal all of us at the foot of the Alps, ready to climb.

All of us except Roger.

"Shit!" I exclaimed in a very un-nun-like fashion. Nice staring at a murderer so he knows you're onto him, Ivy. I ran offstage left. No Roger in sight. "Call 911," I yelled to Candy as I ran through the greenroom. I made it out the stage door in time to see Roger start his car. I went to jump in mine, then realized my keys were in my purse in my dressing room. Double shit! I sprinted back inside the theater as fast as my bare feet would allow, grabbed my purse off the dressing room counter, slung it crosswise over my body, and raced to my car. Even so, by the time I zoomed out of the parking lot, Roger's car was nowhere in sight.

Where would he go? What would I do if I were a killer?

I'd destroy evidence. I headed toward Marge's house and the Pet Cam photos.

CHAPTER 55

I squealed into Marge's drive, slammed the car into park, and jumped out, passing Roger's car as I ran to the front door.

Locked.

Marge's set of keys was separate from my car keys. I fumbled in my purse, pulled them out, and unlocked the door, but not before I realized I had a weapon in the bag. Good, I might need it.

I sprinted toward the kitchen, which was now empty of Pet Cam photos. And empty of my laptop. And, I realized with a start, empty of Lassie.

Yip!

Lassie. I ran toward the sound. As I flew out the open patio door, the nun's habit twisted around my ankles and I tripped, smacking my chin on the rough concrete patio. I tasted blood. Must have bit my lip, but all I could think about was Lassie.

He was on the other side of the pool, struggling to get free from Roger, who held him tightly—too tightly—under one arm.

"It's too bad." Roger shook his head at me in mock sorrow. "Just too smart for your own good. You were almost on a plane to New York."

I scrambled to my feet. "No, I wasn't." I'd been a fool but I wasn't any longer. "All of this producer jazz, your mentoring—that was just to distract me, wasn't it?"

"And hopefully get in your pants." Roger gave a mean laugh and squeezed Lassie, who yipped in protest.

Why did he have Lassie?

I edged toward them, keeping my distance from the black

expanse of water that separated us. Roger must have turned off the pool lights.

"You're not that talented, Ivy." Roger's hair shone silver in the moonlight, but his face was dark. "You're nowhere as good as me, and if I couldn't make it, you don't stand a chance."

I crept closer. Under the black water of the pool, a blacker rectangle. My laptop. Underwater.

Underwater.

Water, over and on top, pressing down.

I couldn't breathe. I stopped stock still, willing myself to not hyperventilate. Blood from my split lip filled my mouth.

"Pity about that little phobia you have." Another laugh from Roger. "'Cause I thought we'd go swimming." He held Lassie out over the water. "But come to think of it, pugs don't swim." He let go of him—a splash and the dark water closed over Lassie's head. "They sink."

CHAPTER 56

"You son of a bitch!" I shouted as I leapt into the pool.

Luckily Roger had thrown Lassie into the shallow end. My nun's habit floated around me as I struggled the few feet to the middle of the pool, where the pug's dark shape was just visible. I scooped him up. He coughed a little when he hit the air, then licked my face. I hurried to my edge of the pool, away from Roger, and bumped Lassie up and over onto dry land. Then I tried to do the same.

No dice. My wet nun's habit weighed a ton.

I turned toward the pool steps. The pool steps that Roger, fully clothed, was slowly descending. Shit! I tried again to hoist myself onto the edge. Not a chance.

The ladder was the only other way out, and it was across the pool in the deep end. No way I could swim there with the dead weight of the habit dragging me down.

"I did think about using fire, given your propensity for it." Roger took another step down into the pool. "I even gave it a little test run. Or didn't you notice your car fires were getting worse?"

Another step down. "But fire is messy and noisy, and I didn't want the neighbors to get wind of anything too soon."

Having reached the pool floor, he walked toward me.

"Of course, I could have used the idling vehicle trick, but it was getting a little old."

He was closing in. Where were the police?

"And then I thought, doh!'" He mockingly hit himself on the forehead. "Drowning. It's nice and quiet and a completely believable accident."

Shit. Roger had thrown Lassie in the shallow end to make me think I could get out. Instead, I was right where he wanted me—confined, terrified, and headed toward deep water.

"Your costume," Roger's teeth glinted in reflected moonlight, "is an unexpected bonus."

As if on cue, my nun's habit grabbed at my arms and legs like a fishing net. If it didn't kill me, Roger would. I had no illusions about that. He was a murderer, after all.

I stepped backwards, out of my habit's grasp, away from Roger, and into deeper water. "I think I know how you did it," I said—Roger was the catalytic converter thief, landscaper, and killer. "But why? Why did you kill all those people you don't even know?"

"I knew the last one I attacked. You know, the one who kept me from real fame? In fact, I saved Marge for last. Sort of like dessert." Shadowed eyes in a grinning face, like a death head. Closer.

I took another step backwards, trying desperately to not think about the drop-off to the deep end, just a foot behind me. I had to keep Roger talking while I came up with a plan. "But why the rest of them?"

"Money." Roger's skull face loomed nearer. "You didn't really think that house in Mexico was built on actor's wages, did you? Oh." His eyebrows shot up in mock amusement. "Maybe you did. After all, this house," he gestured back at Marge's house, "was built on theater." His words dripped with disgust.

"I thought you loved the theater." The water was up to my shoulders.

Roger snorted. "I gave my life to the theater and where am I? Fifty years old—"

"Sixty." If I was about to die, I wasn't putting up with any bullshit.

Roger took another step toward me. "And basically homeless, moving from town to town, living from paycheck to paycheck."

I swore my costume was alive and trying to drag me down. "Who paid you to murder all those people? Bitsy? Arnie?"

"Bitsy? She's just a malicious nymphomaniac. And Arnie..." Roger's voice actually softened. "Arnie's just a guy like me, duped by the illusion of theater. In fact, I don't think I would have killed him even if I had been contracted to do it."

The habit tangled itself into the purse slung across my body, threatening to throw me off-balance. "I've been duped by the illusion of theater too. How about not kill me?"

"Nice try."

Balanced on my tiptoes, I desperately tried to untangle the habit from my bag.

Oh.

My bag.

"Who did contract you?" I grappled underwater with the bag's clasp.

"Debra, my agent. She decided to quit show business and invest in real estate. Needed to make some real money. Then we both got a little drunk one night and started talking about how traveling actors have the perfect cover for crime. We have aliases—like 'Ivy Meadows'—no permanent addresses, no long-term ties, and we're in and out of a city in three months or less."

I let Roger get nearer. He had to be close for my plan to work.

"We even have the perfect motive," Roger said. "We're always broke."

He took another step toward me. I forced myself to stay where I was. "You killed all those people for your agent? Just for money?" I grasped the weapon inside my bag. The pool bottom sloped away beneath my feet. I struggled to stay upright. And to breathe.

"It's not such a bad thing," he said. "I only kill people over seventy. They've had their chance at life."

I thought of Charlie Small. I thought of Marge and Arnie and my other friends over seventy. I thought of all the older performers who made me laugh and cry and dream. I looked at Roger, smug with his rationalized belief.

And I shot him.

CHAPTER 57

"Good thing that worked after being submerged." Hank pointed at the lipstick pepper spray I still held in my hand.

"Nice job with the pool toy," I replied.

Hank had figured something was wrong when I ran offstage. Being a logical sort, he started his search for me at Marge's house and arrived just after I'd shot Roger in the face with the spray. While Roger was still yelling and thrashing around in the pool, Hank grabbed an inner tube and shoved it over Roger's head, pinning his arms to his sides and making him look like a big fat fool.

Hank helped me out of the pool and stood guard until official help arrived just a few minutes later. Now he stood (sans sunglasses for a change), in front of the patio chair where I sat with Lassie in my lap.

"Seriously, I'm fine," I said to the young redheaded EMT who was kneeling next to me, checking me out. "It's just a scrape." I lifted a hand to feel the gash on my chin but Hank grabbed it. "Don't. You probably have some pepper spray on your face." There was no probably about it. I'd held my breath and closed my eyes when I shot Roger, but I could still feel a sting on my face.

The EMT straightened up. "Neither your chin or your lip look like they need stitches. You're lucky, Sister."

Sister? Oh, I still wore the habit. "Thanks be to God," I said, with a sideways smile at Hank. He smiled back, a first.

"We do want to get that pepper spray off you, though. I'll be right back." The EMT disappeared inside the house, probably to get something from the fire truck parked out front. The police had already left, taking the dripping red-faced Roger with them.

Lassie, who had sat up straight in my lap while the EMT was near, now curled into a ball with a big doggie sigh. Poor little pug, all tuckered out.

Hank sat down across the table. "You know," he said slowly, "when I found out you were investigating the suicides, I was really pissed off. Thought Bob wasn't taking me seriously, you being so green and all."

I didn't tell him that my uncle hadn't taken him seriously, or that he thought Hank was just being paranoid, or that he was worried about him acting "hinky." I also didn't tell Hank that the investigation would never have happened without Marge's call to Amy Small. Which brought me to another question.

"How did you know it was Marge who had the accident? You know, that day at the 7-Eleven when you got the call from the posse?"

"You mean the day you followed me dressed in that nun outfit?" He nodded at the costume I still wore.

I cringed. "Yeah, then."

"I recognized the address, because...well, it was sort of an unusual situation." He looked at me, a question in those silvery gray eyes.

"I know about Marge's confusion, if that's what you're wondering."

"Yeah. Well, see, the posse has this program to keep watch on folks who tend to wander away. Works with a personal GPS unit they wear that connects to our computers at the station and to a home computer. It's almost always a spouse or caregiver who requests it. Marge asked for one for herself. I admired her for that—thought it took guts to admit something like that—so I kept an especially good eye on her."

Hank cleared his throat. "And, I, uh, admire the job you did too. Even though I'm pretty sure you suspected me." Lassie, on the edge of sleep, snorted. "See," said Hank, with a nod to the pug.

"Even the dog's smarter than that."

I was about to protest when I saw the twinkle in his eyes. "You *were* always first at the scenes, and..." I decided to take advantage of our newfound camaraderie. "It was your sunglasses."

He looked at me, his eyes flashing silver in the light from the full moon. If I had cool eyes like that, I'd show them off all the time.

"Uncle Bob thinks you wear them all the time because there's something wrong with your eyes." I took a deep breath. "I think you wear them to hide the fact you're high."

Hank paused, but his face didn't change expression. "You're both right. I have glaucoma, acute angle-closure glaucoma. Sometimes it hurts like hell. The pressure builds up in your eyes, and you feel like your head is going to explode. Painkillers don't help. One day, my doctor said he'd 'heard,'" he made air quotes with his fingers, "that marijuana could help with the pressure and the pain. It does. But..."

Good PI-in-training that I was, I waited for him to go on.

He sighed. "Medical marijuana may be legal now, but it's not well-accepted yet. Hell, even my doctor was reluctant to write the prescription. Plus I shouldn't be driving if I've...taken a dose." Hank tipped his head back toward the sky. I wondered if he could see the stars above us. "I guess I need to quit the posse."

The first time I'd ever heard emotion in Hank's voice, and it was sadness.

CHAPTER 58

"But Hank didn't have to quit." I updated Marge and Arnie over celebratory drinks at Marge's house a couple of days later. "The posse said he could work dispatch when he was feeling okay. And his doctor's looking into a new treatment." I had told them about Hank's glaucoma, not his pot use. Hadn't told anyone, not even my uncle. Legal or not, it didn't seem like something Hank wanted spread around.

The two lovebirds sat close together on Arnie's sofa, Lassie snoring away at their feet. Marge's doctors had determined that her dementia was medication-based, not organic. That's what we were celebrating. Or so I thought.

"Time for a toast," said Arnie, standing up and refilling our champagne glasses. "To Ivy, the great detective."

"I'm not such a great detective." I clinked glasses with them anyway. "I never even suspected Roger."

"You thought it was Bitsy, didn't you?" Marge smiled at the bubbles in her champagne.

"I thought she might have paid someone to do it. I couldn't figure out her motive when it came to everyone other than you and Charlie, but I knew she had something to hide." That something had turned out to be her husband in Nebraska, whom she had tried to ease out of this world a little early. No one had been able to prove what she had done, so she'd been let go with a slap on the wrist and the restraining order, courtesy of her now-estranged son.

"You suspected me too, didn't you?" asked Arnie. My face grew hot, but he didn't look the least bit offended. "I mean, I installed that security system to keep an eye on Marge, and I did commit fraud once." He held up a hand in his defense. "Albeit for art, but fraud all the same." I wasn't sure a swamp-themed amusement park was art, but decided to give him this one. "Between my history, the theater being in trouble, and the life insurance policy, I made a pretty good suspect." He managed to take a sip of champagne with his cigar still in his mouth.

"Yeah," I admitted. "And speaking of insurance, I've been saving this for you two." I put my phone on speaker so they could hear the voicemail I'd received a few hours earlier. "Guess what?" My uncle's voice filled the room. "Carl Marks was picked up a few hours ago. Had the audacity to show up at a military funeral in Yuma. I guess he..." His voice took on the tone he had when he was reading, "'Wore Ray Bans with a Class A uniform, which is not military protocol.'" Back to regular Uncle Bob voice. "A couple of real Marines took exception to an imposter at the funeral." He chuckled. "He's in the Yuma jail now."

"Here's to that." Marge raised her glass. "Asshole."

"And I have one more toast." Arnie's voice cracked as he lifted his glass too. "Damn it." He swiped at his teary eyes.

"To Desert Dinner Theater?" I guessed. Once the local media picked up on the "Captain Vaughn Katt Tries to Drown Cabaret Dancer" news, the show was so popular the theater had to add two weeks to the run.

"That's not it," Arnie said with a sob.

"Aww, chickie." Marge gave him a tissue. "Let me do it." She clinked her glass with his. "To the new Edelweiss team."

"The Edelweiss...? Oh!" I hugged Marge around the neck. Marge Weiss, that is, who sat next to the tearfully happy Arnie Adel. "The Adel-Weiss team."

"Yeah." Marge's eyes glimmered too. "We're getting hitched."

CHAPTER 59

Tears were on the menu, it seemed. I'd emailed Amy Small right away after learning that Charlie's death was not suicide, but when I finally got to talk to her on the phone at my uncle's office, she had a hard time making it through the conversation.

"I just knew my dad wouldn't do that." She snuffled. "I mean, it's horrible, but I'm...relieved." I had already told her that Charlie hadn't suffered. "If he had killed himself, I would have felt like I didn't really know him." She began crying in earnest. "Oh, Dad..."

I hung up quietly so Amy could grieve on her own. Besides, I had work to do.

I had Roger's admission that he had killed those retirees. His shoes were in the incriminating Pet Cam photos (which I had emailed to Uncle Bob right after downloading them). I even found seven different bank accounts in his name with large semi-regular cash deposits. But none of that was concrete proof. And Roger and his agent had made sure they had no obvious connections to Underwood Holdings. It was going to be tough to pin the Sunnydale murders on Roger. I searched through my notes again. Surely there was something...

"Olive." My uncle got up from his office chair, and walked over to me. "You've done everything you could. It's time to let the police handle the rest." He gently closed my new laptop. "Good thing that Roger guy tried to kill you. They'll keep him in jail for that."

"Yeah, good thing." I knew I was lucky, but it didn't really feel that way.

He went back to his desk and opened the top drawer. "Come over here. I've got a few things for you."

I walked the few feet to his desk.

"First of all, I owe you an apology."

Wow. My family did not do apologies.

"I should have filled you in about Hank's suspicions. I thought he was just being paranoid. I didn't want to get you headed down the wrong road."

"Secondly," Uncle Bob's chins tripled as he tried to hold back a smile, "someone else owed you a little something too. I wasn't sure your landlady could ask you to pay rent while they fixed your apartment. It's a little complicated, since it looks like you might have caused the fire, which you will never, ever do again—"

"Never," I agreed.

"But a nice letter from a PI on the official letterhead of Franko, Hricko and Maionchi did the trick." He handed me a check from the account of Mae Freeman, my landlady. "The rent money you paid."

"Thank you!" I ran around the desk so I could hug my uncle.

"One more thing." Uncle Bob took a small cardboard box out of his drawer and handed it to me. This time he didn't try to hold back his smile. I opened it to see a stack of business cards, printed with "Duda Detective Agency, Olive Ziegwart, Assistant Investigator."

I didn't know what to say so I hugged him again.

He made some "aw gee shucks" noises, then looked at me. "Hey, I like your peacock earrings. They go really nice with your blonde hair. Now," he patted me on the head, "can I take my ace detective out for a beer?"

"I'd love to," I said, "but I've got a date."

Water sparkled in the pool at my feet, cascaded in waterfalls next to me, and reflected the setting sun in the canal below. Water, water, everywhere—and I wasn't afraid.

"I guess the baptism by fire cured me," I said to Matt, who sat on a sculpted "boulder" near me at Arizona Falls, a way cool hydroelectric generator-turned-art installation.

"Any other issues cured?" He looked over at the couple who stood hand in hand gazing through a sheet of falling water. Cody reached out to the waterfall and splashed Sarah, who squealed in delight.

"I'm working on it." I knew I needed to recognize Cody as more than just my kid brother with a disability. He was a full-fledged adult with a girlfriend. "Really."

"Thanks for coming. Cody really wanted a double date." Matt's smile didn't reach his eyes. "I think it would have been too much like having a chaperone if it was just me."

"I'm sorry about Candy."

"I'm not sure we would have ever worked out long-term." Matt watched Cody and Sarah as they walked toward us. "This acting life in L.A....it's what she wanted."

"Yeah." Spray from the nearest fall misted my face. I closed my eyes and thought about what Jeremy had said, about acting precluding any romantic relationship.

"What about you?" Matt must have read my mind. I was so comfortable with him. Maybe I didn't need romance, as long as I had friendship like this. "Don't you want that too?" he continued. "Fame and fortune?"

I tried to picture myself onstage in a fancy theater in New York. I wanted it, oh, I wanted it, but the photo in my head was fuzzy. "Not yet." Roger might be a despicable man, but he was right about one thing. "I'm not good enough yet. I think I can be, but I've got a lot to learn."

I opened my eyes and turned toward Matt. "And I like working with Uncle Bob." I thought again of Roger and how I didn't suspect him until it was nearly too late. "But I'm not a great detective yet, either."

"What are you guys talking about?" I turned to see Cody behind me, Sarah by his side.

"I was just telling Matt that I'm not a great actor or a great detective—"

"But you're a great sister." Cody hugged me around the neck.

Not yet.

But I'm working on that too.

Author's Note

You won't find Sunnydale on an Arizona map, though you will find several very nice retirement communities that look a bit like Marge's hometown. A couple of these communities in Maricopa County (which is on a map) have posses, staffed by volunteers who help their neighbors and even save lives.

The Phoenix Fire Department is thankfully very real, though the annual Fire vs. Police tug-of-war is not. That said, Guns and Hoses events across the country raise money for charity and include not just tug-of-wars, but golf tournaments, bouncy ball races, and jelly donut-eating contests. Go out and support your local first responders!

Cindy Brown

Cindy Brown has been a theater geek (musician, actor, director, producer, and playwright) since her first professional gig at age 14. Now a full-time writer, she's lucky enough to have garnered several awards (including 3rd place in the 2013 international *Words With Jam* First Page Competition, judged by Sue Grafton!) and is an alumnus of the Squaw Valley Writers Workshop. Though Cindy and her husband now live in Portland, Oregon, she made her home in Phoenix, Arizona, for more than 25 years and knows all the good places to hide dead bodies in both cities.

In case you missed the 1st in the series

MACDEATH

Cindy Brown

An Ivy Meadows Mystery (#1)

Like every actor, Ivy Meadows knows that *Macbeth* is cursed. But she's finally scored her big break, cast as an acrobatic witch in a circus-themed production of *Macbeth* in Phoenix, Arizona. And though it may not be Broadway, nothing can dampen her enthusiasm—not her flying cauldron, too-tight leotard, or carrot-wielding dictator of a director.

But when one of the cast dies on opening night, Ivy is sure the seeming accident is "murder most foul" and that she's the perfect person to solve the crime (after all, she does work part-time in her uncle's detective agency). Undeterred by a poisoned Big Gulp, the threat of being blackballed, and the suddenly too-real curse, Ivy pursues the truth at the risk of her hard-won career—and her life.

Henery Press Mystery Books

And finally, before you go...
Here are a few other mysteries
you might enjoy:

BOARD STIFF

Kendel Lynn

An Elliott Lisbon Mystery (#1)

As director of the Ballantyne Foundation on Sea Pine Island, SC, Elliott Lisbon scratches her detective itch by performing discreet inquiries for Foundation donors. Usually nothing more serious than retrieving a pilfered Pomeranian. Until Jane Hatting, Ballantyne board chair, is accused of murder. The Ballantyne's reputation tanks, Jane's headed to a jail cell, and Elliott's sexy ex is the new lieutenant in town.

Armed with moxie and her Mini Coop, Elliott uncovers a trail of blackmail schemes, gambling debts, illicit affairs, and investment scams. But the deeper she digs to clear Jane's name, the guiltier Jane looks. The closer she gets to the truth, the more treacherous her investigation becomes. With victims piling up faster than shells at a clambake, Elliott realizes she's next on the killer's list.

LOWCOUNTRY BOIL

Susan M. Boyer

A Liz Talbot Mystery (#1)

Private Investigator Liz Talbot is a modern Southern belle: she blesses hearts and takes names. She carries her Sig 9 in her Kate Spade handbag, and her golden retriever, Rhett, rides shotgun in her hybrid Escape. When her grandmother is murdered, Liz high-tails it back to her South Carolina island home to find the killer.

She's fit to be tied when her police-chief brother shuts her out of the investigation, so she opens her own. Then her long-dead best friend pops in and things really get complicated. When more folks start turning up dead in this small seaside town, Liz must use more than just her wits and charm to keep her family safe, chase down clues from the hereafter, and catch a psychopath before he catches her.

Available at booksellers nationwide and online

Visit www.henerypress.com for details

NUN TOO SOON

Alice Loweecey

A Giulia Driscoll Mystery (#1)

Giulia Driscoll has just taken on her first impossible client: The Silk Tie Killer. He's hired Driscoll Investigations to prove his innocence and they have only thirteen days to accomplish it. Talk about being tried in the media. Everyone in town is sure Roger Fitch strangled his girlfriend with one of his silk neckties. And then there's the local TMZ wannabes stalking Giulia and her client for sleazy sound bites.

On top of all that, her assistant's first baby is due any second, her scary smart admin still doesn't relate well to humans, and her police detective husband insists her client is guilty. About this marriage thing–it's unknown territory, but it sure beats ten years of living with 150 nuns.

Giulia's ownership of Driscoll Investigations hasn't changed her passion for justice from her convent years. But the more dirt she digs up, the more she's worried her efforts will help a murderer escape. As the client accuses DI of dragging its heels on purpose, Giulia thinks The Silk Tie Killer might be choosing one of his ties for her own neck.

FINDING SKY

Susan O'Brien

A Nicki Valentine Mystery

Suburban widow and PI in training Nicki Valentine can barely keep track of her two kids, never mind anyone else. But when her best friend's adoption plan is jeopardized by the young birth mother's disappearance, Nicki is persuaded to help. Nearly everyone else believes the teenager ran away, but Nicki trusts her BFF's judgment, and the feeling is mutual.

The case leads where few moms go (teen parties, gang shootings) and places they can't avoid (preschool parties, OB-GYNs' offices). Nicki has everything to lose and much to gain – including the attention of her unnervingly hot P.I. instructor. Thankfully, Nicki is armed with her pesky conscience, occasional babysitters, a fully stocked minivan, and nature's best defense system: women's intuition.

DINERS, DIVES & DEAD ENDS

Terri L. Austin

A Rose Strickland Mystery (#1)

As a struggling waitress and part-time college student, Rose Strickland's life is stalled in the slow lane. But when her close friend, Axton, disappears, Rose suddenly finds herself serving up more than hot coffee and flapjacks. Now she's hashing it out with sexy bad guys and scrambling to find clues in a race to save Axton before his time runs out.

With her anime-loving bestie, her septuagenarian boss, and a pair of IT wise men along for the ride, Rose discovers political corruption, illegal gambling, and shady corporations. She's gone from zero to sixty and quickly learns when you're speeding down the fast lane, it's easy to crash and burn.